Cave of
the Moving
Shadows

Thomas Millstead

Cave of the Moving Shadows

The Dial Press   New York

Published by
The Dial Press
1 Dag Hammarskjold Plaza
New York, New York 10017

Copyright © 1979 by Thomas Millstead
All rights reserved. Manufactured in the U.S.A.
First printing

Library of Congress Cataloging in Publication Data
Millstead, Thomas. Cave of the moving shadows.
Summary: A 12-year-old boy living in Cro-Magnon
times must choose between his training in
sorcery and his desire to be a hunter.
[1. Man, Prehistoric—Fiction.
2. Cave dwellers—Fiction] I. Title.
PZ7.M63988Cav [Fic] 79-10890
ISBN 0-8037-1388-6
ISBN 0-8037-1387-8 lib. bdg.

Foreword

Four hundred centuries ago—long, long before written history—there were men and women living in the caves of western Europe. Much of what we know about these distant ancestors of ours comes from the beautiful and mysterious paintings they drew on the walls of their caves. These images tell us of an adventurous and dangerous period when animals that are now extinct roamed the earth and when human beings lived in small tribes and hunting was their only means of survival.

This is a tale of those times.

Cave of the Moving Shadows

the great valley

FORBIDDEN MOUNTAINS

the Others' cave

Sabo's caves

the notch

Kimba's
home cave

stream

S

E — W

RIVER

N

It is 50 miles from Home Cave to Forbidden Mountains.

Chapter

1

A hawk swooped so low, he could almost touch it. Then upward it sailed and all but vanished in the glare of the sun.

Sprawled on top of the cliff, the boy shielded his eyes to watch it soar. How he thirsted to wheel and skim through the sky like that, to peer down at all there was below. Perhaps if he imagined intently enough that he *was* the hawk, the Power that Utrek spoke of would actually enable him to look out through the eyes of that now-distant bird.

Then he would see far past the river winding in the distance. Then he would see what lay beyond the Forbidden Mountains far to his right. Then he could detect the movement of the herds of animals that his Tribe so badly needed to sustain them.

And then he would lead the Tribe to the game and be first in the hunt that would follow!

It might even be a herd of the Mighty Ones!

He returned to his task, chipping with a flint point upon a soft, flat stone. He was sketching the form of a Mighty One. That was the name his people gave to the mammoth—the giant woolly elephant.

He bore down carefully. This was the hardest part, reproducing the long, wide curve of those fearsome tusks. His tongue stuck out at the edge of his mouth as he concentrated.

There! He had them right, the tusks sweeping in a great arc toward the bulbous head.

And he had done it entirely from memory. It had been many, many days since his people had seen a Mighty One. Or any other of the large animals they hunted for food: the bison and the wild horse and the reindeer.

He gazed again at the rumpled plain below. There was no sign of game anywhere. By stretching, he could look down to the base of the limestone cliff. In its side was the cave the Tribe had made its home.

Some of his people were walking about and working

near the mouth of the cavern. From here, they looked no bigger than ground squirrels.

They had lived in the cave during the almost endless winter. It had sheltered them from the elements and protected them from their enemies. But now, with the time of thawing, they would have to move on. For when the game departed, the Tribe must go, too. It was a hard thing, to leave the warmth and familiarity of the cave. But already stomachs were hollow for lack of meat.

The boy returned to the slab of stone. The likeness was a good one. Proudly, he scratched on the corner of the stone a symbol he had taken to signify that this was his work. It was a straight up-and-down line with a point on the end. He meant it to indicate a spear—for he thought of himself as a hunter.

Not yet a great hunter, it was true, since he had seen only twelve summers. He had never, in fact, hunted any large game. But he knew he would be a hunter, and a good hunter—perhaps the best of them all.

Every boy of the Tribe became a hunter. That was the only way of life that a boy could conceive of. There was no other. But Kimba was different. He was not born of the Tribe and he was being raised in another manner. The Tribe did not expect Kimba to become a hunter.

Gripping the flint tightly, Kimba retraced his drawing of the mammoth. They were immense, the Mighty Ones. But that would not stop him. He would yet show the Tribe that he could be a hunter.

He imagined himself clenching his spear, circling a

Mighty One, measuring it, dashing in with a ringing cry.

Kimba lay on his back, staring at the sky, visualizing his victory. Movement flashed before his eyes and roused him. It was a hawk, gliding onto the lowest branch of a stunted black oak rooted in the sandy soil.

It was a small hawk, earth brown with red markings at the wing tips and near its eyes. Was it, he wondered, the same bird that had flown so low only moments before? Its unblinking eyes were fixed upon Kimba.

He pursed his lips and whistled. The hawk cocked its head, still staring at him, and sounded an identical whistle.

Again Kimba whistled—a long, sweet trill. Hesitantly, the bird fluttered to the ground. It took several nervous steps toward him.

Kimba extended his hand. He made his mind go blank, letting it be filled with feelings, not thought. They were the feelings that a small hawk would experience, feelings of freedom, ferocity, and the joy of flight. He let himself be one with these feelings and with this living creature.

The hawk studied Kimba's hand, then walked to it. The boy lightly stroked the silken feathers. The bird shivered but remained still.

He had always been able to do this, to imitate the calls of birds and small animals, to charm them, to compel them to draw near. It had nothing to do with hunting. The Tribe required herds of large animals in order to subsist. The tiny, bright-eyed bird had no reason to fear him, and the boy knew this gift of his was of no practical use.

He did not question how he was able to do it, but Utrek said it was another sign that Kimba had the Power.

Suddenly the hawk shot into the air. A shadow fell across Kimba's body.

The boy reached for his spear.

"Kimba!"

An old man loomed over him, angrily shaking a long staff. His legs were spindly, and gray, dirt-stained hair all but covered his eyes. He was bent like an ancient tree. This was Utrek, sorcerer of the Tribe.

Utrek picked up the stone on which Kimba had been sketching. He looked from it to Kimba and back again.

"You were forbidden to come here today!" His voice was a screech that sent shivers down the boy's spine.

"Yes, Utrek."

The sorcerer held out the stone with a trembling hand. "And I did not tell you to make a Mighty One."

It was so. He had assigned Kimba to sketch a bison. But the boy's mind was alive with visions of the majestic Mighty Ones. He had meant to draw a bison. He had just not gotten to it yet.

Utrek pointed a finger at Kimba—the forefinger of his left hand. He had only two fingers and a thumb on that hand, and he knew that this had always awed Kimba. The boy had often wondered in what dreadful way the other two fingers had been lost.

"You must not dream your own dreams," Utrek shouted. "You have the Power. But you must learn to use it for the Tribe. You must not waste it!"

Kimba bit his lip. He dared not talk back. It could be most dangerous. Utrek could do strange and marvelous things. It was the Power that enabled Utrek to paint so

7

skillfully, to summon game, to interpret dreams, to heal, to recount the Tribal legends, to work wonders.

Someday Kimba would do these things, too; someday he would master the Power. So it had been decreed long before, when Kimba was so young that he could recall nothing else.

But as he grew older the prospect bewildered him. To have the Power was a great gift, Utrek said. But how was it great? Kimba wondered. The other boys did not spend their days carving on stone. Or mixing clay to make paints. Or carrying heavy loads of Utrek's masks and ritual implements. The other boys were free to roam, free to practice spear throwing, free to perfect their skills as hunters.

"I must punish you, Kimba. You must learn."

Kimba's eyes dropped to the ground. He had been told before by Utrek that he was a dreamer, an idler. Let someone else be trained then, he thought. Let someone else be found who has the Power.

"This will be your punishment. . . ."

Kimba knew he would not be struck. Utrek had never done that. But his punishment would be working longer in the Grotto with the sorcerer, hours when he could be outdoors. He would rather be beaten and be done with it.

More dreary hours in that dank chamber! On such a fine, clear day. He turned for a final look at the plain below. His gaze swept over the great expanse, then stopped abruptly.

"A Mighty One! There!"

Utrek squinted. "Where?"

"There! There!"

"Ah! Tell the Tribe! Hurry, Kimba!"

The boy bolted for the rocky path. Utrek hurried after him, leaning on his staff, wheezing as he made the steep descent.

Kimba was already far below, sliding, running, kicking loose a torrent of pebbles. He was shouting before he reached the bottom of the cliff.

"A Mighty One! I see it! A Mighty One!"

The people of the Tribe greeted him with shouts of their own. "Where? Where, Kimba?"

"There! Across the river!"

Excitement gripped them. Game sighted! After so many days of only roots, moss, and the inner bark of willows. Meat! Fresh meat for all!

"Hunters! Prepare!" Rab's voice carried over the tumult. He clapped a hand on the boy's shoulders. "Good work, Kimba!"

The hunters dashed for the cave to fetch their weapons. Rab, with Kimba at his side, led the way.

Rab was Spear-Maker for the Tribe. It was he and his mate, Urda, who had taken Kimba in when the Tribe had found him ten summers before. Now Rab took his longest spear—a hardwood pike with a large, sharp bone point securely lashed to it. He would need this rather than a flinthead spear to penetrate the thick hide of a Mighty One. The throwing sticks and javelins the hunters carried when hunting smaller game would be useless.

Rab, Urda, and Kimba lived in a small niche near the mouth of the cave. Their fur bedding, their few utensils,

9

and the many stone tools of Rab's trade littered the area. Other families occupied their own plots of territory throughout the wide cavern. No group would attempt to take over the space claimed by another. That was the rule of the Tribe.

Rab's face shone. "A Mighty One!" he told Urda excitedly.

"Hunt well!" Urda smiled. She was taller than the other women of the Tribe, almost as tall as the men. Yet she was small-boned and graceful. Chestnut-colored hair fell to her shoulders and her face was delicate and good-humored.

"Hunters! Come!" Rab cried as he ran back out into the sunlight. The other able-bodied men of the Tribe, little more than a score, assembled around him.

Now Utrek made his way toward the hunters. His ribs rose and fell rapidly, for he was still fatigued by the climb down the cliff.

Kimba grasped his spear tightly with both hands. It was one that Rab had made for him the previous autumn. The spear was as tall as he was, yet nowhere near the length of the weapons held by the others.

Utrek shook his staff and the hunters fell silent. Kimba, taking small steps to make his movement inconspicuous, sidled up to the edge of the cluster of hunters.

Eyes gleaming wildly, Utrek uttered a piercing howl. It hung on the air, shrill and terrible, for a moment. Then it ended and Utrek's staff lunged in the direction of the Mighty One.

"Hunt and kill!" he shrieked.

The hunters let out a roar and began running toward the distant river. His throat dry with excitement, Kimba raced with them.

"Kimba!" It was Utrek shouting. "Come back!"

Rab spun around and saw him. The Spear-Maker let the other hunters stream past him.

"Go back!" he commanded Kimba.

"I saw the Mighty One first."

"You are too small to hunt yet."

"But I was first to—"

"Go back!"

There was impatience in Rab's face. Kimba stamped his spear on the ground, angry too. But Rab could not be defied. Kimba turned slowly and made his way back to the cave. Utrek took him by the ear, pinching it hard. "You will work in the Grotto from sunup to sunset tomorrow. I did not permit you to join the hunt! Your place is here with me!"

"I saw the Mighty One first."

"That does not matter! You are not a hunter!"

Chapter

2

Kimba strode stiffly past the women and smaller children, conscious of their stares. Urda put her cool hand on his shoulder, and together they entered the cave.

He sat cross-legged on his bearskin sleeping robe, keeping the spear in his hands. Brooding, he would not look at Urda.

She smiled slightly, and resumed her work: using a flint scraper to clean the flesh and fat from the hide of a small hare. It would be made into a pouch for Rab to carry flints with him as he hunted. The hare had been the only meat that Urda, Rab, and Kimba had tasted for a week.

Urda offered Kimba the bulbs of some lilies that she had dug up that morning. He shook his head grumpily, even though they were succulent-looking and he would have liked one. Urda bit off a piece of one of the bulbs. "Oh, good," she said, trying to tempt him.

Kimba grunted. It was no time to think of food dug from the earth, when a Mighty One was being hunted. But he was still not a hunter, Utrek had told him. He who had been first to see the Mighty One!

Not a hunter? They would see! He would be a hunter yet. He did not want the Power. What good was it, this Power, if it meant working here with women and children while the hunters were out on the trail?

"Tabok, have some."

Urda extended a lily bulb to a snub-nosed boy who had joined them. Tabok was Kimba's closest friend, and now he nodded eagerly and quickly began chewing it.

"Kimba?" Urda inquired, offering them again.

Once more, Kimba shook his head.

"Would you like to practice with the throwing sticks?" Tabok asked.

Again Kimba shook his head. To *practice* the ways of the hunters with one who was a summer younger than himself! While the hunters were after real game!

But it was a good time to use the throwing sticks, Tabok pointed out. Utrek had left Kimba free for now.

13

A good time for children to play their games, Kimba thought. But what had that to do with real hunting? He also realized that Tabok might hit the target more often. This was because Tabok had more time to practice than Kimba, because Tabok did not have to attend Utrek for the better portion of each day. The prospect of being bested today by a younger boy would not improve his belief in himself as a hunter, Kimba knew.

But then another thought came to him and he jumped up.

"Very well. We will do as you say."

He reached over and scooped up one of the bulbs. "Come, Tabok," he said quickly.

The base of the cliff curved into a smooth and grassy glade, and here had been set up a life-size replica of a cave bear. Kimba himself had molded the bear two summers before out of the umber clay that was so abundant after the melting of the snows.

Utrek had pronounced it an excellent likeness. Kimba had always been proud of his handiwork.

The bear was gigantic, even on all fours, and seemed to snarl frighteningly. However, its coat was a mass of pockmarks from the spear and javelin thrusts it had absorbed, and part of its face had been obliterated.

Tabok, son of Odlag, had brought his father's throwing stick. A throwing stick was a small, stout piece of wood with a rawhide strap attached. The heel of a javelin—a shorter spear, almost a dart—was placed on this loop. With a deft thrust of the throwing stick, the javelin could be hurled faster and farther than if thrown by hand.

Kimba and Tabok were the only males of the Tribe past the age of childhood who were not yet hunters. There had been a third boy named Mrodag. But just one summer ago—when he was the age Kimba was now—Mrodag had been initiated into the ranks of the hunters. Now he would scarcely speak to his two former companions.

Tabok dropped to his knees and began creeping toward the clay animal. When he was twenty paces from it, he leaped up, shouted, brought back his right arm and unleashed the javelin.

It wobbled in flight but struck the bear's right shoulder and remained loosely embedded. Tabok gave a thin, yipping call of triumph.

"Now you, Kimba."

But Kimba was looking back at the cave. Ordinarily, many of the Tribe would be visible. Now the hunters were gone and others were within the cave, busy with chores or discussing the possibility of obtaining fresh meat. No one was to be seen.

"That is *my* Mighty One, Tabok," Kimba said, pointing in the direction the hunters had gone. He walked farther along the base of the cliff, toward some rocks that would block him from sight of the entrance of the cavern.

"You must not tell anyone what I am doing," he instructed the younger boy. "Especially Utrek."

Tabok stared in wonder.

15

Kimba raised his spear and shook it ferociously, as hunters did. Not a hunter? They would see!

He broke into a run. The other hunters had a long start on him. But he would catch up!

Chapter

3

The land where the Tribe lived was plateau country—a series of huge, flat-topped, limestone cliffs that were separated by broad, winding valleys. Much of this lowland was tundra, thick with grass and moss and with occasional patches of dwarfish trees.

The ground was wet from the melting of the snows. In places the earth seemed to suck at Kimba's feet, slowing him.

Had the hunters found the Mighty One yet? Were they even now stalking it? They must not slay it before he joined them!

Never hunt alone—that was a prime rule of the Tribe. Never leave the cave or the fire or the company of your kinsmen. Death waited and watched in a hundred different forms.

Kimba pushed the thought to the back of his mind. The Mighty One he had seen, that was all he must consider. That was all that mattered. He must be there to share in the victory over it.

Soon he drew near the wide river. Groves of alder and willow flanked it. More marshy meadowland lay beyond and, farther away, another hump-backed plateau and then another and another past that.

But there was no sign of the Mighty One. Or of the hunters.

Unless . . . There!

He leaned forward intently. Figures were emerging from the thickets bordering the river. The hunters? No, they moved too fast.

He realized then what they were: wolves. It was a large pack.

And with game as scarce for them as it was for the Tribe, they would be famished.

Kimba hesitated. They were not heading his way. They followed the flow of the river, moving northward, toward his left.

But he did not want to attract their attention. Stooped over, he imagined himself a shadow streaking across the ground. You must imagine yourself to be what you want to be, Utrek had said. You can do nothing until you imagine yourself doing it first.

He stopped again and stood erect. The wolf pack was growing smaller in the distance. But there, across the river, something blurred the line of trees.

It looked like a dark hill that had not been there before. And then it moved.

The Mighty One!

His heart thumped as though it would smash his ribs. He had found game, and now he would join the hunters and lead them to it!

He went on more cautiously. He must be alert, calm, sharp-eyed. He reached the water's edge and looked downriver. The wolf pack was nowhere in view.

Only the head of the Mighty One was visible above the treetops. The mammoth must be eating leaves, Kimba thought. Good. That meant it was not aware of being stalked.

Crouching at the bank, the boy waited until his breathing became regular. He took a long drink of water. It was refreshing but very cold. The river would be frigid, but it was the only way to get to the Mighty One. It had to be crossed.

Kimba grunted at the first touch of the icy water. He stood a moment, shivering. Then he plunged straight in, up to his neck.

It all but paralyzed him. He had to move through it rapidly or it would never release him. The current was swift, fed by the snows at the source of the river high in the Forbidden Mountains. It shoved him and spun him and tried to push him under.

He could take only tiny, laborious steps. He knew the hunters must have forded the river in a shallower place. And he was much smaller than the smallest of the other hunters. Even for his age he was small—a spare, slight boy not much more than a stunted willow, Utrek had said.

Suddenly his feet were yanked off the bottom. His arms and legs thrashed madly. He could not swim, beyond the crudest paddle stroke. None of the Tribe could. They feared deep or swift bodies of water. Monstrous creatures were said to lurk in their depths.

Water gushed into Kimba's mouth and he felt himself choking. He pawed and kicked harder. His hand loosened on the spear. No, he commanded. Hold on to the spear. It would be necessary when he joined the hunt for the Mighty One. He must not let go.

And then his feet touched solid bottom again. His legs buckled, but he forced them forward. Two steps, three steps—while the current tried to pluck him back—and he was on the far bank.

Coughing out the water in his lungs, he threw himself down on the grass.

He was gratefully aware of the sun warming and drying his skin. For a long while his limbs seemed unable to move. They looked to him like branches washed ashore, as though he had no control over them.

But one thought resounded in his mind: This was his first real hunt! He had found the Mighty One! He must not let it escape him now! The hunters would still be searching. Now, when he led them to it, they would have to permit him to participate in the kill.

Gingerly, he sat up. With the spear, he pushed himself to his feet.

Strength returned as he walked. He passed the trees where the Mighty One had browsed. Fallen leaves and broken boughs marked the trail. He saw hawks circling in the sky. They were like the one that had approached him on the cliff above the cave. Again he thought how simple it would be to see the Mighty One from their vantage point.

He left the shelter of the trees that fringed the riverbank. Here he could see far across the plain to the crusty spines of earth that grew gradually into the next plateau. It was not a high cliff, but it was very long, with snakelike ribbons of rock extending along the length of the base.

The breath hissed out of Kimba's body. For the Mighty One stood near a ravine in the lower reaches of the plateau. Its huge trunk was gliding over and picking up the lush, newly greening vegetation.

Where were the hunters? Kimba wondered once more. He sprinted upriver, hidden by trees and underbrush. At a point considerably beyond the Mighty One, he swiftly crossed the valley floor to the first levels of the plateau. Stealthily, he maneuvered himself along the outcropping over the twisting ravine.

If the Mighty One continued on in the direction it had been facing, it must pass here.

Yes! One slow, clumping foot at a time, the mammoth was moving along the floor of the ravine.

This was Kimba's closest look yet. It had, he noticed, only one tusk. The other was a mere stub, probably broken off in battle. But the remaining tusk was sharp and glinting, and it looked as though the mammoth had learned well how to use it alone.

All Mighty Ones were big, but this one must tower over the others of its breed. Though he had never been so near a living mammoth before, he had watched the beasts from a distance and he knew he was not mistaken. The One-Tusk's woolly, rusty-brown coat was shaggy and torn. The creature walked regally, deliberately, as though it knew that no creature on earth had ever bested it in combat and none ever would.

Kimba chewed his lip, suddenly uncertain. He had located the Mighty One, but what good was that if he could not lead the hunters to it? And all of the hunters would be needed to slay a beast of such size.

The Tribe seldom even hunted the Mighty Ones. The risks were too great. Only when meat was scarce would they attempt it. When they did, it was all of them pitted against one mammoth.

Should he call out? he asked himself. Perhaps the hunters were not far away.

But he might cause the Mighty One to flee. In a matter of moments, the Mighty One would pass him, go on its way, and the Tribe would remain hungry.

He must do something, and at once.

A thought came to him, so stunning that it was almost like a blow.

No hunter could face a mammoth alone in open battle.

22

But one hunter—one small hunter—could trick a Mighty One.

The very boldness of the idea shook him. But it also sent a surge of excitement and anticipation through him.

Yes! It could be done by trickery!

Did he not have the Power? Utrek assured him he did. No other hunter did. Could not the Power accomplish as much as a score of hunters?

Yes!

His eyes flew over the terrain. Yes, there was a way! The ravine sank abruptly at a point where a small gorge hacked into it. The drop-off was twice the height of the Mighty One's body. If the beast fell, it might well be killed.

Kimba could not drive the Mighty One toward this drop-off. But he could lure it. A mammoth would not normally attack a hunter. It was not a flesh eater and knew enough to avoid these dangerous two-legged creatures.

But the Mighty Ones were short-tempered, easily angered. He could play on this weakness.

There was a thin shelf of rock just below the edge of the drop-off. If the Mighty One pursued him, Kimba could jump to this perch. The mammoth then would hurtle down.

But he must be quick. Now, Kimba told himself—before there was time for fright!

The boy rubbed his hand over the wolf tooth he wore on a sinew around his neck. Utrek had given it to him six summers before when he had become apprenticed to the sorcerer. It is powerful, Utrek had told him. It will bring triumph.

Let it be so, Kimba breathed to himself.

He rose and ran forward, straight at the Mighty One.

The mammoth halted and lifted its trunk, almost as if not sure for a moment what to make of the tiny figure scurrying toward it.

Then it bellowed, a sound that bounced and reechoed off the walls of the ravine and of the plateau above.

Kimba shouted as he ran: a small, ragged yelp. The Mighty One's eyes, he saw, were red rimmed and blazing with fury.

The boy stopped and raised his spear as if to hurl it. The Mighty One started forward, bellowing again.

Kimba whirled and ran.

The rapid pounding of the mammoth's feet was like thunder. Its frightful trumpeting seemed to explode only a few steps behind him.

Too close! He had come too close, he told himself. He should have turned and run sooner. The precipice was too far!

In his mind he could see that long, long sweeping tusk. Right behind him now!

Sobbing for breath, he made a final, desperate effort.

The drop-off lay before him. One quick glance—to find the toehold—and he leaped.

His feet slipped, then steadied. He was safe on the out-cropping. He hugged the side of the precipice, not look-ing up. Not daring to watch the enormous body that would suddenly blot out the sky above him. And then come crashing down.

He held his breath, but the heavy tattoo of the mammoth's gallop had stopped. He heard another bellow, directly above him.

The Mighty One's trunk, like a deadly snake, slithered down. It probed and groped, feeling the cracks and knobs of the precipice, searching for Kimba.

He squeezed closer to the rocky wall. The One-Tusk had eluded his trap! Its hairy trunk swung furiously to and fro. The two rough lips at the tip of the trunk fiercely gyrated and snuffled, brushing his leg.

Kimba imagined himself a tiny lizard, so tiny that this sensitive antenna would bypass him. His chest hurt from the agony of holding his breath. He was tiny, he commanded himself, so small that he was all but invisible. Tiny!

There was a last disdainful trumpeting and then the slow, heavy tread began again. The One-Tusk was leaving.

Kimba took a deep swallow of air. He stood on tiptoe and peered up into the ravine.

The mammoth was retreating, back the way it had come.

Kimba pulled himself over the ledge. But as the One-Tusk disappeared, a figure came sliding down one side of the ravine.

The boy knew the outline, the gait, even before he recognized the face.

It was Rab.

And instantly Kimba knew what had happened.

Rab and the other hunters had been hidden just beyond him on both sides of the ravine. They had intended to roll boulders down upon the One-Tusk as it passed.

They must have planned the ambush carefully. Meat for the Tribe depended on it.

And now the Mighty One was heading the other way. It was too late to prepare a new trap. It would be difficult—and very perilous—to chase the mammoth and hope to corner it now.

As Rab approached, Kimba could see his face. There was anger in it, more anger than Kimba had ever seen there before.

The boy turned and fled.

His feet, shod in bison skin, flashed over the ground. He ignored the fatigue in his muscles, the trembling in his legs.

He ran on and on, conscious only that he could not face Rab and the Tribe just now. He ran because he knew if he stopped, the realization of his failure would choke him as the river water had.

He was stumbling often, weaving to his feet, and pushing on. His legs felt wooden, but he reminded himself that when he had raced with Tabok and Mrodag, he had always been the fastest. He had been able to run effortlessly, as though a wind undetected by anyone else was propelling him.

He let this thought enter his mind, giving him comfort. If he thought of those races and of his two companions, it would erase thoughts of the terrible thing he had done and of what would become of him now.

It had pleased him particularly, he remembered, to defeat Mrodag. For Mrodag was older than Kimba and Tabok and was forever trying to vanquish them. Mrodag was large for his age—already as heavily muscled as several of the older hunters. Though Kimba was slight in comparison, he was wiry and highly energetic. It was never hard to outrun Mrodag.

Then there would be a look in his face that Kimba could remember vividly—a look of anger and of fear. It was a look that said: You won, but it does not matter because you are not of us; you are different.

When Mrodag had become a hunter Tabok had been grateful, because they would no longer have to put up with him in their day-to-day activities. But Kimba had only said: "If Mrodag can be a hunter, *I* can be a hunter."

The memory stung Kimba now. Had he destroyed forever his opportunity to be a hunter? He was barely able to remain on his feet and he did not know how far he had come. There were still steep, blocky limestone tablelands all about him, but they were unfamiliar to him. Here the grassy plains were dotted with clusters of trees.

Branches fluttered in a dell ahead of him. It was only some breeze, he thought, even though he could feel no wind. But the branches moved once more and he saw what they were: the towering, palmlike antlers of a brown fallow deer.

The boy shook his head to clear it. A fallow deer! He

might yet bring back meat to the Tribe. It would not compare with a Mighty One. It would mean little more than one meal for all. But it would at least atone to some degree for what he had done.

The stag's head lifted; its nostrils were twitching. It had caught his scent.

Kimba flung himself forward as the deer bunched its muscles and jumped, easily clearing a deep crevice. Kimba rushed up a moment later. The crevice was wide, but the game must not elude him this time!

He jumped, missed the far edge, and clawed wildly for an instant. The spear flew out of his hands and he slid to the bottom of the crevice.

Bruised, he rushed from one wall to another. All were too high and steep; the crevice was a natural trap. There were bones scattered around its floor. Many small animals had fallen in and never gotten out.

Kimba slumped down. He must rest; he must think! It occurred to him that the Mighty One he had stalked today had not been clumsy enough to topple into such a trap. But now he, the hunter, had.

A rumble jerked him upright, a low, throbbing growl.

A sabertooth, limping slightly, paced along the edge of the crevice.

Chapter

4

His spear was gone. All he could find to defend himself
was the gleaming skull of a hyena. Kimba grabbed it and
cocked his arm, ready to throw.

He knew it would not stop a sabertooth. But he could
not just wait there, empty-handed.

The tiger's yellow eyes measured him; its enormous
fangs were bared. The beast was tormented by hunger,
Kimba could see. It was old and partially lame. Perhaps

that was why it had been unable to bring down prey for so long. The boy realized it was willing to concern itself later with getting out of the crevice. First it would eat.

Suddenly he heard a new sound. The cat spun around, hissing, spitting. Something large and red, roaring ferociously, flashed into Kimba's vision.

The tiger hopped backward, one foreleg slapping at its attacker. The other animal dodged, whipped its head and bit savagely. Then it leaped aside, evading the tiger's two fangs.

A wolf, Kimba thought, one of the biggest he had ever seen. It was fast and powerful, with a shaggy, red-speckled coat and blunt, heavy jaws.

The tiger sprang, but the attacker swerved and took another nip. The tiger screamed in pain and fury.

It was not a wolf, Kimba now saw. It was a wild dog, one of the marauding breed that his Tribe feared as much as wolves or lions.

The dog, with a booming growl, lunged and then dodged. The cat clawed at empty air and the dog's teeth slashed the tiger's hindquarters. The sabertooth twisted around, but the dog was out of reach again.

Confused by the dog's speed, wounded and bleeding, the tiger hunched down. Its tail, swishing angrily, sent pebbles sprinkling onto Kimba.

The tiger had no time to gather its wits. The attacker rushed in, feinted, veered, and tore off a chunk of shoulder flesh. As the big cat howled, the dog darted in once more.

This time the tiger was not off guard. Its tawny forepaw

caught the dog's midsection, raking it from spine to belly.

The dog yelped and, in a sudden frenzy, vaulted onto the tiger's back. The sabertooth shot sideways, squirming and squawking. Its massive head swung wildly as it tried to reach up and stab with its deadly fangs.

But the dog bit deeply, twice, and leaped off, out of range once more.

Its muzzle flecked with the tiger's blood, the dog growled steadily. The tiger snarled back, but in it was a whining note, not the chilling ferocity of a few moments before.

Then, like a blazing red torch, the dog flew forward again. The tiger squealed, lashed out with its twin sabers, and missed. As the dog spun about, the cat, with a high-pitched scream, bolted. The dog pursued, snapping and growling.

In seconds, all sound of them had vanished. Kimba leaned limply against a wall of the crevice. He let the hyena skull fall from his hand.

Why, he asked himself, had a wild dog taken on a sabertooth like that? For food? The dog had not looked starved. A sabertooth, even an old and somewhat infirm sabertooth, would ordinarily be too much for any dog, no matter how fast and strong.

Could the dog have wanted Kimba as its own prey? Was it merely putting a rival to rout?

And then it was back. Kimba gasped, looking up at the animal. Its large, smooth-muscled body seemed even redder in the light of the fast-dying sun.

Kimba retrieved the hyena skull, never taking his eyes

off the wild dog. The dog's tongue lolled, and it panted loudly from the exertion of battle. The claw marks along its side looked raw and ugly. Its eyes were brown and un-blinking, expressionless as they fixed on Kimba.

The boy had no idea how long the two of them stood like this, staring.

Suddenly the dog whirled and was gone.

Kimba still did not move. He kept looking at the spot where the dog had stood. It had been a strange experi-ence. Never had he imagined a look such as this passing between himself and one of the Tribe's natural enemies.

Soon it would be dark. He was still trapped in this cleft in the earth, but, oddly, fear had left him after his confrontation with the red-speckled dog.

He knew he must find a way out, and quickly. His hand, exploring the face of the wall, froze at the sound of a soft footfall.

The sabertooth again? Or had the strange wild dog come back?

Rab's face peered down at him.

"Kimba!"

The boy could not believe it. Not after what he had done; not after the way he had harmed the Tribe.

"Rab," he said at last.

"Come!"

Rab poked Kimba's spear down into the crevice. The boy grasped it, braced his feet against the wall, and began climbing. Rab's thick arms tightened as he pulled back on the spear. With a quick heave, Kimba was up and over the edge.

32

Rab lifted him to his feet. He looked the boy over, briskly, to see if there were any serious injuries.

"Rab," Kimba began again.

The hunter slapped the spear into Kimba's hands and, without a word, turned and strode off. Kimba watched, not moving. Rab wheeled. "Come!" he commanded.

The boy trotted after him. Rab was alone, he saw, and he realized what this meant. The Spear-Maker too had broken the Tribal rule never to travel alone.

It was foolhardy of Rab to have followed his trail. It was never done. If someone wandered off, or became too sick to continue the journey, the person was abandoned. It was not cruelty. The Tribe simply could not spare anyone to care for those who could not or would not remain with it.

Stay with the Tribe or perish—that was the rule.

Kimba was hard put to keep up with Rab. But they must not be out long after dark. That would be the most foolhardy mistake of all.

Kimba remembered the anger in Rab's face after he had chased away the One-Tusk. Rab could have slain him then and there. Or at least banished him from the Tribe.

But Rab had defied the Tribe to find Kimba and to save him.

Rab's mouth, he saw, was set in a hard line. Perhaps the Spear-Maker was scolding himself for his weakness. By all rights, the boy should have been left alone to suffer whatever fate awaited him. Now neither of them might ever see the Tribe again.

He would repay Rab, Kimba resolved. He would yet do

something fine and good to show his gratitude! He would yet be the Tribe's ablest hunter!

Seldom did Rab say much. But he was often smiling. Now he was stony faced in the gathering twilight. Kimba, on the verge of collapse, knew only in the most general sense where he was. It was all he could do to keep Rab in sight. They crossed the river at a sandbar. The water was up to Kimba's waist, but Rab did not look back to see if the boy was still behind him. When they reached the cave, Kimba did not realize it at first. It was merely another high bluff, another obstacle to go around. But Rab took him by the neck, pushing him forward, and Kimba realized they were home.

To alert the lookout, Rab gave the Tribe's special whistle—a staccato burst, like a nightbird, followed by a long, trailing-off note. The two of them wound their way around the hearth. The wood fire was ashes now. No one stirred, but Kimba was sure that their late return had brought everyone to wakefulness. He looked into the cave's dark interior, where Odlag's family slept, and he knew his friend Tabok must be watching, wide-eyed and relieved.

Then Urda clutched the boy tightly. "Kimba!" she whispered, and he noticed, despite his fatigue, that there was a quaver in her voice. She gently eased him into his fur blanket. In the moment before he fell into a deep sleep, he touched the wolf tooth hanging from his neck. Perhaps it had helped.

The mutter of quarreling voices woke him. Light was streaming into the cave. His body still ached from the rigors of the day before. Kimba yawned and stretched. Sleep was hard to shake from his system this morning, which was why it took him so long to listen to what the voices were saying.

"His Power is bad! He must go!"

The boy sat upright. Were they talking of him?

"No!" It was Rab. "He has good Power! He will stay!"

"He must go! He must go!"

Kimba slipped over to the wall which separated their sleeping area from the rest of the cave. He peered around. The Tribe had formed a semicircle around Rab and Urda. Many were shouting. Others waved their arms. So jumbled was the noise—like the loud buzzing of infuriated hornets—that Kimba could discern only occasional words.

"We have no meat! He is to blame!"

"He let the One-Tusk escape!"

"His Power is bad! It will harm us all!"

"He is not of the Tribe! He is different!"

"He must go!"

Others took up the cry. It became a chant.

"He must go! He must go! He must go!"

"No!" Rab's voice cut through the din. "No! He will stay!"

"He is young," Urda joined in. "He has much to learn. He will bring us good Power someday!"

"His Power is bad! He must go!"

"He will stay!" Rab took a fighting stance, leveling his spear. "I say he will stay!"

Kimba saw Mrodag, his former companion, in front of the circle. His voice was among the loudest.

Horrified, Kimba shrank back. They wanted to banish him! His people! The Tribe he looked upon as his own!

"He must go!" The other hunters pushed in closer. The older men and women on the fringe, Kimba noticed, had joined in the chant, too.

"He must go! He must go!"

"He will stay!"

"We will watch him," Urda pleaded. "It will not happen again."

"He must go!"

"He will stay!" Rab insisted.

Not only had he given them reason to cast him out, Kimba realized, but now he had caused Rab to be pitted against his own kin. Rab had saved Kimba, and in return Kimba had given him only misfortune.

Better that Rab had not found him! Better that the sabertooth had gotten him!

He had not cried, facing the One-Tusk, facing the sabertooth. Now tears trickled down his cheeks. No one must see them. A hunter did not weep.

Hugging the cold limestone wall, Kimba slipped away from the front of the cave. The men and women, engrossed in their heated argument, did not see him.

The passage turned and Kimba walked faster. They must not find him weeping, that was all he knew. They might banish him, but they would not see his tears. He must bring himself to act like a man and a hunter.

It was dark now and the cave floor was uncluttered. Members of the Tribe lived near the entranceway. They seldom ventured far into the cavern.

The passageway narrowed and assumed the shape of a coiling serpent. But Kimba knew every twist of it. Many hundreds of times he had come this way with Utrek. For Utrek's domain was deep within the cave. There he practiced the most mysterious of his arts.

Kimba felt the coldness and the darkness as a comfort. Here he could find refuge—briefly, at least.

But he remembered his first trip this far into the interior, when he was made Utrek's apprentice. Then it had prompted only fear in him: the stillness, the obscurity, the never-ending chill. Even now, at times, it made him uneasy, but he would never dare admit this.

The tunnel widened into a high-ceilinged gallery that the sorcerer had covered with paintings. Each of them Kimba knew intimately. He had held the torch—a flat piece of rock with a wick in a lump of grease—and mixed the ochre clay powders to produce colors ranging from bright yellow to vermillion red. All the while, he had watched Utrek's every move.

Other paintings he had studied alone, observing each line, tracing them with his fingers, soaking in the knowledge that he must have when, someday, he filled Utrek's role. True, he did not wish to become like Utrek. But the paintings had a quality that enthralled him, that always caught him in a snare of wonder.

He had no torch now, but enough light entered through several tiny slits in the high ceiling to illuminate the marvels upon the walls. Here was a Mighty One, in livid red, its humped head lowered, its massive legs slanted as though it were charging. The painting was larger than the tallest member of the Tribe. Kimba fingered the long tusks and shuddered, recalling yesterday and the sound of the mammoth bearing down on him from behind.

Nearby was a bison, boldly drawn, complete to the bushy fur on its back and the hair beneath its muzzle. It was so real that Kimba could almost catch the animal's pungent scent.

He wandered on among the pictures. They were like old friends, while, out there in the world of sunlight, those he had thought of as friends might now be preparing to expel him from their midst.

Here was a stag's head. And beside it a sturdily built horse, its mane outflung. And then a woolly rhinoceros, ponderous and threatening. And an aurochs, an ibex, a panther. All were painted with sure, masterly strokes. Utrek's bony finger would dance over the wall. He would first use his feather brush, then switch to tufts of fur for certain effects. And in mere moments, Kimba remembered, the animal would seem to come to life.

There had been time to put many paintings on the walls. The Tribe had wintered in the cave as long as Kimba had been with it, and for long before that.

He walked on, through another tunnel. It was very narrow, and the light had faded. The passage dipped and his feet splashed through a frosty puddle formed by a continual dripping from the ceiling.

Beyond it was the Grotto, the largest of the rooms in the cave. This was where Utrek performed his most elaborate rites. Most hunters entered it only half a dozen times a year, beginning with their initiation into manhood. No woman had ever entered it. Because their visits were rare, few of the hunters ever got over their awe of the vast, echoing chamber.

Kimba stepped into it, guiding himself more by memory than sight. The Grotto was almost completely black. Torches had to be used when he and Utrek worked here and when rites were held.

These walls, too, were covered by paintings. Though Kimba could see none of them now, he could go unerringly to any part of the chamber and touch the wall and name the animal reproduced there.

Here was another Mighty One, he knew, feeling a knobby area above his head. Utrek had used that natural swelling to represent the mammoth's forehead. It showed the hump of the head thick with fat, as it was in the autumn—the fat that enabled the Mighty One to live on less food during the season of cold and blizzard. Utrek had constructed the rest of the painting around this bulge. Kimba rubbed the dampness where he knew the tusks were drawn.

Somehow he would still succeed in hunting the Mighty Ones, he told himself. He would yet make the Tribe proud of him.

But how could he if they would not permit him to stay with them?

He must return. He could not let Rab continue to be denounced for his own foolish actions. He must face the

Tribe. The tears had long since ceased, and it was not the way of a hunter to cower and hide.

But in this darkness he felt protected. Surrounded by the animals of the Grotto, he felt safe.

Sighing, he stepped back toward the entrance to the Grotto.

The blackness suddenly erupted in a bright shaft of light. Kimba whirled.

A form moved toward him, shimmering a whitish green. It had wide, spreading antlers, outthrust claws, a long and flaring tail. Its face was bestial, but it walked on two feet.

Chapter

5

For an instant, Kimba froze with fear. He knew this figure, knew it well. But momentarily he had been taken by surprise. And the sight was a terrifying one.

"Utrek?" he asked, and was aware his voice sounded like the peep of a newly hatched bird.

"Why are you here, Kimba?"

The boy backed up until he felt the cold wall behind

him. The sorcerer—in the most sacred and mystifying of his costumes—loomed over him.

Utrek had appeared from his secret den, Kimba realized. The boy had never seen it, never been in it, as often as he had worked with the sorcerer in the Grotto. It was a place permitted for Utrek alone.

Kimba turned his head away. He could not look directly into that awful, gleaming, beastlike face.

"The Tribe," he said. "They will banish me."

"What?"

"They will banish me."

He heard the heavy snorts that were Utrek's manner of breathing. "Come," said the sorcerer.

Bathed in the whitish green color, Utrek seemed to float along the cave floor. He carried a juniper-bush torch that burned brightly without emitting the sooty smoke that a pine branch would. They passed through a thin slit that Kimba had never before noticed and climbed a narrow passageway that ended in a small chamber.

In the flickering light, Kimba saw furs, tools, and other shadowy objects scattered about. The stalactites on the roof, like irregular rows of teeth, hung down just over Utrek's head. The sorcerer handed Kimba the torch.

"Is it because of the Mighty One that was lost to us?" he asked.

"Yes. They will banish me."

"Do not tell me what they will do. You still thirst to be a hunter?"

"Yes."

"Even after yesterday?"

"Yes."

"You have the Power, Kimba! You must use it for the Tribe! Let the hunters risk their skins! There are many hunters. But the Power is rare! Do not let some Mighty One—"

The pitch of his voice rose and the words grew indistinct. Tufts of his beard had gotten into his mouth, as they often did, and caused him to sputter as he talked. Utrek never seemed to be aware of it until he had finished what he had to say. Then he would make a face and rub his hand over his lips, clearing the strands away.

He pulled off the bear cuffs and claws covering his hands. Gripping the antlers, he lifted off the mask. It was made of the hide of some animal, with evil-looking eyebrows and mouth and a hideous nose painted on in red and blue. Then he removed the bison robe with its sewn-on wolf's tail. Kimba stared at the glowing bits of costume on the cave floor.

Utrek stooped, his knees cracking, and raised a skin covering. There, on the floor, a small nest glittered with the same sort of light the costume had given off.

"Do you know it?" he asked.

Kimba leaned closer. It was fox fire, the luminous fungus he had seen growing around the thick roots of certain trees.

Utrek picked some of it up and demonstrated how he smeared it over his mask and robe. Kimba hesitantly touched the gleaming mask.

"Remember," Utrek said, "not to let the Tribe see you gathering it. They must not know how it is done."

43

Groaning, the old man lowered himself onto a thick pile of hides. "There is much you must learn yet." He pointed with one of the two fingers on his left hand. "Bring me that," he ordered.

Kimba tugged a large, leathery bundle over to Utrek. It felt like the pelt of a woolly rhinoceros.

"I have never carried this," said Kimba. During the summer, when the Tribe left the cave to travel about in pursuit of game, it was Kimba's task to carry many of Utrek's possessions.

"It remains here, in the secret place, even when the Tribe is gone. No one else dares enter here." He undid the thong around the bundle while Kimba squatted close by.

There were furs and paints and masks and whistles, the boy could see. Then Utrek lifted high a smooth, curly-haired skin. It was that of a bison. The black horns still projected from the head. Utrek shook it out, then thrust it at Kimba.

"Yours," he said.

Kimba held the bison hide at arm's length, admiring it. "Eh! Eh!" Utrek motioned to him to put it on.

It was much larger than he was. It engulfed him when he slipped into it, and he had to let almost half of it drag behind. He pulled the hood low over his face. It was warm and stifling, but immediately he felt different: powerful, mysterious, able to work wonders.

He began a slow, shuffling dance. He had not intended to, but something seemed to possess him. It was as though he had gotten out of his own skin and into the bison's.

44

His feet jerked forward in quick, prancing steps; his head bowed and rose rhythmically.

Feelings welled up in him as he danced—feelings of strength, of speed, of oneness with all the creatures that thundered over the grasslands.

Afterward, he was quiet. He allowed the awareness of who he was and where he was to flow back in.

In that costume, in that dance, he had been something other than himself. With the memory still fresh, he became confused again. Was this the Power? Had the Power worked through him?

"Good," Utrek said. "Good."

He instructed Kimba to put the costume in a corner that now was his. He was free to enter the secret den whenever he chose. And Utrek would come here with him. For now he would learn the deeper mysteries.

"Why now, Utrek?"

"Because now is the time. The Tribe must know that you are to remain with us. I have chosen you to follow me and they must know that this is how it will be. I have not taught you as much as I might have. Now I will do so. There is still much more for you to learn."

The skills of the sorcerer, he went on, must be worked at continually. The paintings were most important, for it was they which would magically produce game for the hunters. But Kimba would also be taught the rites to transform boys into men and the rites to send the dead on their long journey. And he would learn the ways of healing, the ways of foreseeing the future by gazing at the

45

heavens, and the legends that must always be kept alive and told to the Tribe as new generations appeared.

Already Kimba had much of the Power, Utrek said. It was born in him, just as it had been born into Utrek. It took a long, long time to learn to manage the Power so the Tribe would reap its benefits. But it had been born into Kimba, and this had been clear from the beginning.

The sorcerer reminded Kimba of how he had joined the Tribe. It had been during this very season, a warm day in a series of chilly days when rain mixed with snow had fallen. The Tribe had been following a game trail and, suddenly, there ahead of them had appeared a child.

It was a boy who did not look to be beyond two summers of age. He was seated on a rock and his hand was outstretched. Standing on it was a ground squirrel that was not many days old itself. The boy was smiling and chuckling at the little animal. It kept looking at him and seemed to have no fright. He did nothing to trap it or prevent it from running away.

"I did not understand," said Utrek. "But I felt the Power at work in you."

The child had smiled at the members of the Tribe, no more afraid of them than the squirrel was of him. The hunters had fanned out and searched the area, warily, with spears ready. Eventually, they had found the body of a man, partially buried by a large rockslide. There must have been others under there, but the boulders were too heavy to move. The little boy must have wandered off from his party just before an avalanche of melting snow had loosened the rocks.

"That, too, was an omen," said Utrek. "You had been spared—and no one else. And the Tribe came to you almost at once. If we had not arrived . . ."

The boy had been able to speak a few words in a tongue they understood, and he had given his name as Kimba. He had not known what had happened to his people. He could not say if they had been part of a larger party. He had cried, at last, when the Tribe had taken him along on its journey.

But he had adapted quickly to his new situation. To the Tribe he remained a mystery—a child with strange, wide-set green eyes. All others in the Tribe had eyes of brown. He was a child who at five summers was demonstrating the ability to scratch on boulders and make amazingly accurate likenesses of game animals. He was a child who manifested the Power more surely than Utrek had at the same age.

"I have wondered if others among you had the Power, too," Utrek said. "I have wondered what sort of tribe they were."

"I remember only a woman who held me often," said Kimba, "and a man who picked me up and threw me in the air and whose face was rough when he rubbed it against mine. I remember being carried on long marches and being awakened once by shouts and screams. I remember a river and fish caught and thrown, flopping, beside me. I remember nothing else of that time.

"I remember well," he said, "only you and Urda and Rab and the rest of the Tribe. I remember no faces from before you found me."

47

Utrek recalled that the Tribe had inquired about Kimba's origins of every other band it had met. None had ever heard of such a boy or known who his people might be.

"I have no other people!" Kimba exclaimed. "I am of the Tribe!"

And then his voice fell so that Utrek could scarcely hear him. "But now they will banish me."

"They will not," the sorcerer said.

"They say my Power is bad. How can you show them it is not?"

"You will see." It was necessary at times, Utrek continued, to do what some birds do when their young are threatened by a hungry animal. The bird pretends to have a broken wing. The predator, thinking she will be easily caught, follows her. She leads it away from her brood. And then she suddenly flies away.

What he meant, Utrek explained, was that in some situations there is a need to prevent trouble by diverting attention.

"Come along," he told Kimba.

Back they went, through the dark, looping corridors, until the light became clear and Kimba could see a cluster of people. Silence fell as Utrek and Kimba appeared. Urda moved toward the boy, as though to shield him, but the sorcerer motioned her away.

Utrek and Kimba stood at the entrance to the cave. Members of the Tribe began to gather around them. There was a loud shout from Narik, Mrodag's father. He

48

was with a group of hunters spread out in a line and searching the broken flatland in the distance.

"There he is!" Narik shouted, and the hunters ran back toward the cave.

"We have been hunting him," Narik said to Utrek. He was a huge, grizzled man, next only to Utrek in age. His body was a mass of battle scars. "He must go! His Power is bad! It will kill us all!"

"He must go!" repeated Mrodag, joining the crowd. "He must go!"

Rab pushed to the front of the throng to stand near Kimba. But Narik shouldered his way past Rab and poked a thick finger at the boy.

"He is not of the Tribe! It was wrong to take him in! He has brought bad Power!"

Swiftly, Utrek swung his staff, filed to a needle point, so that it all but touched Narik's heart. The big hunter, startled, took a few steps backward.

"His Power is not bad!" Utrek declared. "Only I can judge whose Power is good and whose is bad! Kimba's Power is good. My final journey must start soon. Who will summon the game then? One of you? None of you has the Power. In winters to come, Kimba's Power will mean the difference between life and death!"

"He cost us the Mighty One!" Narik protested. "We have no meat!"

"We will have meat," Utrek said. "I will summon game today! I will use my Power! And Kimba's Power will help! I will hold a Summoning Rite! Today!"

Cheers rang out, and there were cries of: "Good! Good! We will have meat!"

"Make ready," Utrek said, "for the Summoning Rite! Make ready! Come, Kimba!"

He led the boy back into the cave. The Tribe watched, quiet now, respecting the privacy and the responsibility of these two who had the Power.

Kimba noticed that Narik was scowling. But the rest of the hunters seemed elated, and Kimba's friend Tabok had broken into a wide grin.

Utrek had not called a Summoning Rite for a long while, although the Tribe's need was great. It had seldom happened that at this season the herds they fed from were so hard to find. With the melting of the snows, game ordinarily would be more plentiful.

Some of the hunters had suggested a Summoning Rite, but without stating their wish bluntly—for no one could make demands of the sorcerer. All in the Tribe were conscious that there were only rare periods when the rite could be effective, and that these times were known only to those with the Power.

Utrek, by announcing the rite, had made it clear that at last this was the proper time. So it must be, Kimba decided. Surely Utrek would not have made the decision just because of Kimba's predicament. Surely the decision was based on Utrek's secret knowledge of the ways of the animals. It must be, the boy surmised, that the fortunate timing of the Summoning Rite was but another example of the sorcerer's Power.

It was a ceremony Kimba had grown to know well. As

usual, he would be concealed behind a large, square boulder that bulged out of one wall in the Grotto.

Just as the sun stood directly overhead, the men began filing into the cave. They had daubed their bodies with paint, as Utrek had directed, and each held a spear or club.

They hesitated on the threshold of the Grotto, then stepped in. Two fires were burning on the red clay soil. The hunters' shadows seemed to leap about the huge chamber, sometimes mingling with the figures of the beasts painted on the walls.

The hunters seemed awed and alone in the hushed chamber. Mrodag, especially, who had seen few of these rites, cast his eyes about nervously. His jutting jaw was held high, but Kimba noticed—with some pleasure—that the young hunter's hands were shaking.

Then a high, weird crooning began. It seemed to have no source. It rebounded off the walls and the vaulted roof. It stopped, but its echo persisted.

Suddenly Utrek stood before them. He had entered through the hole to the secret den, and appeared so swiftly that he might have materialized out of nothingness. He wore the same glowing costume that had so surprised Kimba. The hunters had seen it before, yet it always brought a gasp from them.

The sorcerer uttered a piercing howl, gesticulating with his bear-claw hands, doing a rapid jig with his feet. Gone was the slowness and stiffness of an old man. For this rite, for these few moments, he had made himself into something ageless.

He whirled about the room, glistening with the radiance of the fox fire, his shadow monstrous on the dim walls. Before the painted portrait of a mammoth his dance stopped. He faced the Mighty One, shrilling even louder. He flung his hands out at the creature, as though his gesture had caused it to come into being. The sounds he made rose to an inhuman peak. They became a bloodcurdling shriek, and he lunged at the Mighty One on the wall, clawing it fiercely.

This was Kimba's signal. Hidden behind the boulder, he dropped grass and shredded birch bark into the fire near him. The flames shot up, vividly illuminating Utrek.

Utrek danced back a few steps, then once more screeched and clawed at the mammoth. Again Kimba, unseen by the hunters, dropped tinder on the fire. The flames soared.

The hunters leaned forward, almost hypnotized. Who could doubt the sorcerer's Power? Who could doubt he would produce game for them?

Now Utrek motioned to the hunters. They let out ear-shattering yells and waved their weapons. Hopping from one foot to the other, they surrounded the Mighty One's picture.

Utrek slipped to the edge of the tightly pressed mass of men. His loud, insistent voice goaded them into faster, more abandoned sounds. The tempo of the dancing picked up. Soon they were hurling their bodies to and fro, their throats taut with the force of their savage cries.

Kimba's blood seemed to thrum with excitement. He

longed to join them and lift his voice in a fearsome, numb-
ing shriek.

"The Mighty One!" shouted Utrek. "The Mighty One!
It is ours! It is ours!"

He signaled Kimba. The boy dumped the last of the
grass and bark onto the fire. It flared up, almost licking
the ceiling.

The hunters roared, filled with a sudden sense of their
prowess and invincibility.

They thrust their spears at the mammoth and struck
their clubs at it, screaming in fury and defiance. Again
and again, they attacked.

"Now!" Utrek cried out. "Now!"

The hunters turned from the beast on the wall. Still
shouting, they dashed from the Grotto, eager to begin the
chase, sure they would find game, certain they would succeed in downing it.

"You thirst to go along?" Utrek asked, his voice low
and hoarse after the strain he had put upon it.

"Yes," said Kimba.

"You are not to hunt, as I told you yesterday when you
sought to disobey me. But I must remember that you are
still a boy and the ways of the hunter stir your blood. And
it is necessary that you know the animals."

He handed Kimba a flint and a limestone drawing
block. "You must go near them if you are to learn to
make them come alive on the walls. To make them know
it is their lot to feed and clothe the Tribe, you must feel
your kinship to them."

He paused a moment. "And it must become clearer to the Tribe that you have the Power. Go then."

"Yes!" Kimba agreed enthusiastically. He ran from the chamber and raised his voice in imitation of the yell the hunters had given.

"Kimba!"

The boy looked back.

"But do not go too near," Utrek said.

Chapter

6

There was a doubtful look on Rab's face. If Kimba had disobeyed Utrek again . . .

"He told me to come," the boy said, hastily displaying the piece of limestone and the flint he was to sketch with. Kimba fell into step beside Rab.

Narik frowned, still not assured that the boy's Power was good. He grumbled in a muted voice to his son, Mrodag. What did they know of Kimba, despite what

Utrek had said? Nobody knew whose whelp he was. Nobody knew what he would grow into. It was like adopting a bear cub. Later it would turn on those who had pitied it. Better to slay it at once.

Kimba felt the old hunter's anger. He realized he would be blamed every time Narik's hungry stomach growled for meat.

The boy hefted his spear. Of course he would obey Utrek. He was here to sketch, not to hunt. Yet, he thought, once game was seen, many things could happen. There might be a chance for him to rush in. Maybe he might beat them all in the attack.

The hunters were moving in an irregular line, several paces apart. Their eyes roved back and forth. They were all tall men and beside them Kimba looked small. Skins of wolf, reindeer, or bison covered their bodies and were lashed about their feet.

Most had taken their largest spears, anticipating a chance to meet another Mighty One. Others were armed with throwing sticks and axes—short clubs with heads of sharp, pointed stone—for hunting smaller game.

They had gone again to the wide river, proceeded north beside it for some distance, then crossed at a spot where glacial rocks were scattered in a bridgelike formation. They pushed onward in the direction of the sun's rising. Here the meadowland was rough. Small patches of forest offered easy concealment to hunted creatures.

Rab, on the far left, stopped. He cocked his head, touched his ear, and pointed toward a jumble of rocks and gullies.

Narik listened and shook his head. He had detected nothing.

But he was older and his sense of hearing was weakening, the others knew. One hunter nodded at Rab and began to run toward the rocks. This was Odlag, the father of Kimba's friend Tabok.

Kimba heard a noise, too. It was a faint snuffling, hard to distinguish.

Odlag clambered over the rocks and into a small ravine. He came to an abrupt halt. Something streaked toward him, then quickly turned and dashed off. The hunters took up pursuit.

The narrow ravine permitted only two or three men to stand side by side. Odlag gestured at something on the ground, but he did not stop running. The others saw what it was: a dead boar. Whatever had slain it had just begun to tear off hunks of flesh when the hunters had surprised it.

Now they would have the boar—and the flesh of its slayer, too! "After it!" Narik cried. Then he stopped so suddenly that those immediately behind crashed into him.

This was the head of the ravine, a high barricade of rock. There was no exit. Odlag, the first man to follow the killer of the boar, crouched, facing the trapped beast of prey.

There was a menacing growl. Odlag yelled and hurled a javelin from his throwing stick.

Kimba wiggled through the knot of hunters to see what had happened. Odlag had missed. The animal sprang.

It was the large, red-speckled dog.

The onrush bowled Odlag over. He tried to grip the

dog's throat, to fend off the snapping teeth. The two rolled over in the confused fury of close combat.

The hunters pressed forward, but were unable to act. They might easily have hit Odlag instead of the dog.

Suddenly Odlag was knocked flat on his back. The dog looked up for an instant, to glare defiance at the men crowding in with raised spears.

Then its eyes met Kimba's.

The snarl died. A strange look, a look of familiarity, passed between them. It was the same look they had exchanged after the dog had routed the sabertooth.

"Kill!" Narik shrieked.

"The Mighty Ones!" Kimba shouted.

"Where?"

"There! I saw them!" The boy pointed toward the east, toward the closest table-shaped plateau.

The hunters whipped about to look. The dog darted forward in a dizzying burst of speed. Powerful legs propelled its huge body through the ranks of the hunters, tossing them aside.

They cried out in surprise. Mrodag alone reacted quickly enough to jab at the blur of red. But it was too late. The dog was past them. Two unleashed their javelins, but the casts were too hurried. The dog bounded up the rocks out of the ravine and was gone.

Never mind, Rab told them. Let the dog go. The Mighty Ones had been sighted.

"I do not see them," said Narik.

"Where?" Mrodag demanded.

"There," said Kimba.

58

"That is not where he first pointed," Narik put in.

"That is the way they were going," said Kimba.

"Come," said Rab.

Kimba felt suddenly weak, as though he would not be able to walk. For he had not seen any Mighty Ones. He did not know why he had shouted that he had. He only knew they had been about to kill the dog, and he desperately had not wanted them to.

So he had yelled the only thing he knew that would distract the hunters long enough to let the dog escape.

And why should he let the dog escape? he asked himself. The Tribe needed meat. One such animal would not satisfy the entire Tribe. But wild dogs were fair game, just like bison and reindeer.

He had again acted contrary to the interests of the Tribe. True, the dog had saved his life. But why must the Tribe lose because he chose to repay a debt of gratitude?

It was a hunter's part to kill wild game. Did he not still thirst to be a hunter?

Shame drenched him. They would soon know he had seen no Mighty Ones. He had disgraced Rab once more.

Odlag struggled up. He was torn and bleeding from his fight with the dog, but able to continue. Maybe Utrek would have something to put on the wounds later. Until then, Odlag would have to endure the pain in silence and keep up with the rest. There was no time for pity from the others, and no hunter would waste energy pitying himself. Thoughts of pain were shoved aside at once.

Narik looked at Kimba suspiciously. Now they would know, he said, if the boy's Power was good or bad.

And if it was bad . . . He left the threat unspoken.

Kimba lagged behind the others. Maybe his Power *was* bad. He had not intended to hurt the Tribe. But that was all he seemed to be doing. Maybe his Power was so bad that it made him do these evil things in spite of himself.

He should tell Rab, he knew. Tell him there were no Mighty Ones, that it had been a made-up story. And then he must let them do to him what they felt was just. Utrek was not here to protect him. Now those who wanted to banish him might have their way.

Banishment would almost certainly lead to his death, he was aware. No one could survive for a long period without the assistance of kin or companions. For someone alone, death might not be immediate. But it would certainly come.

Yet Kimba could not continue to lead them astray. He tugged at Rab's elbow.

The Spear-Maker placed a hand on the boy's shoulder, as he often did.

"Rab . . . Rab . . ."

A hunter waggled his spear in great glee. "Mighty Ones! Mighty Ones!"

To Kimba, it was as though a heavy boulder had been lifted from his back. He, like the others, squinted at a ribbon of light green. It was a grove of poplars that seemed to stitch together the choppy meadowland and the foothills that led to the next steep plateau. Something was moving among those trees.

Yes! It was the Mighty Ones.

They were very near the spot at which Kimba had

pointed. Rab grinned at Narik, as though to say: You see, the boy *did* sight them!

Now, Kimba realized, he need not admit his deception. But was it a deception? Could the Power actually have caused him to point as he had, even though he had not known it at the time?

Such thoughts made his head whirl, as it did when he stared too long at the moon. Such thoughts were too complicated, too unnatural. He knew the hunters would never understand. Even Rab would not. They were good, simple men. They left such thoughts to those like Utrek who dealt with the unseen.

Almost at once, the Mighty Ones—for it had looked like a herd of the shaggy giants—were lost to sight amid the faraway trees. When the hunters reached this thin stretch of forest, the mammoths were still nowhere to be seen. The men began to climb the lowest of the plateau's foothills.

Then they heard a sound that stopped them instantly. It was the angry, thunderous trumpeting of two bull mammoths.

Only for a moment did the men pause, glancing furtively at each other. Then, knowing the Tribe had to have meat, they continued up the sand and thick grass of the hillside. Once at the top, they lay down flat and stared into the valley.

They made no effort to quiet their grunts of wonder. The noises below were so loud that their voices could not have been heard.

The sight was one that not even Narik had witnessed

before. Two immense bulls were battling to the death for the supremacy of the herd. The other Mighty Ones, ten or fifteen of them, watched from a safe distance.

The valley was a natural arena, wide and open except for sparse patches of vegetation and clusters of rocks. The hillside where the hunters lay formed one wall of the arena. The other wall—the far slope of the valley—rose steeply until it joined the sheer cliffside of the plateau.

The rounded, wrinkled heads of the bulls butted together. Their hairy trunks gouged at one another. And their curving tusks, longer than a man was tall, hooked and stabbed cruelly.

One of them, Kimba observed, was the One-Tusk! He poked Rab, but the Spear-Maker had seen it, too.

The One-Tusk, despite its handicap, was bigger and more aggressive. Its legs were as thick as tree trunks. Its gigantic humped body moved lightly. Its lone tusk was everywhere, slashing from both sides, pulling back, thrusting from the front.

The One-Tusk had been alone before. Now evidently it intended to destroy this bull mammoth and take over for itself the herd of females and their young.

There were bright stains of blood spattered over the long, stiff, hairy coats of both beasts, but there were not so many on the One-Tusk. Its opponent shrilled powerfully, but the One-Tusk's bellow was even louder.

Their heads smashed together once more. Their tusks locked and they stood, pushing and swaying, trumpeting into each other's faces.

Rab leaped up and signaled the other hunters.

Now was the time! While the two bulls fought each other, the rest of the herd would not expect an attack.

The hunters were not close enough to rain boulders down on the animals, and there were no deep holes below to use as traps. They would have to engage the Mighty Ones at close range. When they had been compelled to do this before, they had usually cut the leg tendons of the lumbering creatures. This either brought them down at once or so crippled them that the hunters could follow until they fell. But it was dangerous and very uncertain work.

Kimba rose, too, but Rab pushed him down. He grinned and pointed to the boy's sketching block. There would be much to draw! There would never be a better chance to see so many Mighty Ones!

The boy sank back onto the sand at the top of the hill. He watched the hunters wind their way into the valley. Then he turned back to the bulls and began sketching. With quick strokes of his flint, he reproduced their battle on the flat stone.

The two mammoths were still locked together by their tusks, hurling their tons of weight against each other, pulverizing the ground under them.

The hunters were slipping up on the nearest cow mammoths now, approaching from the off-wind side, spreading out like a noose about to be pulled tight. Popping up and down in the bushes and behind rocks, they drifted toward their target.

Kimba tensed. The sight of the mammoths was vivid in his mind. He could sketch them later in greater detail.

Now would be the time for him to join the hunters. Now he would not be stopped! He would do as Utrek had directed—make likenesses of the Mighty Ones. But he would participate in his first hunt, too!

There was a sudden bellow. The One-Tusk had pulled free and with one rapid movement had sunk its lance of ivory deep into its enemy's throat.

The roars of the dying Mighty One turned to squeals, and its gigantic bulk leaned sideways and crashed to earth.

The victor raised its trunk in triumph. Its blood-covered tusk shimmered in the late afternoon sun. It trumpeted again, and this time no rival dared offer challenge.

Kimba looked back at the hunters. The cow mammoths still had not detected them. They were very close now. In an instant, they would race in, spears flashing. Kimba began to run down the hillside.

Then the One-Tusk bellowed once more. But not in victory this time. There was rage in the sound.

Horrified, Kimba realized that the large bull had seen the hunters. It came bursting toward them, shrilling its anger.

The hunters scattered, while the rest of the herd began to echo the One-Tusk's trumpeting. The bull mammoth bore down on the nearest man. Its trunk picked him up and smashed him to the ground. Without stopping, the One-Tusk changed course and started after the next hunter.

The man stumbled, fell, and screamed as the huge

body galloped over him. The One-Tusk turned and made for its next victim.

The hunter ran desperately for the hillside. But for such a clumsy-looking beast, the mammoth's speed was startling. It closed the distance quickly.

As the Mighty One was about to trample him, the man whirled. Kimba saw, with a shock, that it was Rab.

He pushed his spear into the mammoth's charging body and dodged to one side. The Mighty One screeched in pain and savagely hooked its tusk up, catching Rab on it.

Chapter

7

The pace set by the hunters was far too slow for Kimba. As soon as the cave fires came into view, he had begun running. He had to tell Utrek at once, so the sorcerer would be prepared when they brought in Rab.

It had been a mournful journey from the valley where the One-Tusk had defeated them. Two of their tribesmen lay dead there. Rab still lived, but just barely. He had leaned on the shoulders of two fellow hunters during the long journey back. He had lost much blood.

The Mighty One's tusk had gone in through his shoulder and out through his back. After goring him the mammoth had tossed Rab aside and had gone after other hunters. Kimba had rushed down and dragged the Spear-Maker to cover in some underbrush. The One-Tusk, only scratched by Rab's spear, had sounded its victory call again and led its herd away.

In spite of the deaths of their two companions and Rab's serious injury, the hunters had taken time to hack off pieces of meat from the fallen bull mammoth.

Kimba had fretted and pestered them to start back, but he did not blame them. Here was meat, and the Tribe needed meat. The dead could not be helped now and the condition of one man, Rab, could not outweigh the needs of the Tribe.

Still, as shaken as they were, they had done their work briskly and rapidly. They ate some of the meat raw to strengthen themselves for the return march. Then each was given a large piece to carry back.

Several times on the trip home it had seemed as though Rab would have to be abandoned. But Kimba had talked to him, urging him to open his eyes, to stay on his feet. Each time, fighting hard to remain conscious, the Spear-Maker had kept going.

Now the boy ran up to the cooking fire. The women and children hurried to meet him, anxious for news of the day's hunt. They smiled when they saw the chunk of rib meat that Kimba carried. Then they noticed the desperate look on his face and their smiles disappeared.

"What is it, Kimba?" his friend Tabok asked. "What has happened?"

"Utrek!" Kimba called, brushing past the questioners.

The sorcerer got up from the fire. He leaned heavily ôn his staff, for at night the aches in his bones grew worse.

"Utrek!"

"It is Rab," the old man said quietly, not needing an explanation. He hobbled back toward the Grotto, where he kept his remedies.

That night the clammy walls of the cave rang with sobs and laments for the two men who had fallen to the One-Tusk. The members of the Tribe had eaten well at last, but this did not compensate for the loss they had suffered.

Urda said nothing as she sat beside Rab, holding his hand while he tossed and moaned. Utrek knelt beside him, changing the poultice of leaves and mud he had put on the wounds.

Kimba squatted at Rab's feet. The boy's arms were clasped about his knees and he peered, unblinking, into the face of the Spear-Maker.

Utrek's Power must work, Kimba told himself. It must. Rab must live. Utrek would know how to make him well again.

Kimba placed another branch on the fire. It was his task to keep it going throughout the night, as though while the flames still flickered so would the life of the wounded man.

Narik strode over, looking from Rab to Utrek. "The Power was bad," he said.

"A cloud covered the sun after the Summoning Rite," Utrek replied. "It undid the good Power."

"Your Power was good," said Narik. "We found meat." He pointed at Kimba. "*His* Power is bad! His Power made the One-Tusk attack! His Power undid the good of yours!"

"No!" Utrek insisted. "It was a cloud covering the sun. A large, dark cloud. I saw it after you left. It was too late to call you back."

"Two hunters lost!" Narik exclaimed. "And Rab?"

The sorcerer gently lifted the fur blanket and studied the shoulder wound. "It does not go well."

"Ha!" snorted Narik. His frown was ugly and twisted. "The boy's Power is bad. It will be the end of us all!"

Urda's face was pale and beseeching as she looked up at Utrek. "What can save Rab?" she asked.

Utrek got up stiffly. He kept his back to Urda and Kimba. He fingered his beard a long while.

"It will not be easy. Sometimes there is nothing that can be done to keep a hunter from the final journey."

"But Utrek," Kimba pleaded in a trembling whisper, "there must be a way. And *you* would know it!"

The sorcerer was silent a long while. "Unless . . ." he said at length.

"Yes?" Urda asked quickly.

"If anything is to save him, it would be the tip of the tusk that gored him. Only that. It must be touched to his wound."

69

"And that will heal him?" Kimba said.

"Yes."

Urda lowered her head. "There is no way then," she murmured.

"Without the piece of tusk," Kimba said very softly, "Rab will begin his final journey?"

"I cannot say for certain. Rab may be as he is now for many days, and his fate cannot be known yet. I know only that nothing more of my Power will help."

"But the tip of the tusk . . . ?"

"Only that would surely bring recovery. Only that."

Instantly Kimba was on his feet.

The One-Tusk! There was hope then!

He scurried over to the nearest hunter, excitedly reporting what Utrek had said.

"We must go in the morning! After the One-Tusk!"

The hunter only stared at Kimba, then turned his face away. Kimba hurried to the next man. He, too, did not answer.

Narik overheard the boy's pleas. "Go after the One-Tusk?" he shouted. "After today? Would you have us lose all our hunters? Is that it?"

"We go back for more meat from the slain Mighty One," Odlag called over. "It will feed the Tribe for days. But the One-Tusk? No."

Narik now shook the boy violently. "You hear? We will not hunt this One-Tusk! This is a trick of yours! Your Power is bad! You would do away with us all!"

He flung Kimba aside, as he would a gnawed bone he

was done with. "Better to lose Rab than to give more hunters to the One-Tusk!"

Kimba crept back to the fire. He was stunned. They would not even attempt it! Not even to save Rab. He could not believe it.

As the night wore on, the fire burned low. And Rab became more ashen, more still. All were asleep within the cave now, except Urda, Utrek, and Kimba. Finally the sorcerer, too, dozed off by the fire. Kimba sat cross-legged, brooding.

Rab had saved his life. More, Rab was like his own father. He could not just wait day after day, sitting helplessly here or calmly painting pictures, knowing nothing was being done. Someone must try, at least. Someone must go after the One-Tusk.

Very cautiously, his hand slithered out and closed on Rab's reindeer antler knife. Utrek had unslung it when he had first probed the wound. Kimba concealed the knife with both his hands and stole away from the flames.

Urda had her eyes fixed on Rab and did not notice him leave.

Swiftly, the boy went to his sleeping area. He hung Rab's knife around one shoulder and snatched up his own spear. What else would he need? He pondered a moment, then picked up a handful of flints and two handfuls of moss to use as a fire starter. He put these in the small deerskin bag tied to his waist.

Kimba recoiled at a slight, sudden noise behind him. It was Tabok, and he was clutching his father's throwing stick and javelin.

"I am coming," he whispered.

"No!" Kimba said.

"Let us go now."

"No!" Kimba repeated. "You are too small. You are not a hunter yet."

As he said it, he realized how the hunters must regard him. Not a hunter yet! He had been told that often. How could he refuse Tabok in the same way they had refused him?

Yet he believed that he could succeed in this mission. Did he not have the Power? But he knew he had to attempt it by himself. Tabok would be of little help, and he must not let the younger boy endanger himself. Besides, he lived with Rab. Tabok did not.

Nevertheless, he felt comforted that his friend was willing to take this risk. He touched Tabok on both shoulders. "You will be a hunter soon!" he whispered.

It was just after dawn. The lookout at the cave entrance would be brought to full attention by anyone or anything that approached. But his senses were not attuned to being alert for anyone inside who might wish to slip out.

So Kimba, moving stealthily, was unseen as he left. Shortly after midday he was a great distance from the cave.

Padding along briskly, he retraced the route the hunters had followed the day before, crossing the river and traveling in a straight line toward the valley where they had last seen the One-Tusk.

He had violated the Tribe's rule again, he knew. What he was doing was inexcusable—unless he succeeded. If he did not, even Utrek could no longer shelter him from their anger.

He trotted on into a small, dark forest of chestnut, black oak, and sharp-needled firs not far from the ravine where the dog had attacked Odlag. Kimba pushed the branches aside impatiently.

There was a whisper of movement across the sodden leaves covering the earth.

He ignored it. There would be birds and rodents here. It was nothing more than that. He hurried on.

A branch snapped.

He turned, saw nothing, and went on. But now he was running.

He heard a soft, swishing noise. It seemed close behind him.

Kimba thought of what he had heard the hunters say: Beware that when you are stalking something, something else is not stalking you.

He batted the branches aside. There was a clearing, and he raced through it. Then the trees closed in again. The sound behind him was more insistent now, the soft sighing sound of something moving rapidly through the dense underbrush.

Branches slapped his face, but he did not slacken his pace. This was not a large piece of woodland, yet it seemed never to end.

And then he tripped on a twisted oak root, his spear dropped from his hand, and his face met the soft, wet dirt.

Squirming around, he groped for the knife.

He heard a ticking, slavering sound almost on top of him.

He cleared his eyes. The large red dog was there, panting hard, its tongue dripping. Flat on the earth as he was, he thought the animal looked as big as a bison.

Its eyes were on him again.

Kimba remembered how viciously the dog had fought the sabertooth, how it had slashed Odlag.

He swung the dagger free. He pointed it at the dog's thick, matted chest. He waited, trying not to let his hand tremble, staring as hard as the dog was.

The animal did not move either. Its muscles did not tense. Its fierce muzzle gaped open, but there was no snarl.

At last Kimba realized that the beast was not going to spring on him.

Careful to make no quick movements, the boy regained his feet. He kept the knife ready. Still the dog did not stir.

Kimba backed away, two paces, three, four. The dog was immobile.

He retrieved his spear and began walking. So did the dog, close to his side now.

The boy picked up his pace, and still the dog was beside him. Uneasy, Kimba kept glancing to his right. The dog maintained its distance, seldom looking at the boy. Yet no matter how often he changed his course, it tagged along near him.

After a while, he slung the knife back over his shoulder and relaxed the tight grip he had been keeping on the spear.

Chapter

8

Soon Kimba no longer bothered to look when the dog strayed from his line of sight. Perhaps, he thought, it was not hungry. When it felt its appetite rising, then he might have cause to fear it.

But somehow he did not think so.

Surely it meant him no harm. Soon it would wander off and let him be.

The wind grew stronger and sharper. On such a day, many scents were blown about. Kimba noticed the dog sniffing first the air, then the earth. It loped forward purposefully toward a bushy clump. A small antelope bolted out into the open. The dog gave chase.

The antelope was swift, probably too swift for its pursuer. But the red-speckled dog would not give up. Kimba remained motionless long after the two had disappeared among the trees.

The dog would not return, he was sure. He need no longer guard against any abrupt change in its behavior.

The knowledge that the dog had gone should have pleased him. It did not, he realized. It only made him more aware that he was alone.

But he must not linger. He had his quest, and there was not a moment to lose.

Kimba continued on, concentrating on the urgency of the task. He would begin his search where he had last seen the killer mammoth: the valley where the two tribesmen had perished. He made himself picture that long, deadly shaft of ivory and the mammoth's dreadful rampage.

What could he do if he met the One-Tusk? What could he possibly do?

He was small and alone and had yet to sink his spear into any wild creature.

And he was hungry, tired, and—the truth he had been avoiding dawned on him clearly—very afraid.

Kimba touched the wolf tooth hanging about his neck.

But he felt no wave of courage revitalizing his body. What could he possibly do, he asked himself again, even if he met the Mighty One?

He stopped, acutely conscious of how open to attack he was. He longed for the safety of the cave, for the security of the Tribe.

A cold wind riffled through the high grass like a prowling beast. It moaned in the distance like an angry, wounded animal.

He had his spear, at least, he reminded himself. It had been made for him by Rab. By Rab, who had always defended and cared for him, and who now desperately needed his help.

Kimba shrugged off his fears. After all, he had the Power. Utrek had so frequently told him so. And he believed he had felt it himself at times.

Exactly what the Power was, or how to employ it, still puzzled him. But since he had it, he must be greater, in some way, than the other hunters of the Tribe.

Where they failed, he could succeed. And he had to. It was Rab's only hope.

With long, sure strides, Kimba approached the valley.

He climbed the hillside from which he had watched the ghastly battle. His eyes swept the bowl-shaped terrain. Two jackals flashed briefly into view. There was no other sign of a living creature.

He went down the slope cautiously, intent on what might lurk below. So the large, bounding shape that hurtled past him from above caught him by surprise.

His spear arm flew up, but he recognized at once what it was: the dog.

A peculiar feeling of heightened confidence welled up within him. The red dog had returned! True, it virtually ignored him as it sped down the hill, swinging in first one direction, then another. Soon it would run off again, probably to be seen no more.

But for now it was back.

There, he saw, were the two rock cairns that marked the graves of the tribesmen the One-Tusk had sent on their final journey. The other hunters had done their best to protect the bodies from predatory animals and to pay their farewells to their kinsmen. Usually there were solemn rites for sending hunters on their final journey. The bodies would be painted and Utrek would pronounce special words to guide them on their way.

But Utrek had not been there when the hunters had been killed. And Kimba had not yet been instructed in conducting the proper rites for such an occasion.

"Hunt well," Kimba now said softly. This was the custom when passing the burial place of fallen hunters.

The moist earth of the valley floor was pitted in many places by the feet of the mammoths. It would not be a difficult trail to follow.

He paced along beside the traces of the One-Tusk. Its tracks were bigger than any of the rest of the herd. Here it had struck Rab. Here it had rushed at the other hunters. Here it had driven its followers out of the valley.

Kimba's fingers touched the outline of one of the One-

Tusk's tracks. It was larger around than the width of his circled arms.

He plunged his spear into the footprints again and again, shouting.

No matter the size of the One-Tusk! It could not stand up to the Power!

The One-Tusk had a day's start on him, Kimba reminded himself as he left the valley. The herd was headed toward the Forbidden Mountains, which were dark and hazy in the distance but appeared to climb right to the clouds.

If the mammoths had meandered slowly southward, stopping often to browse, they might not be far ahead. But if the One-Tusk had taken alarm, the herd might be days away by now.

He followed their trail intently, until the sun sank over his right shoulder and turned from gold to red. He would not find them by nightfall, he realized. And he must not be overtaken by darkness. For then he would be easy prey. Then he would be of no more use to Rab or anyone else.

He passed a tall, pillarlike boulder. Kimba hesitated. The light had grown dim and a deep chill was creeping up through the earth. Soon it would be impossible even to see the footprints. It would be best to take no chances.

He gathered a few twigs and boughs from some slender poplars and dropped them inside a hollow area at the base of the boulder. Then with loose rocks he built a small semicircular wall.

He sat back on his heels and began striking a flint on a

rock. He had solid support behind him, and with a fire to the front he should be reasonably safe.

The flint drew the sparks and the sparks ignited the dried moss he had brought with him. The dog tensed, startled by the fire. It stared at Kimba suspiciously, then wandered off into the darkness. Kimba threw twigs onto the flames and soon had a satisfactory fire going. He banked the blaze with pieces of turf, and allowed only one branch at a time to burn. The hunters had taught him never to build a large fire needlessly. It wasted wood and it might be seen by some whose curiosity was not to be encouraged.

He wedged himself against the boulder and put the spear across his lap. Beyond his weak and smoky fire, darkness shrouded the land. High above, the first stars were appearing.

Was someone, Kimba wondered, striking a flint up there in the heavens? Was that what the stars were— small, protective fires set by hunters in the far distance who huddled, as he did, in fear of the night and its terrors?

He wished Utrek would explain it to him. Sometimes the sorcerer would go to the mouth of the cave and study the night sky and nod approvingly. Other times he would gaze long and hard at certain stars and their distances from each other, and reenter the cave shaking his head gravely. Then the members of the Tribe, too, would look at each other in deep concern, knowing the signs were bad and they must ready themselves for the worst.

Kimba stared a long while into the lazily crackling fire,

then swung his eyes up once more to the stars. Some of them seemed to have moved a bit. They would remain steady while he studied them, but appeared to change their positions when he took his eyes away. Instead of being campfires, were they torches carried in some slow procession? And who carried them?

Utrek would know. But he might never see Utrek again. He might never be given an explanation.

The realization brought his attention back to his immediate surroundings. He laid another branch on the smudgy fire. He would have to sleep in snatches, waking often to be sure the blaze still burned. He dared not let it go out.

Drowsiness swept over him in a great rush. Kimba's hands slipped from the spear. His head rolled back against the base of the boulder.

A muffled growl jerked him into wakefulness. He reached frantically for the spear. The fire, he saw, was almost dead.

He heard the growl once more. It was just beyond the low wall of rocks.

A vicious snarl answered the growl.

Kimba recognized it as the snarl of the red-speckled dog.

Suddenly there was a tumult of growling and snapping and thrashing about. The grappling bodies thudded against the rock wall, knocking it partway down. A howl split the night. And then there was silence.

Above the pile of rocks, he saw the dog's huge head. Its jaws were open, its eyes glistening.

The battle, Kimba knew, had been with a prowling dire wolf. It had crept up close, waiting until the fire went out. The dog had slain the marauder in seconds.

There was always this natural hostility between wild dogs and the dire wolves. They looked much alike and from a distance it was difficult to tell them apart.

They are of a kin, Utrek had remarked, but they are different. And whatever the difference was, it would inevitably prompt them to kill each other on sight.

Kimba scurried out, grabbed the dead wolf's legs, and hauled the carcass back into the enclosure.

A chorus of high-pitched howls throbbed through the crisp night air: the rest of the wolf pack. Rumbling from deep within its chest, the dog swung around to face the danger head-on.

Kimba poked a branch into the coals, but the stick was slow to ignite. The wolf pack edged closer. Now he could see the occasional glint of intently staring eyes.

From his pouch, Kimba scooped out more of the kindling. He tossed it onto the fire and blew on the small tendrils of flame. The blaze suddenly flared, wood popping and sparks dancing.

He was determined not to be caught unaware. He fed a large branch onto the fire. Before long the wolf pack—whining and yowling—began to withdraw. Their eyes remained visible a long while. Then at last they faded into the darkness.

Kimba quickly cooked the slices of loin he slashed from the slain wolf. He could scarcely wait for the heat to penetrate and char the meat. As he ate, he felt his body crying for sleep. But the wolves could always return. He could not relax his guard. They might be waiting for that. . . . Waiting . . .

Were they back? In confusion, he sat up. He realized he had dropped off to sleep again. And something big and furry touched him. . . .

Panic pulled him to his feet. And then he saw it was the dog.

It had overcome its fear of fire to cross over the rock wall. It paid no attention to Kimba as it devoured the last of the meat he had roasted.

It dawned on the boy that the dog had never eaten cooked meat before. It rolled its eyes up to Kimba, imploring him for more.

Kimba laughed. It was such a piteous, begging look! From a beast that had just dared to face a pack of savage attackers.

He roasted more meat, threw it to the dog, and leaned back against the boulder.

He could sleep now, he knew. The dog would awaken him if danger arose. The dog's presence meant new, undreamed-of security.

He was not alone anymore.

Chapter

9

The next day dawned chilly and bleak; the sun was so pale, it seemed to be draining away into invisibility. Kimba's breath frosted in the air—something it had not done since the earth entered the thawing season the full course of a moon ago.

Kimba picked up the trail of the One-Tusk with no trouble. As he followed it, the dog made its usual wide-ranging excursions.

Its flanks were streaked with dried blood from the battle with the wolf. There would be new scars on that tough body. But the animal moved with fluid grace and suppleness, head high, as though it had suffered not so much as a scratch.

This was land Kimba had never before seen in his travels with the Tribe. His eyes skipped over it and he fixed every feature in his mind. Now he must not be the dreamer that Utrek said he was. He must know exactly how to make his way back.

The great meadows continued to spread before him, slanting upward to yellow limestone cliffs. Marshy grass—some of it up to his chest—carpeted much of these long stretches. There were times when he could not see the dog, but he could tell where it was by the movement of the grass.

In low-lying areas, the grass thinned to a few rank weeds sprouting out of black, muddy bogs. Kimba avoided these carefully. They were unpleasant to walk in and occasionally the clinging muck was strong enough to hold a hunter or even a large animal immobile, as honey could trap a fly.

The track of the Mighty One remained easy to follow. The grass was crushed flat where it had passed with its herd. It could not be far now, Kimba felt. The One-Tusk would not be hurrying. It would not know it had such a persistent pursuer.

The day did not warm up as it should, and dark-purple clouds formed in the sky where the sun would be setting. While the shadows of afternoon were still short,

Kimba knelt by a shallow, sluggish creek and drank deeply. Beside him, the dog dipped its muzzle in the cold water, then looked up, snuffling. The hackles on its back rose.

Kimba stared along the dog's line of vision, down the long flow of grassy plain.

Something moved, some creature or other. Then he saw more movement. There were many of them, whatever they were.

One of the creatures stepped onto a slight rise, and Kimba knew what they were, although he had never before seen them.

The Others!

He threw himself down, out of sight.

The hunters had told him of this breed. They had warned him that there was nothing more dangerous to face.

For the Others were much like Kimba and the members of his Tribe. They walked on two legs, they spoke among themselves, they carried weapons which they made, and they knew the secret of producing fire.

But they were squat and hairy, with flattened heads and beetling brows. They moved in a shambling fashion, swiftly, but bent over and furtive. They were powerful in combat, although they had to move in close to deal with their enemies with spears or knives because they did not have knowledge of the use of the throwing sticks.

And they had a fierce hatred for beings like those of Kimba's Tribe.

The Others were near the mammoths' trail. Kimba

counted seven of them. He began to make a slow, careful arc, hoping to cross the trail further ahead.

He snaked along on hands and knees, stopping often to peer over the top of the high grass. The Others were hunting, Kimba saw. Game would have been hard for them to find, too.

In a thicket of tangled bushes Kimba was able to stand without being seen. The Others, he observed, were moving in his direction. They beat the ground, hoping to stir some small animal into flight and expose itself to their spears and clubs. And they grubbed in the earth for seeds or pods, small lizards or insects to eat.

Suddenly the wind shifted. It was stronger and colder, and now it was blowing toward the Others.

Kimba wondered if it would carry his scent to them. Because he had never encountered these beings before, he did not know what they were capable of—and this further increased his fear.

The hunters had told him that the battle cry of the Others was more terrifying than any other charging creature's. They said that their stumpy legs were tireless and swift.

He must leave this place. He motioned to the dog.

"Come!" he called.

It was the first time he had spoken to the animal.

Chapter

10

Keeping low, Kimba continued to make a wide loop through the spongy sea of grass. When at last he dared look up, the Others were nowhere to be seen.

But the wind had intensified. It was as frigid and cutting as it had been during the winter days when the Tribe stayed within the cave. Kimba shivered. The big dog sniffed the air uncertainly. The sky was even darker now and more ominous, although nightfall was still far off.

He must rediscover the trail before the storm struck. The huge prints of the One-Tusk had to be nearby, he was sure. But the light was growing misty. Kimba squinted, his eyes sweeping back and forth. He trotted faster, moving his arms briskly to keep warm.

The first snowflakes began drifting down.

Never had he known it to snow this late in the year. The season of cold and snow and scarcity already was a lengthy one, but now it seemed to be extending its grip even further. Why this was so only one as wise as Utrek could explain, Kimba thought.

But Kimba did know that he had to find the trail of the One-Tusk before it was entirely covered.

He ran harder, peering through the white haze, knowing that his frantic efforts might very well be carrying him farther away from the trail. But he was ridden by the urgency of his quest. Soon the ground would be nothing but a blur.

He spotted a series of wide indentations in the earth. Examining them, he decided they were the tracks of a woolly rhinoceros.

When he looked up, the dog was no longer visible. Above him was a vastness of white, slowly and perpetually descending.

Even doubled over, Kimba could scarcely see the ground.

Something erupted in front of him, an explosive flapping. He stumbled back and saw the object, brown and yellow, quickly disappear. It had been a large bird nesting in some bushes.

If he could not see the bird before almost stepping on it, he knew he would probably not detect the One-Tusk's footprints unless he actually fell into one. There was no purpose in continuing. He had to find shelter until the snowfall ended.

Apprehension filled him. During the season of cold and snow, the Tribe always stayed in its cave. He had never been caught in a snowstorm alone, never before faced the prospect of spending the night out in one.

He called the dog, shouting "Hoooh!" as the hunters did when they were cut off from view of each other and wanted to communicate.

He waited, hearing nothing but the droning rasp of the wind. The snow blinded him now. Everywhere he turned it was like a gigantic white pelt, suffocating him.

Again he shouted to the dog, until his lungs were emptied of air. Again nothing answered.

He was not sure why he called the dog. But it seemed important that the animal be with him now. It seemed important that he not be alone at a time of such great danger.

Lurching about, he put the lashing wind to his back. He knew there were no protective caves or even large boulders in this region of flatlands and grass. There was nothing but the wind and the snow and the ever-fiercer cold.

His chilled hands were losing all feeling. He rubbed them together vigorously, flexing his fingers. There was a painful tingling in them, but he knew that in this wind it would not be long until they froze.

His thoughts flew to Utrek's hand and those missing two fingers. Had the cold and not some mortal enemy been responsible? Kimba folded his arms over his chest, tucking his hands under his armpits. It helped some, but his whole body was shaking uncontrollably.

Should he call the dog once more? the boy wondered. But his breath was short. He could not suck in enough of the frigid air to utter a shout.

Above the keening of the wind he heard it then—two sharp bursts of sound. It was the bark of a wolf or a dog.

Kimba faced into the wind, hurrying toward the sound. The barking seemed closer, and then it ceased. Kimba reached up and touched a coat of snow-covered fur. It was the wild dog.

He put an arm around the animal, drawing near to feel the warmth of its body. But the dog pulled away. Kimba rose to his feet and stumbled after it. The sharp fear seized him that the dog might vanish once more and this time he would never find it.

But the animal had halted. Kimba rushed up to it, and then he saw what was stretched out on the ground: a large roebuck, its magnificent antlers almost covered by snow.

The dog must just have brought it down, for the stag's flanks were still warm. And there was a gaping wound where the dog had paused to feed.

The boy knew what to do. Though he sometimes let his mind wander, he had listened carefully to the hunters' stories.

With his knife, he cut a slit along the stag's belly. He dug out the entrails clumsily, for he was unskilled at this sort of job and his hands were all but frozen. It was a gory task, but he was not squeamish.

He and the members of the Tribe had great respect for the beasts they killed. It was a feeling of kinship. All shared life, Utrek had said: Both the people of the Tribe and the animals they pursued were the magic carriers of life.

And when the hunters killed an animal, it was as if its life became theirs. So the hunters killed without regret and had no time for delicacy. Their need was far too strong.

Brother, I thank you for this shelter, Kimba silently told the roebuck.

He climbed into the still-steaming carcass. There was room for the dog to crouch beside him. Huddled together, they let the stag's hide serve as their tent.

They were cold, but not so agonizingly cold as they had been. The wind picked up, but they were out of reach of its wicked, biting edge.

Tight against the dog, Kimba tried to forget his discomfort by concentrating on the One-Tusk. All traces of the mammoths' passing would be concealed beneath the snow. They might veer off in any direction. Where was he to start looking in the morning?

Behind his closed eyes, he let his mind go blank, as Utrek had taught him. At first it was not easy, for images of the storm, Rab's plight, and the dog all appeared in rapid succession. It was as though these images were in

92

a race to gain his attention. Then calm prevailed, and with it a sense of moving swiftly through space.

He felt detached from the body that was shivering within the frozen remains of a roebuck on a desolate, snow-choked night. Instead, he felt free, dimly conscious only of what Utrek had tried to convey to him: We must know deeply those we hunt—know them outside and inside; we must *become* them.

He no longer felt free; rather, he became aware of a sense of confinement. Confinement within a body that was lumbering, powerful, huge. He could see, but his vision was not sharp. His hearing was keen and his sense of smell was acute. There was a strong odor all about him. It was the easily recognizable reek of the Mighty Ones.

Ahead of him marched the One-Tusk. Behind him he heard the grunts of the other Mighty Ones. He was one with them.

The heat of the sun felt good on his flanks and broad back. They were headed toward a plateau rearing up out of the snow-covered flats. There would be more foliage there; green and tender shoots were budding on the trees along a small stream that trickled through the land ahead. His eyesight swam when he peered into the far distance, but he could make out one distinctive feature. It was a triangular notch cut into the square-shaped top of a distant plateau.

It was toward this pass that the One-Tusk led the herd.

The trunk of the One-Tusk was never still. It tested the air; it scoured the ground; it sucked up snow; it tore up whatever was edible beneath the crust. The One-Tusk turned and the tiny, reddened eyes—all but hidden under the overhanging brow—surveyed the herd, assuring itself that all were still obediently following. The herd felt fear. . . .

Kimba awoke with a sneeze. His face was pressed into the dog's soggy neck. He ached from the cold and his arms and legs were stiff.

But it was morning and the storm had ended. As the boy stretched, the dog wriggled out of the makeshift shelter. Kimba followed, blinking in the weak sunshine.

The land was an unbroken sheet of glistening white. Had it been the Power he experienced during the night, placing him among the One-Tusk's herd? Or had it only been a dream? Or was there a difference?

He was only mildly hungry. Anyway, the cold had turned the stag's flesh into the hardness of rock, and Kimba was in too great a hurry to build a fire.

If it had been a dream, its impact was not dwindling. What he had seen and smelled and felt remained vivid in his mind. The herd had been traveling roughly in the direction of the Forbidden Mountains, and the sun had been to his left.

Kimba shaded his eyes and slowly scanned the horizon. The Forbidden Mountains were a gray, jagged smudge against the sky. Between them and where he stood were a large number of limestone cliffs. They were of various heights and shapes, and he knew that some of the closer ones blocked his view of those that lay beyond.

He was bothered by the glare of the sun on the snow. But then excitement burst out of him in a sudden cry.

94

There!

It was a triangular-shaped notch in the level silhouette of a high plateau!

It was as he had seen it during the strange experience he had had during the night.

There need be no more questioning about which way to proceed! The next leg of his journey was clearly laid out for him, and it was not a long one. He would face the One-Tusk this very day.

Kimba and the dog set off at once toward the notched plateau. They moved swiftly, letting exertion warm their chilled bodies. Before the morning was half over, Kimba detected a series of dents in the snow. They were the prints of the Mighty Ones!

With his spear, Kimba drew in the snow a picture of a mammoth with one tusk. Hopping from foot to foot, he danced around the Mighty One. His voice grew louder and louder and seemed to him to come from some source other than his own body.

The picture of the Mighty One became a blur as he whirled around it. The trunk, the swollen head, the monstrous body, the ugly eyes, that lone tusk. There was the enemy! There was the creature that stood between Rab and life!

With a yell, he hurled his spear into the snow. It sank deep into the mammoth's side.

Kimba yanked the spear out and waved it. Now he would meet the One-Tusk! Now at last he would be a hunter!

Now he would do what must be done to save Rab!

Chapter

11

Already the snow was melting. The valleys and meadows Kimba walked through were bogs of cold slush.

Late in the morning, he came to the stream he knew the Mighty Ones must be following. It was narrow, slow-moving, strewn with pebbles. The thick belt of under-brush that lined its banks clearly traced its course. He saw that the stream twisted about in large and sweeping arcs, but that it came from the direction of the plateau with the triangular notch.

The mammoths would travel vast distances as they wound back and forth along the stream. Kimba realized that if he went in a straight line toward the notch, he could be waiting there for the herd to appear. And he might even have time to prepare a surprise for the One-Tusk.

"We will be on our way back to Rab this night!" he called to the dog.

He waded the zigzagging stream many times, pushing through the willows, alders, and rushes growing along its sides. He was mindful only of the need to keep the notch in sight.

His progress was steady, unswerving. He took no time to relax or to search for food. And so before it was yet midafternoon he stood at the foot of the plateau, gazing up at the notch that he had first seen in his dream or his imagination or his vision—whatever it had been.

Here, he found, the stream bed narrowed and the water emerged from under a tiny crack in the base of the cliff. Many of these limestone bluffs were undercut by bodies of water, and Kimba knew the stream must originate on the far side of the plateau.

But how would the Mighty Ones pick up the course of the stream? They could endure the long journey around the plateau, true. But he did not think it was their custom to do so.

Kimba sat on the side of the stream near the cliff. He

let his feet dangle just above the cold water while he stared at the heights above.

The triangular notch was really a natural pass slicing through the middle of the plateau. The land leading to it tilted upward gradually. It looked as if a game trail had been worn there by the continual passage of animals.

He suspected that the trail was part of the Mighty Ones' feeding pattern, and that they frequently used this pass to enter other favored areas beyond.

A small fish glided just below him. Absently, he thrust his hand at it. He felt its fins within his grasp, and then he let it dart away. At the splash, the dog's ears perked up, and it watched Kimba intently.

Somewhere up there, the boy thought, there must be the right boulder, big enough to kill or stun the One-Tusk and yet loose enough to be easily dislodged.

He plucked a small, flat stone from the bottom of the stream. He flung it sideways so that it skipped across the surface of the water four, five, six times before sinking.

True, once the herd had passed through the notch, there might be other opportunities for an ambush. But he could not rely on it. He must first try to find some means to attack the One-Tusk on the approach to the notch.

Kimba held the wolf tooth tightly, closing his eyes a moment and inviting the Power to show him what he must do.

Then he bounded up to the trail, the dog behind him. The angle of incline was not severe, and Kimba was hardly conscious that they were gradually moving upward.

His eyes scanned the slopes on either side. The steep stretches of limestone were littered with rocks and boulders. Would one of these be large enough to destroy the One-Tusk? He looked at each calculatingly.

At a sharp turning of the trail, he spotted a boulder that looked promising. It was as large as a reindeer, but poised precariously on a small overhang. It looked as if one shove might send it rolling.

While he peered at it, the dog snarled. Almost at once, Kimba heard another sound that he knew would always haunt him, should he live to be older than Utrek.

It was the trumpeting of the One-Tusk.

From around the bend of the trail a mammoth appeared, its enormous body rocking along at a gallop.

The One-Tusk! Kimba thought. But no. He saw then that it was not.

Then the earsplitting trumpeting sounded again and another Mighty One lumbered into view. This was the creature he had come to slay.

Kimba stood stock-still, frozen by the sight. The One-Tusk was in a rage. The fleeing mammoth must be one of the females of the herd. Perhaps it had dared to try to break away from the One-Tusk's dominion.

Kimba dropped down into a thicket of brambles as the cow, squealing in fright, thundered past him.

The One-Tusk could not see him if he remained hidden, he told himself.

But the giant Mighty One seemed to be pounding directly toward him, as though it would trample both Kimba and the thicket underfoot and never notice it. The boy's eyes fixed in horror at the tusk and its sharp, wicked tip.

He jumped to his feet and dashed for the slope.

Instantly the One-Tusk turned its fury from the terrified female mammoth to the smaller creature that had so suddenly materialized in its path.

Kimba picked a section of limestone that was gouged with steplike projections and began to scurry up it.

He knew that safety lay only a short distance upward, that the slope was too steep for the One-Tusk. Mighty Ones could not jump, he knew. Yet he felt a desperate need to be as high as he could above that snaky trunk and bloody tusk.

In his haste, he stepped on an unsteady stone covered with slush, and his feet went out from under him.

He toppled down the slope.

Frantically, he grabbed a rock, trying to slow his descent. But the rock came loose and he continued to fall.

It was the spear that saved him. It caught between a boulder and the trunk of a dead, stunted poplar. The sudden stop almost jerked his hand loose, but he managed to keep his hold on the spear.

The cascade of rocks and pebbles had alerted the One-Tusk, he knew. How far had he fallen? Driven by fear, he pulled himself to his feet.

The trunk of the One-Tusk uncoiled toward him, flicking and weaving. Though Kimba was still too high to be reached, he was chilled by his closeness to the great beast.

The One-Tusk took two small steps up the slippery

slope, and Kimba shrank back. But the mammoth's feet slid as it attempted to go higher. Trumpeting, it retreated.

Kimba cautiously climbed several steps higher. His fear was less now, although the pounding of his heart still resounded as loudly in his ears as the Mighty One's bellows.

A streak of red caught Kimba's attention and then the One-Tusk's. It was the dog, crossing the trail. The mammoth made a rush toward it. The dog spun around, snarling, as though it might actually meet the attack. Then it swerved away and ran up the slope to be beside Kimba.

At once Kimba felt bolder. He was scratched and bruised from his fall, but he and the dog were out of reach.

They were safe for now. But that was not enough. That was not nearly enough! To save Rab's life, he must yet obtain the piece of tusk.

And before him stood the creature that had all but sent Rab on his final journey!

Sudden rage filled Kimba. He threw his spear, knowing as he did that it was a useless gesture.

It hit the beast's forehead and bounced off as though deflected by a granite slab. But the One-Tusk had felt the impact and blasted out its wrath. It sucked up the wet snow and blew it at Kimba in a great wet torrent. The boy hurled a rock back at the mammoth. Then he threw another and another, screaming at the One-Tusk, giving full vent to his fury.

The One-Tusk stamped about in a frenzy, bellowing back, looking for something, anything, to step on and crush. But there was nothing except the snow and the rocks. With much trumpeting, the One-Tusk departed.

Kimba let his fury ebb away. In its wake he felt only excitement. He had faced the One-Tusk! He had not beaten it, but he had not been beaten by it either. The next time he would have a plan. The next time he would not flee in panic.

The next time? The next time must be soon! It must be today!

He went back on the trail and recovered his spear, "Come," he said to the dog.

The slopes seemed to press in closer. But there was no real sense of climbing. So it was with surprise that Kimba noticed they had almost reached the notch.

At this point, the trail widened considerably into a flat glade before continuing on to the pass. The eastward edge of this shelf ended in a long, thin gap just where the trail met the side of the plateau. He gazed down to the yellow-brown soil of the ravine below.

If the One-Tusk could be driven from this drop-off, the quest would be ended.

He paced about the open expanse. It was so large that a lone hunter would have trouble stampeding the herd toward the precipice. The space was not confining enough.

So again he must scout the trail further ahead. He sprinted up the final, easy ascent to the pass. Here, in the shadow of the ridges still above, he obtained a sweeping view of the land beyond the plateau. The stream appeared once more. The trail sloped down to it and followed it through a series of small forests and meadows in which plumes of brown grass waved high above the melting snows. Along this route, continuing upstream, the herd would be accustomed to good browsing.

But it was on a spot only a few steps below the pass that Kimba's attention became riveted. The trail grew very narrow, and the cliff wall on the east fell away abruptly, exposing a sheer drop to a gully far below. Above this section of the trail a lone hunter could wait, concealed, until the Mighty Ones marched past beneath him.

Here he might somehow frighten several of the One-Tusk's herd. They would rush forward and push against their leader. There would not be room for the One-Tusk to move out of their way.

It would be shoved to the very edge of the trail. And then off it.

Here, Kimba exulted, he would have his final meeting with the One-Tusk!

He scrambled up the wet grooves in the limestone wall and hid behind a craggy outcropping. The dog watched from the trail below, but the boy felt no concern that its presence would give them away. The dog would vanish quickly enough when the Mighty Ones made their appearance.

The Power had not guided him when he had faced the One-Tusk farther down the trail. But, he decided, it must have led him to this place. He let himself be filled with the knowledge that the Power would work through him, that he represented a force greater than himself.

Then he heard that familiar, shrill trumpeting. It was

the One-Tusk. At once, his heart thumped with fear and his mind seemed paralyzed.

Rab's life depends on me, he shouted silently at himself. And the Power is working through me! I have the Power!

This seemed to unlock his thinking processes. He began to consider how he would cause sudden surprise and panic in the herd as it passed him.

The One-Tusk cried out again, and this time the herd began squealing. Then Kimba heard a sound that he could not quite believe.

It was the shouting of many men.

There were hunters back there! Probably back at the widening in the trail just before the pass. They must have leaped out of hiding, yelling and swarming around the herd.

The boy clambered down and ran to look. They were not the Others, he saw at once. They were hunters like those of his own Tribe. He had seen bands of people who resembled his own breed many times before. Sometimes they were friendly. Sometimes they were not.

This group had done just what Kimba had intended. The men had created an uproar that surprised the woolly mammoths and set them to milling about.

The One-Tusk wheeled, prepared to take on the attackers. It had fought the two-legged breed before!

But the cows had panicked. Like a mountainous mass of bone and muscle they hurtled forward, directly into the One-Tusk.

It shrieked, stabbing at them to force them to stop.

But their momentum was too great.

Kimba's eyes widened and he sucked in his breath at the sight. The One-Tusk's rear legs slid off the trail. Still bellowing, still slashing, it tried to regain solid ground.

The pressure from the herd intensified. The One-Tusk's struggling body slowly slipped backward.

With roars as loud as thunderclaps, it dropped into space.

Chapter

12

Kimba watched as the immense, shaggy form struck the rocks below.

The hunters cheered and charged the rest of the herd, hoping to force more of the mammoths over the ledge.

His pursuit was ended, Kimba realized.

For long moments, he stared down at that awesome body. The One-Tusk had been destroyed. It was hard to grasp the fact.

But it was so. The One-Tusk was dead and Rab would live!

Joy suddenly surged within him. It was so! The enemy had been conquered! Now Rab would live!

Now Kimba would accomplish what he had set out to do!

Now he would repay Rab! Now the Spear-Maker would live to hunt again!

But he must hurry. Kimba let out a whoop of victory and scampered wildly down the slope to the gully below.

There would be little time, he knew. These hunters would quickly claim their kill. And they must have seen him passing on the trail above while they waited in ambush for the mammoths. They knew he was somewhere about, and they might very well search for him.

Even in death, the One-Tusk looked menacing. It almost seemed as if the monstrous body might suddenly arise and utter that horrifying bellow.

The dog sniffed the One-Tusk warily, as if it, too, could hardly believe that the raging Mighty One had been vanquished. There was a low rumble in the dog's throat as it paced around and around the fallen monarch.

But there was no time to marvel. The hunters on the trail had ceased shouting, and no more mammoths had come crashing down. The rest of the herd apparently had escaped.

That meant the hunters would soon appear. And the tip of the tusk would not be easy to obtain.

Kimba rubbed his hand over the long, smooth curve of the tusk and made a discovery. The ivory had been badly

107

cracked by the fall. It was all but broken off already.

Rejoicing, he hacked at the shattered tusk with Rab's knife. The tip was very loose. He tugged at it, working it back and forth. Suddenly it tore free.

The boy stumbled backward, clutching it tightly. In wonder, he held up the jagged sliver. He had it at last!

"Come! Quick!" he called to the dog.

He ran to the head of the gully where he could climb back up the slope he had descended and return to the game trail.

He would make a half circle around this plateau until the afternoon sun was on his left cheek. Then he would set a straight course for the Tribal cave. If he did not tarry along the way, he could be there in two days.

Kimba felt fresh, invigorated, triumphant. The dog caught his spirit and rushed past the boy, frisking like a puppy.

Then the dog slid to a stop in the melting snow and its muzzle wrinkled in a snarl.

A man advanced on them with a throwing stick and javelin in his hand. Behind him was another man, then another.

Kimba whirled, darting off at a tangent. Another hunter materialized in front of him.

The boy turned back in the direction of the One-Tusk. But three more hunters appeared from a clump of scrubby pines only a few paces to his left.

It seemed clear to him that these hunters had seen him descend to the gully and had quickly and stealthily followed.

The dog vaulted at the nearest man, downing him. A second circled them, looking for a chance to lunge at the animal.

A third hunter came for Kimba.

The boy raised his spear and the hunter stopped. He had his throwing stick poised, the deadly javelin was ready. Each studied the other cautiously.

There was a rush of footsteps. Kimba was grabbed from behind by the throat. His spear was wrenched from him. He reached for Rab's knife and it, too, was torn from his hand. Then he was pushed to the earth.

Above him stood half a score of hunters—big men like those of his own Tribe—wedged shoulder to shoulder. One of them brandished a knife and stooped toward the boy.

"No." Another hunter stopped him.

Kimba hastily tucked the ivory tip from the One-Tusk into the pouch containing his fire kindling. They must not take it from him!

The hunters allowed him to rise. The dog had eased closer to the stunted pines. The hunters now turned from the boy and began to move slowly toward the dog. They crouched, readying their weapons.

One man launched his javelin. But the dog was off with the flash of the hunter's arm.

The javelin quivered in the ground. The second hunter made his cast, aiming ahead of the dog. But the animal's speed was too great, and it was instantly out of sight.

Grunting angrily, the man with the knife again bent toward Kimba. Once more he was pulled back.

"No!" yelled a man whom Kimba had not noticed before.

He was taller and slimmer than the rest of the band. His forehead was high and bulging, and the skin of his face was taut, like animal hide that has been stretched to nearly the breaking point.

The hunters stood aside as this man approached Kimba.

"He is young. He is quick. We can use him."

The man's voice was soft and musical, like the cooing sound of a songbird.

"He is bad," declared the man with the knife. "He is not like us. He and the dog are of the same pack."

"We can use him," said the slender young man.

Kimba found he could understand what they said, although the accent was different from his own Tribe's.

"One dog escaped. We will kill the other," insisted the hunter with the knife.

"No." The young man spoke with authority. He was not armed. He wore across his shoulders a mantle that was white as snow. His arms and legs were painted with bright-colored circles, dots, and snaky lines.

Then Kimba knew that the young man was to this tribe what Utrek was to his: the sorcerer, the wizard, the healer, the prophet.

He leveled his cold gaze on Kimba. Suddenly he seized the boy's cheek, cutting into the skin with fingernails as long as claws. He pulled Kimba's face closer to his own and studied it a long while.

"We will take him," said the sorcerer. He swung around and pointed in the direction of the One-Tusk.

"There is meat! As my spell provided! A Mighty One! Which I created for you! Which I led you to! Go—get the meat! Tonight the tribe will feast!"

When the hunters began the arduous task of slicing up the One-Tusk, Kimba discovered how they would use him. He was to carry a solid slab of meat cut from the mammoth's back. The load was much heavier than the one he had carried to his own Tribe from the Mighty One slain by the One-Tusk. The weight of this load nearly doubled him over.

Each of the hunters hoisted a chunk of the same size onto his back. Four men were required to transport the meat from one leg alone.

Darkness was approaching, but they were in a merry mood, chortling, tearing off pieces from their kill, and eating as they walked along. Kimba wondered what his fate would have been if they had failed to down a Mighty One and had been filled with hunger and irritability.

He would have to pass the night with these hunters, he knew. This would be the third night he had spent away from the Tribe, and it was becoming more and more urgent that he begin his journey back.

Perhaps the hunters would let him leave when he had finished carrying this load; perhaps they would permit him to be on his way.

He tried hard to keep concentrating on the need to bring the piece of ivory tusk back to Rab. But it became harder to do so because the huge mound of dripping meat grew heavier with every step.

Soon he could think of nothing but reaching the place

where they would permit him to drop his burden and rest beside it.

It was shortly after dark when he became aware that they had arrived at their destination.

Shouts burst from the hunters' throats. Shrill, excited cries answered them.

Women, children, and elders of the tribe ran up, rejoicing at the prospect of fresh food. And enough meat to last for many, many days!

More squeals went up at the sight of the stranger. "A young one! A young one!" some of the women yelled.

"A two-legged dog," said a hunter, laughing.

The meat was pulled from Kimba's back and he slumped to the ground. But the sorcerer's foot thumped him in the ribs. He motioned the boy to stand.

"I carried the One-Tusk's meat," Kimba said. "Now let me go. My friend Rab—"

The sorcerer gestured sharply, annoyed. He indicated a group of chattering women.

"Go with them. Do what they tell you. Do not try to flee."

His eyes narrowed and fixed on Kimba, reminding him of a sabertooth's. Then the sorcerer turned and stalked away.

As tired as he was, Kimba yet looked closely at his surroundings. The people of this tribe lived in a series of caves burrowing into the side of a limestone plateau. Like his own cave, they faced south to give shelter from the freezing winds that blew northward in the season of snow and cold.

None of these caves, he noticed, was very large. They appeared to be little more than cramped holes.

A stout woman dragged Kimba to a raging fire that had been built in a deep pit. Small children giggled and stared. Older ones pinched him, laughing, or pointed to his eyes—glinting green in the light of the flames.

An old woman with stringy hair that hung to her waist seemed to be in charge of preparations for the feast. She brushed the children aside and jerked a finger at Kimba.

"Get wood!"

He ambled off, searching the ground.

"Fast!"

Forcing himself to move more rapidly, Kimba went to the fringe of the camp. As he gathered up a pile of branches, he began to entertain a flicker of hope. Might not this chore provide him with an opportunity to run off in the darkness?

But almost at once he observed that several young men of the tribe had strolled after him, and were watching from only a few steps away.

"Wood!" the old woman shrieked. Kimba hastened back with the armload he had collected.

It would not do anyway to slip away tonight, he realized. He was far too weary.

The burden he had carried seemed to have put a permanent crimp in his spine. The faces of his captors suddenly looked like fuzzy blobs. Their words became a meaningless babble.

The cookfire sent smoke and sparks high into the night sky. No one ordered him on any more errands. He edged close to the warmth of the fire and flopped to the ground.

A gruff voice awakened him and rough hands yanked him up. Many of the tribe were leaping around the fire; others still gorged themselves on the flesh of the One-Tusk. After finishing the meat, they heated the bones and broke them in half to get at the melted marrow.

Kimba was dragged to some low, rounded rocks. No one spoke to him. But, surrounded by so many of them, he knew it would be impossible to escape.

He wondered if he would be given any meat, and then he slept.

The shivering of his body returned him to consciousness. It was quiet now and the fire was little more than embers. The many revelers who had been all around him were gone.

Was he free? The question brought him more sharply awake.

But he knew instantly that the answer was no. Two hunters with their spears held upright sat beside the fire, turning now and then to catch the sights and sounds of the night. He heard a stirring nearby and saw the form of another hunter—probably another lookout—outlined by the half moon.

No, they were alert and ready to stop him from disappearing into the shadows.

He sat up and propped his body against a rock. The night air was cold, and the earth—still layered with snow in many places—was even colder.

"He and the dog are of the same pack," one of the hunters had said. And now they were treating him as little more than an animal—a creature not to be given shelter, food, or warmth.

He would have to creep nearer the fire, Kimba decided. The hunters probably would warn him away, but he must try it. The chill was settling into his bones. Soon he would suffer too much discomfort to sleep. And without rest, without strength, he could not make the journey home.

He felt the piece of tusk within his tunic.

"Rab, I will yet bring this to you," he murmured.

Then he became aware of a savory smell. Bending over him was a small, smiling girl his own age or a season younger, bearing on a stick a smoking piece of meat.

She extended it to Kimba. When he hesitated, she placed his hand around the stick.

"Eat," she said.

Kimba did, first nibbling and then fiercely attacking the food. The girl sat on her heels, smiling more broadly as she watched. When the stick was bare of meat, he licked his fingers.

Then the girl pulled a fur covering over to him. She dropped it beside Kimba, got up, and began to melt away in the blackness.

"Who are you?" was all he could blurt out.

She half turned and only smiled.

"Who are you?" Kimba asked more loudly.

"Nupa," said the girl softly and was gone.

Kimba wrapped himself in the skin she had left. He stretched out, warm and comfortable. "Nupa," he said to himself, and then he slept.

Chapter

13

The next morning, the women of the tribe were first up. Most of them were busily hanging slices of the One-Tusk's meat to dry in the brightly shining sun. Several carried pouches of animal skin to a spring for fresh water. One worked at cutting an eye into a bone needle.

The old woman who had supervised the cooking of the feast ordered Kimba to help a group of children go through the bones discarded the night before. Any bones which looked as though they could be turned into weapons or tools were to be collected and put in a pile.

As he toiled, Kimba searched for Nupa. Finally he saw her. She was tending three children who were just learning to walk. Patiently, she helped them up when they tumbled. And she clapped and laughed when they succeeded in taking a few faltering steps.

She waved to Kimba and walked toward him, smiling. "Did you sleep well?" she asked.

"Away!" cried the old woman. "Away from this one! He is not one of us!" Angrily, she seized Kimba by the neck and sent him stumbling to the bone pile.

At last the hunters stretched, grunted, and listlessly picked at the cold remnants of yesterday's meal. When they seemed ready for the day's labors, one of them gripped the boy's arm. "Come," he commanded. To the old woman, the man said, grinning, "He is ours now."

So Kimba accompanied the hunters back to the fallen One-Tusk and returned wobbling once more under the weight of a heavy joint of meat. Again his spine felt bent and sore, but there was no opportunity to rest. Twice more the hunters and Kimba made the trip. It was late afternoon when they returned to the caves with the last of the meat.

There had been no chance on the trail to bolt for freedom, although Kimba had been alert every moment. Back at the tribe's home he was aware that watchful eyes were continually on him.

A sense of helplessness and fear swept over him. Four days had passed since he had left the Tribe, but it seemed so much longer. And each day meant the possibility of saving Rab had lessened.

Already it could be too late.

"No!" he said aloud. He must not dwell on that thought, he knew. He must not!

Kimba reached down for a soft, yellow-spotted stone. He began hacking at it with a piece of flint. He would make a picture and pour all of his mind into the job. He had done this often in the past, when he was upset or unhappy or his thoughts churned in such a way that he could not think clearly.

It had always distracted him and calmed him. And so it did today.

As he concentrated on the image he was creating, the agonizing fears began to float away. Utrek, he knew, would not approve of the drawing. He was fashioning a butterfly, simply because that was the first object that had snared his attention.

His model was huge and orange winged. It had been fluttering near Kimba among the junipers on the edge of the camp. Now it was still, as if posing. This was because a cloud had momentarily blotted out the sun. Butterflies, Kimba knew, were active only in the sunlight.

It was rare to see one this soon after the season of cold and blizzard. Only the unexpected warmth of today's sun had roused it, and probably only for a short while. This was one of the kind, Kimba realized, that went into hibernation when the chill winds and first snows appeared and only emerged at the time of melting.

There were no other butterflies to be seen anywhere nearby. It had dared to come out when the rest of its kind were not yet ready.

This one is different, Kimba thought. And then it came to him how often he, too, was said to be different.

Was he that different? This thought he also pushed aside, scowling and focusing on his work.

His eyes jumped from the butterfly to the stone. His hand moved quickly, cutting with force and yet with caution. Delicately he sketched the long antennae and the two wide sets of silky wings. There was a round black scratch on the stone. He allowed this to be centered in the middle of one wing, just where the butterfly had a similar mark.

Utrek would frown on what he was doing, because Kimba had been told to draw only the animals that the Tribe needed for food or for skins. The gift of sketching and painting, the sorcerer had emphasized many times, was to be used solely to benefit the Tribe. The artist was not to indulge his own whims.

But Kimba's restless hands seemed almost to have a life of their own. They would scratch out likenesses of trees, of birds, of the moon—and other such useless things as butterflies.

Head low, absorbed in his work, he suddenly felt the presence of someone behind him. The ability to know when this happened also was part of the Power. Or so Utrek told him. Sometimes he had experienced it, and sometimes he had not.

119

He looked over his shoulder and saw Nupa. Her bright brown eyes examined Kimba's drawing intently. Her face, small and fresh as a budding flower, bore an expression of furrowed concentration. She swung her gaze from the butterfly to the boy's depiction of it.

Kimba hastily tossed the stone aside. Perhaps, he thought, she would tell them he was wasting his time and they would put him to work again.

Nupa recovered the stone. Her eyes soaked in its every detail.

"It is . . ." She paused and could find no word to fit what she wanted to say. It pleased her to look on this object, but in her tribe there was no way to express such a feeling. Things were either useful or they were not. If they were not, there was no need to discuss them. So names for them had never been devised.

But now Nupa smiled, holding the butterfly picture to her face.

"Mine?" she asked shyly.

"Yes," Kimba said with surprise. Utrek would have scolded him for producing it. No one else in his own Tribe would have paid any attention to it.

The girl sat down, still clutching the stone. "You have the Power," she said. "Like Sabo."

"Sabo?" asked Kimba, and then he understood. Sabo was the sorcerer—the slender, cruel young man with the slitted eyes. He, like Utrek, would be a painter of animals.

Nupa told him of Sabo. He had been an ordinary youth until, three summers before, the tribe's sorcerer had fallen victim to a lioness. Nobody had been groomed to replace him. So Sabo had proclaimed himself the possessor of the Power. No one else claimed it, so Sabo was chosen.

He seemed, said Nupa, to know what to do with the strange costumes and implements a sorcerer must use. But many in the tribe feared him, for he could be harsh and vicious.

He, too, knew a sorcerer, Kimba said. He described Utrek to her. "He is my teacher," the boy added, and she looked at him with wide eyes.

Kimba paused. Should he trust her? He decided he would.

"Look," he whispered, producing the tip of the mammoth's tusk. Briefly, he told her of its magic properties and how it alone could cure Rab.

She listened to his tales of Rab and Urda, of Rab's courage in rescuing him, of his desire to save his friend.

Kimba stroked the piece of tusk. "This does me no good. Until I can return to Rab."

As she thought about what he had said, Nupa absently twirled the curling edges of one of her two braids of black hair. Pieces of rawhide, painted in red designs, had been tied around each braid, close to the nape of her neck. Kimba thought the ribbons—and her hair—were like the butterfly he had sketched. They caused a delight within him, a desire to gaze even longer. For these feelings there was no word. But Kimba knew that the feelings existed.

"You must return," she said. "I will help you."

"But—how?"

"Away from him!" It was the woman who had put Kimba to work that morning.

"Why? What has he done?" Nupa asked.

"Away from him!" the woman screeched, hurrying up to the two young people.

"He is not an enemy," Nupa said.

"He is not one of us! You are not to talk to him!"

Enraged, the woman shook Nupa violently. The girl had hidden the gift from Kimba in her dress of roebuck skin. Suddenly the stone fell to the ground.

Nupa stooped to pick it up, but the old woman snatched it away. She gaped at it, puzzled.

"Sabo!" she called.

The sorcerer emerged from his cave and marched up to them, solemn and erect. The woman thrust the sketch of the butterfly into his hands. Then she pointed at Nupa.

"Where?" he snapped at the girl.

She must not be involved, Kimba knew. She must not be punished because she had befriended him.

"Mine!" he shouted to Sabo.

"Yours?" The sorcerer stared down coldly at the boy. "You found it?"

"I made it. Then I threw it away. The girl picked it up."

"You made it?" Sabo traced the outline of the butterfly. "You made it?"

His lips curled in scorn. But there was uncertainty in his hostile, hidden eyes. He leveled a ferocious scowl at

Kimba, as though to terrify the boy into denying what he had said. But Kimba gazed back evenly.

Members of the tribe were watching with curiosity. "Come with me," Sabo said in a voice so low Kimba could hardly hear it.

They went to an isolated clearing in the center of a cluster of boulders. Here Sabo ordered Kimba to draw something else on a rock. This time the boy produced the rough likeness of a wild horse.

Sabo followed every move closely. When Kimba was done, the sorcerer again stared at him—but with more bewilderment than hatred.

He took the rock on which Kimba had drawn and laid it flat on his palm. He studied every line and curve of the picture.

"You stay with me," he whispered.

He gestured, signaling the boy to proceed back to the caves. Once more Sabo looked quizzically at the stone. Then, as if it had suddenly turned boiling hot, he threw it into the underbrush.

Chapter
14

"There!" Sabo said, pointing to a niche in a corner of his cave. Kimba threw down the heavy fur covering that Nupa had given him the night before. Now, at least, he would have shelter and a warm place to sleep.

But he did not relish the idea of living in Sabo's cave.

"I have helped you and your people," Kimba said. "Now I must go. Now I must—"

"Quiet!" the sorcerer commanded. "Remain here. Do not leave!"

He stalked out and immediately Kimba saw a hunter slouch down at the cave's entrance. So now, Kimba thought, he was Sabo's apprentice. And he was also Sabo's prisoner.

He went over the cave carefully. There was scarcely room in it to take several score steps, and the roof barely permitted Sabo to stand upright.

At the far end he saw the costumes, tools, and the implements of a sorcerer, but not nearly as many as Utrek possessed. The cave's walls were of the greatest interest to him. They were filled with likenesses of animals, as Utrek's Grotto was. But these drawings were crude, the lines squiggly, the coloring weak. Mammoths were hard to tell from bison or reindeer.

Kimba snorted in disdain.

Late that afternoon, long before dusk, the tribe once again began celebrating the killing of the One-Tusk. There were shouts and laughter, and the smell of roasted mammoth flesh was thick in the air.

At one point, the hunter who guarded him entered the cave and tossed a few strips of meat on the ground beside Kimba. He ate it sullenly, staring out at the cookfire.

The unanswered question repeatedly crowded every other consideration out of his mind: Was it too late to bring the splinter of tusk back to Rab?

He kept trying to grasp the question as though it were a boulder and roll it to one side, out of his way. But it was not easy. It was planted solidly.

To occupy his mind in some other way, he went to Sabo's painting materials. The sorcerer had evidently intended to start another drawing soon. The colors had been prepared.

There were reds, yellows, and browns from the claylike pieces of ochre found in the cliffs, and black cut from lengths of charcoal. Each color had been mixed with a thick binder made of animal fat and was stored separately in the indentations of a flat, pockmarked rock.

Kimba found no brush and decided Sabo had yet to learn to make one. The sorcerer must use only his fingers and hands. Again the boy felt contempt for his captor.

He made a sudden decision and dipped one finger into the red. Instantly he began to draw a reindeer on one of the sections of wall that was still bare.

He compelled himself to consider every small detail of the animal's body, emptying his mind of his fears and concerns. Soon he was utterly lost in the work, unmindful of the noises of the feast as he transferred to the rocky surface the likeness of the beast he so clearly saw in his imagination.

The cave grew more shadowy as darkness fell. Kimba hurried, squinting in the feeble light. He had not had time to do a careful, thorough job. The painting reflected his haste.

Yet when he stood back and evaluated the finished work, he knew it was far more skillfully done than any of Sabo's drawings.

Was it the Power that had guided him as he painted?

If it was, then his Power clearly was superior to Sabo's.

And with that Power, he would still return in time to save Rab!

Tomorrow he would find a way to escape, he resolved. The Power would guide him! The cave was totally dark now, and he lay down on his fur pallet and was asleep within moments.

When he awoke in the morning, the first thing he saw was the sorcerer. He was standing before the painting of the reindeer. Sensing that Kimba had moved, he whirled to face him.

He raised a long thin arm to point at the picture, and he shaped his mouth as if to ask a question. But there was no need. He knew whose hand had drawn the reindeer.

Kimba crouched against the wall. Why had he done it? he asked himself now. He should not have shown up Sabo, not aroused the sorcerer's jealousy. Why had he given in to that impulse?

Sabo stepped toward the boy, his arm back as if to unleash a blow. Then two hunters entered the cave.

"It is time to hunt again," said one of them.

The other gripped his companion's arm and gestured at the newly painted reindeer. Their jaws dropped, then they beamed with pleasure.

"Good!" said one. "Good, Sabo!"

"A good hunt!" exclaimed the other one. He patted the reindeer and then danced in front of it, humming happily.

Surely the hunt would be one of their best, said the first man, with a likeness like that! Surely this painting meant great success for the tribe.

Sabo thrust out his chest and stood tall beside the picture. He made a sweeping gesture.

"You see what I have done! Call the other hunters. Let them see. Let them dance. You will hunt as never before! You see what my Power has done!"

As soon as the two men had dashed out, Sabo shook a finger in Kimba's face.

"You will say nothing!" he warned. "Nothing!"

The hunters of the tribe had assembled for the Summoning Rite. They were packed within Sabo's small cave, surrounding the sorcerer in a tight semicircle.

"I have summoned game!" the sorcerer screamed, raking his clawlike fingernails against the drawing of the reindeer. He was clad in a mantle of pure white and a bison headdress.

"You will find game! You will hunt well! My Power is strong!"

The men cheered and pushed forward, jostling Sabo so that he almost lost his balance. Kimba, almost hidden in his corner, looked on critically. It was so different from Utrek's ceremonies. There were no torches and no dancing shadows, no sudden entrance by the sorcerer, no mounting cadence of excitement and exultation.

There is no Power at work here, Kimba thought.

Yet the hunters waved their spears and stamped their feet enthusiastically.

"Go and kill!" Sabo shrieked.

With jubilant shouts, the hunters left.

When they were out of sight, Sabo walked to the wall

where Kimba had drawn the reindeer. He studied it a long while, then sat down, crossed his legs, and closed his eyes. He began to chant in his high, singsong voice.

But before long his eyes opened and shifted to Kimba. The boy was staring at him. It seemed to annoy Sabo.

"Do not watch me!" he ordered.

His eyes closed again, then quickly reopened. Kimba swung his gaze away, but he knew Sabo was aware he had been staring. He understood that this somehow grated on the sorcerer. Sabo was accustomed to privacy in his chamber, and he also knew that Kimba was not looking upon him with admiration.

But, Kimba thought, now that he had inspected everything else in this cave there was not much else to focus his attention on except the sorcerer.

Sabo realized this, too. Roughly, he took Kimba's arm and pulled him outside. "Do not come back until I order you!" he said.

The boy felt a moment of hope. For with Sabo in his cave and with the hunters gone, today might provide his best opportunity to escape.

But he saw Sabo talking to the women and the elders of the tribe, and he knew they were being told not to let Kimba out of their sight.

He walked idly among them, conscious of the change in their attitudes. He was not one of them, not to be trusted. Yet he was now associated with Sabo in some way they did not understand. Although they no longer glared with dislike or ridicule, they feared to smile at him or talk to him or even catch his eye.

To them, he realized, he was still different.

Nupa was the only exception. For a time, he watched from a distance as she played with the three toddling children. She waved, but he did not go near her. He did not want to cause further trouble for her.

Eventually, pretending it was a haphazard stroll, he drifted toward the outer edge of the camp. He was a fast runner, and given a head start he might well outdistance any pursuers.

He came to the junipers where he had seen the butterfly. Slowly he walked past them.

"No more!" a voice shouted.

He turned to see two men standing not far behind him. One was young and strong. Kimba had noticed him earlier because one of his legs was stiff and he limped noticeably. Apparently he would not resume hunting until his injury was better healed. The other man was elderly and stooped over.

Kimba knew he could easily beat either in a race. But both men carried throwing sticks, and he was keenly aware that he could not outrun the javelins those sticks could hurl.

He smiled, to assure them that he had no plans to go any farther. Then he stretched out on the grass, as though to doze or daydream until Sabo needed him.

But his mind was fully alert. This must be the day he fled! No matter what the risk!

There was a light pinging sound near his elbow, and he shot to his feet.

He heard a ripple of laughter and saw Nupa behind

one of the junipers. He realized she had tossed a pebble at a boulder wedged into the ground beside him.

"You are not asleep then?" she said, giggling.

"No."

"And you have no chores?"

"I await Sabo's command."

She joined him, and he looked anxiously back toward the caves. The two men still watched, but they made no attempt to force Nupa to leave.

"And have you no chores?" Kimba said to her.

"The children rest now." She and Kimba sat down and placed their backs to the large boulder. The day was warm and pleasant. The higher ground was dry now, and there were only a few patches of moist earth where the snow had been slow to melt.

Kimba said little, but only a question or two from him was required to prompt Nupa to tell him about herself.

He learned that her parents were dead, that she had no sisters or brothers, and that her main task—as he had observed—was the care of the few small children who also were motherless. There were no other children her own age in the tribe, but it made no difference. She had her duties, there was always much work to be done, and in a few seasons she would become a hunter's mate.

She did not know if she would be given to one of her own tribe or of another. On occasion, two tribes would meet and share a meal. They might exchange belongings—some colorful shells from a far-off body of deep water for a rare animal skin or a large slab of flint from the chalky cliffs.

131

It often happened then that young women of one tribe would go over to another. It was necessary because the tribes were small and the members were closely related. This was the only way to avoid continual intermarriage.

"Do you fear to go to another tribe?" Kimba asked.

"I do not know. I would try to make their ways my ways. But not to be with my own tribe would be so strange."

"That is so," Kimba said.

"You are thinking of your tribe. And of this Rab."

Kimba nodded. "I must go to him. At once."

Nupa paused. "It may be too late. You have thought of that?"

"Yes. It is possible. I do not know. But I must try."

And it must be today, he was about to tell her. But he stopped because he thought he had seen a streak of color in a stand of willows and birches not far distant. These were the trees that grew near the spring where the tribe went for fresh water.

Kimba had seen movement only out of the corner of his eye, but it had appeared as a flash of red among the pale white and green of the trunks and budding leaves.

He centered his attention on the trees. Again he saw the hint of red.

His heart began to pound. Had he seen what he thought he had?

And then he knew. For the dog stood clearly at the edge of the grove.

Its muzzle was uplifted; it sniffed the air.

Nupa gasped and clutched Kimba. She had seen it, too.

She turned in fright, to call one of the men.

"No!" Kimba whispered. He covered her mouth with his hand and looked over his shoulder.

The two men were busy talking to each other back near the caves. Any sudden movement from Kimba would draw their attention to him, he knew. But for now they had relaxed their guard.

"It will attack us," Nupa said softly, moving her mouth free of his hand.

"No, it will not."

Quickly, Kimba told her of the dog and the adventures the two of them had shared. Her face radiated wonder.

The dog had either seen him or caught his scent. It began taking hesitant steps in their direction.

Nupa shrank back against Kimba.

"No!" Kimba called to the dog, trying to keep his voice hushed. "No!"

It must not rush up to him. It would surely be seen.

He took Nupa's arm and walked toward the caves. On the other side of the junipers, he looked back. The dog had returned to the grove of trees.

"Good!" he said. He grinned. The dog had followed him here. It was waiting, and it would join him when he made his escape.

Nupa glanced back at the trees, and her voice was filled with awe. "It has come close to you?" she questioned.

"Yes."

"Right up to you?"

"Yes."

"You have touched it?"

"Yes."

"And it has not attacked you?"

"It is my friend," he said.

Nupa smiled, hesitantly, her eyes wide at the thought of it.

"I believe you," she said. "Now I must go."

"Farewell, Nupa," said Kimba.

He must not be seen with her anymore, he thought, or after his escape she might be mistreated because of her friendship with him. It was sad that he would speak no more with her. But now he must make his plan. The Power must speed him on his journey this day.

Kimba strolled casually past the series of cave openings. Again he was aware that many eyes were on him.

"Look well!" he muttered quietly. "After today you will see me no more!"

The young hunter and the older man were bound to become careless as the day wore on, he thought. He would return to the edge of the camp and wait for his chance. If he could make it halfway to those trees near the spring before they noticed him, he might be beyond reach of their throwing sticks—provided they missed with their first casts.

It would be a grave risk. But he determined to take it. And then Sabo emerged from his cave. He stretched out his arm to point at Kimba.

"Come here!"

For a moment, Kimba froze. Had the sorcerer read his thoughts?

Then he remembered Sabo's Summoning Rite. No, he

did not think this sorcerer had the Power to discover his intentions.

Sabo motioned him to the cave and had him sit on the floor. He stared hard at Kimba with his eyes that glittered like a bird of prey's.

Then he began to question the boy. What was his name?

When Kimba had answered, Sabo asked where he was from. Kimba gestured to the north and westward.

Sabo did not seem to know of the Tribe. Perhaps the two bands had never met, Kimba decided, because the Tribe seldom hunted to the south. That was the direction in which the Forbidden Mountains lay. And always in the past there had been sufficient game herds to the north of them.

Now Sabo began to question him more insistently. Was there a sorcerer in Kimba's Tribe? Who was it? What did he do? How did he dress? What were his ways?

Kimba answered as best he could. Each time, there was a long pause as Sabo digested the information.

In his replies, Kimba did not restrain himself. He portrayed Utrek and Utrek's feats with more imagination than accuracy. But he did not care. Sabo was inferior to Utrek and must be made to realize it!

Sabo continued, asking what Kimba did to assist the sorcerer. Again Kimba's answers were fanciful. He described himself as more essential to Utrek than he really was.

There was confusion and doubt written on Sabo's face, and again he regarded the reindeer Kimba had drawn.

Kimba could imagine his thoughts: Does this boy have more of the Power than I? Can I learn from him? Can he help me? Or will he try to overcome me and take my place?

The sorcerer pondered these questions, and Kimba grew impatient. None of this was of any concern to him. All that mattered was that he be on his way.

From a distance, he heard a shout. It was the hunters returning, and Kimba's heart fell.

There would be no opportunity to steal away now, at least during daylight.

He quickly began to revise his plan. Perhaps tonight, if there was another feast . . .

Sabo went out to meet the hunters. And Kimba knew at once there would be no feast of rejoicing.

For wails of anguish had gone up from some of the women and the hunters looked grim.

The boy could easily hear their conversation. One hunter had been sent on his final journey, gored and trampled by a woolly rhinoceros. No reindeer were sighted. The hunt was a failure.

"It is the boy!" Sabo cried out.

"The boy?" one of the hunters asked.

"He brought bad Power. It is his doing. My Power was strong. But he made it bad. He has spoiled your hunt!"

Kimba cowered against the farthest wall. He was being blamed again! Just as his own Tribe had blamed him! And now there was no Utrek to flee to for help.

Once more he wished he had no Power, good or bad.

Once more he wondered: Had he really harmed their hunt? Was he really to blame?

Sabo growled some words to a stocky young hunter, who then approached the cave, looked angrily into it, and sat on a boulder near the entrance. He laid his throwing stick on one knee, prominently on view. His other hand rested on the shaft of the knife in his belt.

Kimba was a prisoner in Sabo's cave. He lay down, dejectedly, on his fur pallet. He was trapped here for one more night. He possessed the life-giving piece of tusk. But what good was it to Rab?

The voices rang out loudly, discussing every detail of the day's tragedy. With nightfall they became louder. A fire had been set and more of the One-Tusk's meat was being cooked. But there were no sounds of laughter or pleasure.

He must use the Power in some way, Kimba told himself. He must not brood about the obstacles to escape. He must find a way to use the Power to surmount those obstacles.

"But how?" he said to the darkness surrounding him. How could he use the Power? How could it work through him to show him a way?

The Power—whatever it was—seemed so elusive. The more he thought about it, the harder it was to grasp.

He made his mind go blank so that it would be like a bare wall on which the Power could paint an image.

Within moments he heard a small and friendly voice. For an instant he was convinced it originated within his own mind.

But then he became aware that it came from just beyond the entrance to the cave. It was the voice of Nupa, who was talking to the lookout.

She was bringing Kimba some meat, she told him. He mumbled something in return, and she said it would take but a moment to give it to the boy.

The hunter muttered his reluctant approval.

"See, I bring you meat," she said to Kimba. Her face was a pale, shimmering oval within the cave.

She touched Kimba's shoulder and put her mouth close to his ear. In the softest of whispers she reported what she had just overheard.

Sabo had persuaded the tribe to take Kimba in the morning to the place where the hunter had begun his final journey. There the boy would be lashed securely to a tree and left alone. He would be defenseless, the prey of whatever creature happened by.

Then, Sabo had told them, when some animal destroyed the boy, Kimba's evil Power would enter into the beast. The creature would carry it away and the tribe would be bothered no more.

"You must go now," Kimba said to her when she had finished. "The lookout is waiting."

"But you—"

"I will be gone tonight."

"But they are watching."

"It does not matter, Nupa. I will be gone tonight."

"I have placed a spear there, just outside the cave, for you."

"Good. We will see each other at another time." He smiled, but he did not know if she could see him.

"Go now," he whispered.

He felt her quick, final touch, and then he was alone again.

Chapter

15

The stocky young hunter keeping watch near Sabo's cave had eaten heartily that night. It had been a long, tiring, and discouraging day. Sleep tugged at his eyelids.

Then he came fully awake. A figure had emerged from the cave.

The night was misty and the moon hidden. The young hunter could not see clearly. But he recognized Sabo's white mantle—the skin of an albino bison. It was unusual for the sorcerer to be up and about at such an hour. But Sabo did many things that mere hunters did not understand. It was part of the Power.

The figure in white strode regally forward. The lookout at the edge of the camp also watched in some surprise. But he, too, knew that the sorcerer was not to be questioned.

The figure moved briskly in the direction of the spring beyond the caves. There was something wrong, the young hunter realized. Sabo was much taller than that. The white fur dragged behind on the ground. Had Sabo turned himself into some other form?

Or was it perhaps not Sabo?

The lookout shouted just as the figure disappeared past a row of boulders.

At once someone else appeared at the entrance to the sorcerer's cave. It was Sabo. His face was livid with rage and hatred.

"Kill him!" he screamed, pointing to the boulders.

The hunters hesitated, mystified for a moment. Then they lunged forward, raising their throwing sticks.

Kimba ran desperately, but the sorcerer's robe seemed to weigh him down. He slowed, tore off the costume, and threw it away.

He felt freer then, but it did not help enough. The young hunter was gaining quickly.

He passed the junipers where he and Nupa had stood and ran on toward the stand of trees where he had seen the dog. Perhaps he could elude his pursuers there. But he looked behind and saw that, as fleet a runner as he was for his age, he could never keep ahead of the stocky young hunter.

Just as the slapping of the hunter's feet on the ground seemed directly behind him, the sound stopped. There was a loud, startled grunt.

Kimba looked over his shoulder again. The hunter had braced himself and drawn back his throwing stick and javelin. A large creature, in a dazzling burst of speed, bore down on him.

Too late, the youth hurled the javelin. With the force of an avalanche, the animal bowled him over.

The dog! The red-speckled dog! It had still been waiting for him in the trees beside the spring!

Kimba raced on, and the wild dog quickly joined him. The second hunter was still on their trail, as well as Sabo and perhaps more hunters.

But by the time Kimba was feeling winded, he decided it was safe to halt. He peered back along the way they had come. The moon shone dully now in the mist. No one was visible and he heard no sounds of pursuit.

Sabo must have given up—for the moment, anyway. Kimba sighed with relief. With luck, he would see no more of the sorcerer.

Nor would he see Nupa, he thought with regret. But in some season to come perhaps he would. For he would remember where her people had their caves. And when he was an honored hunter of the Tribe he might well come back and take her away. Then neither Sabo nor any of his tribesmen would stop him.

Kimba felt confident and free. He had the spear that

Nupa had left for him and he had the healing piece of mammoth tusk. Now he—and the dog—would return, victorious.

If only Rab still lived.

Soon he would know. But he must be careful. Sabo would be angry and unforgiving. He would not easily permit the boy to slip out of his hands.

Kimba had told Sabo that the Tribe lived to the west and north. So the sorcerer would believe that was where he was headed.

It would be wiser, he thought, to go southward briefly, toward the Forbidden Mountains. There the land was less open and limestone bluffs merged with the first foothills of the mountains.

After putting themselves out of range of Sabo, he and the dog could swing westward and begin the journey to the home cave.

Now that his initial fear of recapture was over, Kimba realized they must not push on much farther. It was the dead of night, the time that no two-legged creature—even the bravest of hunters—should be away from fire or shelter.

The faint light of the moon revealed a dry streambed that must trace its way down from the Forbidden Mountains. A section of the bank had buckled in, and in this miniature cavern they spent the remainder of the night.

He slept only fitfully, and he had two dreams that were still clear in his mind at morning. One was of two eyes, slitted and evil, that beamed down on him like twin moons. At first they were distant, remote in the night sky.

Then they came closer and grew larger and brighter. He ran furiously, but they kept descending directly toward him with an intense glare, staring at him in unutterable hatred.

The other dream was of freedom, safety, escape. It was as though he were a bird, flying upward, ever upward, knowing that nothing could pursue him if his wings carried him high enough.

He examined carefully his recollections of both dreams. He decided the Power had told him that Sabo would not give up attempting to find him—that Sabo would not be thrown off Kimba's trail and might continue to follow him. And the second dream, he concluded, meant that he must go upward to find security: the risks of the Forbidden Mountains would not be as great as those he'd face if he were to meet Sabo again.

With dawn the mist had disappeared, but it was an overcast day.

They traveled southward through winding valleys, keeping close to the concealing limestone bluffs wherever possible. The lower levels of the Forbidden Mountains were very near. Above them reared the mysterious, jagged pinnacles—so much higher than the sheared-off cliffs of the plateau country that Kimba had always known.

Shortly after midday they reached the first slopes of the mountains. Mingled with the familiar yellow limestone were shafts of heavier, rough-textured, gray-colored boulders.

There were green tiers of pine, fir, and spruce belting

the sides of the mountains. But at their heights there was only rock and snow.

Avoid the Forbidden Mountains, he had always been warned. Their Power was bad. No one had ever approached them.

But he could not ignore his visions. And he would not go far up the slopes, he told himself. Just high enough to be sure he was avoiding Sabo and the hunters of his tribe.

The peak they stood near seemed to Kimba to soar forever into the sky. Yet it was dwarfed by other summits of the mountain range that lay beyond, farther southward.

By midafternoon, Kimba and the dog had passed through several levels of forest and meadow and were picking their way through shale and granite. With each step he glanced upward with some feelings of dread, wondering if they had come far enough to incur the wrath of the mountain's Power. Still, these lower slopes were dotted with the familiar hazel and hawthorn. Birds were all around—ravens especially—and an occasional gray mountain hare darted by. No evil spirits seemed to afflict them.

But there were slate-colored clouds scudding along the tops of the peaks. Soon all was shrouded in semidarkness, and then lightning crackled in the summits.

Was this a warning? "No higher!" Kimba called to the dog.

Sabo would never seek them at such a height, he told himself. He set a course parallel to the ground below.

More lightning flashed, then thunder boomed. Their

passage was easy for a long while, through scrub brush and moderately sloping stretches of stone. Then they reached a steep and slippery section of the mountainside.

They should not, Kimba thought, have climbed even as high as this. His fear of the unknown increased with every bolt of lightning. What if he had interpreted his dream incorrectly? He was not skilled at this, as Utrek was. He descended a bit. But the storm worked its way lower, too. First a cool blast enveloped Kimba and the dog, then torrents of rain began to fall.

They kept moving, one plodding step at a time. The footing was treacherous in the heavy downpour. Kimba halted briefly in the shelter of a rock column.

Thunder shook the mountainside. The dog made a low, whining sound. It was the first time Kimba had seen the animal frightened by anything.

Soaked through and through, he slipped on a rock and skinned his knee. Thunder roared again.

He clung to a boulder, burying his face in his hands until the booming died away. Shaken, he crept forward once more. The wind swung around, whipping the rain directly into his face.

Each step now required great caution. Finding firm footing, he would slowly shift his weight to the new perch. Then the slow process would start again.

The dog whined once more, then barked loudly—somewhere ahead of him and slightly below.

Clutching a spur of rock with one hand, Kimba tried to brush the rain out of his eyes. Then lightning illuminated the whole mountainside vividly.

The dog stood on a wide ledge, beneath an overhang that seemed to offer protection from the pelting rain. Kicking loose a patter of stones, Kimba half hopped and half slid down to the ledge.

At the next flash of lightning, he tried to make out what it was that shielded him against the storm.

It was not a slab of rock or a small overhang. A vast ceiling covered him. He stood in the entranceway of a large cavern.

Was it inhabited? That was his first anxious thought.

But in that flash of light he had noticed no drawing on the walls. As he strained to see further into the interior, his eyes grew accustomed to the dimness. He could discern no sign of movement. Somewhat reassured, he entered.

What immediately impressed him was the height and width of the main chamber. It was much bigger than his Tribe's home. And here the daggerlike rocks hung everywhere from the roof and projected upward from the floor in numerous clusters.

Kimba quickly realized that some sort of tribe either lived here or had recently lived here. Animal hides, bones, branches, piles of flint—all were strewn over the floor. The smell of old food and the dumped dregs of meals was heavy in the air. In Kimba's Tribe, such a litter of dirt and refuse would have been swept out of the cave.

The dog pawed through a clump of bones, crunching them in its powerful jaws. But the bones had been picked clean and broken open for their marrow, and the animal soon turned away.

Above Kimba's head were scratch marks on the wall where generations of cave bears had sharpened their claws. The more recent inhabitants either had killed the bears or had forced them out—or deeper into the cavern. The far end of this chamber narrowed to form a tunnel.

As Kimba examined the cave, he felt the soaked fur tunic that he wore drying on his body. It would be good to linger here, he thought, to rest and spend the night. But to stay would be dangerous.

He must not think of his own comfort. If there was even a chance that Rab still clung to life, every moment could be crucial. They must be on their way.

Outside, the rain tapered off, then stopped entirely. Thunder now rolled in the distance. The sun crept from behind dark clouds, bringing clearer light to the cave's interior.

Kimba took out a flint and very quickly scratched on the wall the outline of a large bison. Below it, with two strokes, he etched in the symbol that was his signature.

Let them wonder who had done that, those who used this cave at times!

As they walked back to the entrance, the hair on the dog's back stiffened. It uttered a warning growl.

Kimba tilted his head to one side and detected the clatter of feet against stones.

They were coming, the inhabitants of the cave. He whipped around, and he and the dog ran to the tunnel in the rear of the main chamber. Kimba had time only to press himself against one damp wall before the Others began entering.

He recognized them immediately as the Others: those stooped, squat, two-legged beings so like the people of his Tribe and Nupa's tribe—and yet so different from them.

They said little to each other, only mumbling in guttural tones that Kimba could not understand. They had been caught in the storm and had been drenched, too, but their spirits seemed high. They had slain an ibex and were gesturing and shouting wildly.

Several women began to build a fire, using rubbing sticks rather than flint. However, many of the men preferred not to wait for the meat to be cooked. They tore at the raw flesh, devouring it with greedy swallows.

Two young hunters fought over the same chunk of meat. The rest ignored them as the pair rolled on the floor, locked in noisy combat. At last, one beat the other unconscious and resumed his interrupted meal.

Grunting contentedly, his belly stuffed, an elder of the group sat back. His eyes fell on the bison Kimba had scratched on the wall. The man hooted in surprise and pointed.

Immediately, the Others gathered about the picture. They had evidently been gone from the cavern on a hunting trip. The drawing had not been there when they left. Yet here it was.

Kimba watched them, fearful, but with some sense of pride. He knew how dumbfounded they would be by such an accomplishment. Drawing was a skill totally beyond them.

He did not notice that a child not yet able to walk

had crawled toward the tunnel. It stopped, staring at the dog—faintly visible near Kimba.

The child let out a wail. Its mother ran up. She, too, saw it.

The woman pointed and screamed shrilly. Instantly, the hunters dropped the raw meat from their hands and reached for their clubs and spears.

Chapter

16

Only a few paces within the tunnel, the sunlight faded. Kimba, withdrawing swiftly, knew he could not be seen here. He stared at the Others hulking in the oval entrance to the passageway.

They muttered and stamped their feet. But they would not venture farther into the tunnel, the boy felt sure. They lived in the huge outer chamber and, like his Tribe and all tribes, they feared darkness.

And then orange light poked through the entranceway.

Torches! They did intend to penetrate deeper into the tunnel!

Kimba pushed himself away from the wall. A savage cry went up. The first torchbearer had spotted his darting shadow. The Others knew now that something more than a wandering wild dog had invaded their domain. They pressed forward, shouting.

Perhaps the tunnel came to a dead end, Kimba thought with fright. Perhaps they knew he was already trapped.

He kept his arms outstretched to prevent his body from smashing into a wall if the corridor should take an unexpected turn. Though absolutely nothing was visible, he still sprinted as if he were running across a meadow at midday. It was a great danger, but to proceed more cautiously—and let the Others catch up to him—would be more dangerous still.

He tried to follow the sound of the dog, the clicking of its claws, the quick intakes of its breath. He heard it veer to the left, and he turned, too.

Something struck him on the forehead so hard that the impact rang out in a clear, deep tone. He reeled back in pain, then reached forward. It was one of the slim stone icicles that filled this cavern.

Behind him, voices grew louder, echoing and reechoing. He sped forward again, aware that he could no longer hear the dog.

He collided with the wet limestone, wrenching his wrist. He swerved, took a new direction, and again banged into a solid wall.

Desperately, he patted the wall, seeking an outlet. This could not be a solid barrier. The dog had somehow gone on from this point.

His hands suddenly slipped through, into thin air. There *was* an opening. Quickly, he traced its limits. It was tiny, but that did not trouble him. The smaller it was, the less likely the Others would be to enter it.

Kimba crawled into the hole. It funneled him into what seemed a larger corridor, perhaps even a large chamber. He was able to stand again, and once more he heard the *tick-tick-tick* of the dog's breathing.

The boy reached out a hand and touched the reassuring bulk of that big, furry head. Then the dog loped on, and Kimba continued after it. He walked now, certain that the Others would not attempt to squeeze through the narrow opening.

Their cries sounded hollow and distant. Kimba paused for a moment to look back. A bright patch of fire swirled into view.

One of the torchbearers had made it through the hole! Another torch appeared. They were still after him.

Again Kimba took flight. They would never stop, it seemed! Arms extended, he ran like a stag pursued by a panther—blindly, numbed by panic.

The voices behind him rose in volume, exultant, crashing fiercely against the roof and walls of the cave.

There was a sudden snarling directly in front of him. Kimba tripped. His head and arms slammed onto the floor and he rolled over twice.

Dazed, but conscious that he had to keep fleeing, Kimba

pushed himself to his knees. His probing fingers encountered the dog.

Why had it so clumsily gotten in his way? he asked himself. Why had it not led them out of here instead of blocking him?

He wobbled to his feet. The torches came nearer, the shouts grew more piercing. Kimba took a step forward and his foot touched—nothing.

He knelt and let his arm dangle. There was nothing. They stood at the rim of a cliff.

If the dog had not tripped him, in his headlong rush he would have plunged over the edge.

But they had to get past the precipice. He scrambled along the rim, groping for a way across or a trail down. There was no telling how high the cliff was. It might be an immense distance to the bottom or it might be only an easy jump.

Like comets fallen from the night sky, the torches whirled toward him. In their light, ugly shadows danced distortedly. The Others saw Kimba, and they roared like hungry sabertooths.

There might be a path around the precipice, but there was no time now to find it. Kimba climbed over the edge. He held on with both hands while his feet kicked and dug into the side of the cliff. But it was sheer, with no chinks to cling to.

The first of the torchbearers rushed up, screeching. Kimba looked into a knotted, hate-filled face.

The boy let go of the edge.

The magic ivory from the One-Tusk, he thought: Now Rab would never see it.

Then he heard a splash and icy water enveloped him.

Kimba's arms and legs flailed and his head popped back up above the surface. He took in air with great, sobbing gulps.

A spear flashed into the water beside him. The Others, waving their torches, capered about on the edge of the cliff, only a short distance above.

Another spear was flung. Kimba ducked his head and paddled furiously with his arms and legs, as he had seen wolves do in crossing a deep stream. He did not know if beings such as he could keep themselves on the surface of the water, or if they would plunge to the bottom like rocks. He cast out this thought and told himself only: I have the Power.

Invisible now in the murk, he tried to slip back toward the cliff. But the torches moved, too, and lined the area where he hoped to reach land. He saw that he was in an underground lake whose length and width he could not judge.

Already the cold water was paralyzing him. He had to thrash wildly to stay afloat. And as long as he made such a noise, there was no way to propel himself back without the Others hearing him and preparing a bloody reception.

From their throats poured jeering abuse. They knew he could not last long in the frigid lake.

Nearby, the water churned and a small wave lapped against him. He was seized by a new fear. Perhaps it was

155

a water monster, a being more dreadful than the Mighty Ones or the woolly rhinoceros.

But by the faint illumination of the torches he saw it was the dog swimming out to him. Its muzzle poked up; its legs paddled frantically. Like Kimba, it was awkward in the water.

They could not return to the cliff where the Others were gathered. And, bobbing helplessly, they could not much longer mark time where they were.

All they could do, Kimba was aware, was head deeper into the lake. Perhaps it was not so wide that it could not be crossed.

Kimba swung his arms like scoops and kicked hard. He would have to be quick. The cold was seeping into his bones, draining him of energy.

Each splash of his arms and legs was an effort. Gasping, he touched the piece of tusk, making certain it was still lodged in the pouch around his waist.

Then he struggled on. Beside him, the dog was breathing with difficulty, fighting to stay afloat.

But the cold had slowed Kimba's wits as well as his limbs. He was dimly conscious of a sense of warmth. It felt pleasant not to move.

His head sank under the water.

Instantly, he shot sputtering to the surface. He redoubled his strokes. He must not do that again! he warned himself. He must keep battling!

He must use the Power! He thought of himself as a fish, swift and powerful, accustomed to these cold waters. With a new burst of vitality, he seemed to slither forward.

The blackness of the water and the blackness of the air seemed stitched into a single choking garment. But he kept envisioning himself as a lake creature with fins, naturally at home in this world where nothing could be seen.

When suddenly there was light, it was for a moment alien to him. He wondered if it was just the sort of colored flashes that he sometimes produced by closing his eyes and rubbing them.

But the light was real. Was it a torch? Were the Others waiting on this side of the lake, too?

But, no. This was the clean, clear light of day. It was faint and faraway, but it was there.

His outstretched hands felt something solid. Numbly, he realized he had made it across the lake.

The ledge on this side was much closer to the water. Grunting, the boy pulled himself up onto it. Only then did he realize that he no longer had his spear.

He heard the dog still thrashing in the water and he called to it. The animal was more fatigued than Kimba and had to be hauled up, almost a dead weight. It lay on one side, shivering and panting.

Kimba, too, wanted only to stretch out and rest. But he had had enough of this dark, oppressive place. He could not bear to remain. The circle of daylight was too close, too tempting.

So he dragged himself toward the light. It poured through a jagged hole in the cave. The patch of sunshine was like a golden hand extended to him.

He ran, stumbling, to the portal. He stepped through it, to the outside, and gazed about in wonder.

He was in a vast, bowl-shaped, green valley. There were gentle hills in the distance. Beyond them, the mountain range vaulted upward once more, and its heights were iced over. But on the nearby hillsides he saw herds of game: musk oxen, bison, and reindeer. The meadows, cut through by a reed-lined stream, were a lush green.

The sun was warm and friendly. Kimba picked for his shelter a hollow, covered with pine needles, in the side of a knoll. He began piling up rocks as a barricade, but before he had placed many of them he was overcome by sleep.

Night came and went without waking him. At dawn he stirred, and found the dog curled up beside him.

They would have been an easy mark for predators, Kimba knew. But nothing had threatened them. This seemed a good place, a place of refuge.

All morning Kimba and the dog roamed the valley. The richness of it and the pleasant snap to the air put new vigor into his wracked body. The thought of the urgency of return to the Tribe never left him. He would not linger here. But he knew he had found a place that the Tribe must be told of.

Edible plants abounded: mushrooms, bilberries, wild lilies with their tasty bulbs. He stuffed his mouth eagerly as he walked. And then the dog pounced on a marmot, and Kimba broiled its juicy meat over a fire. They ate until neither could manage a bite more.

How joyous the Tribe would be to find this haven, Kimba thought. He would lead them to it and its teeming herds.

There were many caves and clefts in the base of the mountain where the members of the Tribe could live. They would be protected by the mountain itself from the angry north winds of winter.

If only Rab would be able to appreciate this valley too! If only there was still time!

First he had obtained the ivory from the One-Tusk. Now he had come upon a land of wondrous hunting. But none of this would help until he returned to the Tribe.

"We go!" he said to the dog.

None of the caves he had found in the valley appeared to run the width of the mountain. From the limited scouting he had done, he could discover no exit—except the way he had entered.

Kimba frowned, nibbling his lip. He could not swim back over that frigid expanse. But he would look it over again.

He went back to the underground lake, taking his time, picking his way along its edge. At last he concluded that what he had suspected was there: a slippery path around the lake.

There had been a trail. If he had known of it the day before, he could have fled his pursuers without that punishing swim.

And had they known of it, they might have been waiting for him on the far side. But he was sure the Others had never gone beyond their side of the lake. It was probably only under extraordinary circumstances that they dared go as far as they had. He doubted if they were even aware of this valley.

159

But now to leave the valley, he must retrace his steps and pass through the stronghold of the Others.

If he did not do that, he would have to keep searching for another route to the northern side of the mountain. There might be one, or there might not. Either way, it would require too much time to find out.

How could he manage to travel through the cave of the Others and not be stopped by them? How could the Power be used to achieve this feat? What would Utrek do?

He thought of Utrek and he remembered something the sorcerer had shown him.

Kimba smiled. He and the dog would return to the Tribe at once. And the Others would not prevent them.

Chapter

17

In the blackness Kimba and the dog followed the narrow trail of sticky mud that skirted the lake.

His foot dislodged a pebble, but he heard no splash. So they were beyond the lake. It had not seemed so enormous, walking around it. In fact, he realized the lake was not really very large at all. Swimming in its cold waters, possessed by fear of the Others, he had greatly magnified its size in his own mind.

Again they traversed the maze of tunnels down which they had fled their pursuers. Finally, they peeped into the chamber where the Others lived.

Enough moonlight shone so that Kimba could perceive the mounds of snoring bodies. An arm or leg stirred at times, but he could see no one standing up or moving about.

Yet there must be a lookout. And possibly many more of the Others would be awake or partially awake. His own people—and Nupa's too, he had noticed—did not sleep soundly the entire duration of the night. Instead, they would sleep for a relatively brief period and then awaken for a similar period. This was their pattern throughout the night. This was how they obtained their rest—but never left themselves totally vulnerable to whatever the night might bring.

He imagined it was the same with the Others.

Someone moved on the ledge just outside the entrance. It was a lookout shifting his weight. Were there two? Kimba could see no one else.

On tiptoe, he threaded his way among the sleepers. The dog followed, silent as fog.

Kimba tried to quiet his breath. His plan was a good one, or so it had seemed during the day. But now? It had to succeed, or these creatures would rise up and seize him in an instant.

He kept his eyes on the lookout. That would be the test of his plan. Kimba knew he would stand no chance if the guard—or anyone else lying here awake—should be too alert or too courageous.

But the lookout's close-set eyes were focused dreamily on the clouds framing the low-hanging moon. All was well. Then Kimba stepped on the hand of one of the Others.

The man cried out, shooting to a sitting position.

The lookout whirled around.

Kimba crouched, almost hidden in the gloom. The lookout and the man who had been awakened stared at the wild dog.

It glowed in the dark: huge, glimmering, spectral.

The man on the floor gurgled in fear, raising a hand to shield himself. The lookout shrank back.

"Tor," he whispered.

The rest had awakened. They saw the dog, and there were gasps and moans of horror.

Kimba dashed for the entranceway. The dog sprang after him.

"Tor," the lookout whispered again, flattening himself against the granite wall of the mountainside, letting them pass. Behind, many more were breathing the word: "Tor! Tor!"

It had worked, Kimba rejoiced, as he and the dog skittered down the slope. The Others had been too terrified to try to stop them. It was good that he had thought of Utrek and the ghostly, glittering costume the sorcerer wore.

Before he had left the great valley, Kimba had gathered the mosslike fox fire from the base of a dead, decaying spruce tree. He had rubbed it over the dog's hairy coat. To the Others, the animal must have resembled an apparition, a ghostly enemy, an evil Power they could not grapple with.

By sunrise they had reached the foot of the mountain. Kimba gazed back up to the tiny speck that was the portal to the cave. He would come back here and lead his Tribe to that pleasant, game-filled valley. He must remember every detail of the landscape.

From this point at the base of the Forbidden Mountains, it would be, he judged, three full days and perhaps half of another until he would be back with the Tribe. But he would hurry and attempt to cut that time.

"We go to Rab now!" he shouted to the dog.

It is too late for Rab, was the thought that came instantly to his mind. It was as though a voice—a sneering voice, such as Sabo's—had said it.

"Go!" Kimba said aloud to this thought. He would not consider it. It would not make its home with him.

He had told Nupa that he must continue to believe that Rab could still be saved. And he meant it. He must continue to believe that the piece of tusk could work its cure.

He must believe this—and so he would!

They saw no game that day, though the dog ranged widely, disappearing for long periods. Kimba settled for roots and edible grasses, but did not feel sorry for himself as he lay down to sleep that night within a small enclosure of rocks that he had hastily built.

By now, he thought, the Tribe must have found meat. Very likely Utrek had managed to summon a gigantic herd of bison or reindeer, and the hunters would have had great success. There were probably stacks of meat in the cave, and they would welcome him back with a hearty feast.

He saw himself sinking his teeth into a tender broiling haunch. That was his last waking thought, and his first the next morning.

Shortly after midday, a fallow deer crossed their path. It had been maimed by some predator and could run on only three legs. The dog gave chase and brought the animal to earth.

Kimba had sliced off only a small chunk of meat when a dozen gray wolves appeared. The pack was lean and ravenous, and Kimba saw that he and the dog would be no match for it.

They pulled back hastily and left the rest of the meat to the wolves.

But they had eaten enough to keep them moving briskly along. They spent that night in a snug sinkhole in the chalky clay adjoining a forest.

The following day they went once more without meat. But there were roots and tender new willow leaves to munch on. Kimba was loping much of the time now, and at dusk he was still filled with energy, reluctant to halt. The stars were out when at last he erected a ring of boulders around them.

On the third day of the journey from the mountains, the sun blazed as if it were the heart of summer. Kimba began to see land he knew well. There was a rolling meadow where he had once watched Rab run down and slay a wild boar. Here was a thin belt of pines where he had amazed the Tribe by softly hooting at an owl until it flew down to him and brushed his cheek with its wing.

That night he slept little. He squirmed with excitement, knowing how close he was to the Tribe. Again and again he stroked the magic piece of tusk.

If only the morning would come!

Somewhere close by, two mighty cats, sabertooths perhaps, coughed and spit at each other, then roared with the fury of open combat. The dog's ears perked up, but the sound of battle did not disturb Kimba. He had the piece of ivory for Rab. Nothing would prevent his return now!

Dawn was faint on the horizon when Kimba arose. By the time the moon had paled to invisibility, he had traveled far from the shelter of rocks where they had passed the night.

He stepped along rapidly, and where the earth was level enough he sprinted. Far in the distance he suddenly observed the bluff which jutted up over the Tribe's cave. It was pink and shiny in the bright light of the morning sun.

Just then the dog streaked after a hare. "Come," Kimba called to it. There was no need of this: There would be food soon when they reached the cave.

"Come," he called again. For the first time, he realized it would be good to have a name to call the dog. He recalled what the terrified Others had said when they saw the animal gleaming in the darkness—"Tor!"

Kimba did not understand their tongue. Tor. What did that mean to the Others? Spirit? Or devil? Or ghost?

166

He did not know. He only knew it must be their name for something awesome and frightening.

Tor. It had a good sound to it.

He cupped his hands to his mouth and shouted once more to the dog. "Come! Tor! Come, Tor!"

The hare skimmed away into the thick rushes along a brook. The dog turned back and hurried up to the boy.

"Tor," said Kimba. He thumped the dog's shoulders. "Tor," he repeated.

Tor was his friend and Tor would be welcomed by the Tribe, Kimba told himself. True, some might be distrustful to begin with. Just as they had been with Kimba. Odlag would not be friendly, and many would have to learn to change their beliefs.

But he would describe to them how much the dog had meant, how it had stayed with him when he had secured the One-Tusk's ivory. And how it had helped him to find the great valley.

They would understand. And so Tor, too, would be rewarded with a plentiful share of meat and would remain with the Tribe from this day forward.

Kimba could not stop himself from running. Every rock, every tree, every grassy swelling of the earth was known to him. At any moment he was sure he would see some of the Tribe.

The cliff was overhead now, and before him gaped the wide entranceway to the cave where he lived.

Kimba paused. The well-worn stretch of ground in front was deserted.

167

Perhaps the men were hunting, he thought. He started forward.

But the women and children should be outside. Could they have been frightened by some animal? he wondered. Perhaps they were remaining inside until the hunters returned.

"It is Kimba!" he shouted as he approached.

No one answered.

He halted outside the entranceway and hollered again. Still there was no reply.

"Urda!" he called. "Utrek!" he called. Only silence greeted him.

"It is Kimba!" he shouted, and entered the cavern.

There was no one there.

He went back out into the sunshine. "Utrek! Urda!" he cried out, knowing it was hopeless.

His voice echoed briefly, then died away.

He should have known, he chided himself. The Tribe would move on. They would already have long devoured the meat from the Mighty One the One-Tusk had killed. With other game so scarce in this region, with the coming of warmer days, it was only natural they had departed.

But somehow he had felt they would wait until he returned—until he brought the ivory that would restore Rab to health.

What a dreamer he was, he thought. Why would they think he would return? The Tribe never waited for those who separated themselves from it.

Kimba slumped down on a rock. What of Rab, so gravely injured? Had they taken him along? Kimba knew well that the Tribe would not risk the safety of all for any one individual.

Had they left him here then? Had Rab begun his final journey?

The boy went to a section of fallen rock at the base of the plateau which the Tribe had set aside as a place of burial.

Here Utrek would praise the virtue of the fallen one of the Tribe, who would be wrapped in ochre-powdered skins with his or her most prized possessions and then covered with rocks to keep away prowling animals.

But the burial place looked as it had when he had left. There was no sign of a new entombment.

The boy's heart soared with hope. Perhaps the Power had kept Rab alive until the One-Tusk's ivory could assure his recovery!

Which way had the Tribe gone? In seasons past it had more often than not been westward, toward the setting sun.

That was the custom, and Kimba could only trust that it was being followed now.

In a short while, the cave and the cliff fell far behind. The boy found no evidence of a trail. Soon hunger began to gnaw at him. He thought yearningly of the valley he had come from and of its vast herds of animals.

On these open, undulating meadow marshes no game was to be seen. A vulture with a wingspan as wide as two men are tall flew low. It, too, was hungry. But it lived off only the carcasses of the dead. Since the boy and the dog still moved, the great bird slowly flapped away.

As the long shadows of late afternoon slanted over the earth, Kimba faced the fact that he might be traveling in the wrong direction. He had no certainty that his Tribe had come this way. He had found no prints to indicate their passing.

Discouraged, he halted beside a creek that was little more than a thin rivulet of muddy water. He drank deeply. The water tasted sour and brackish. The dog just sniffed at it and walked away. Kimba felt sudden weariness. The day had been exhausting, and he had covered much territory.

The dog pounced on something beneath a thicket of brown ferns. Kimba bent to see what it was.

There lay a polished replica of a mammoth. Kimba recognized it at once.

It was one that Utrek had fashioned, one he was so proud of that he frequently carried it with him.

The sorcerer must have dropped it here. That meant the Tribe had passed this way.

Then he had come in the right direction! He would catch up with the Tribe, and soon!

Was it his Power that had led him this way and that had enabled the dog to find the miniature mammoth? The Power had been with him when he had seen in his dreams the notch where the One-Tusk was headed. It had been with him in that icy underground lake.

Or was it Utrek's Power that had guided him to this replica?

Just then his vision began to swim. A clammy coldness poured through his body.

The creek water, he thought. The dog had refused to touch it. Kimba had been warned many times to be cautious about water that was not fresh and clear. But his thirst had been too great, and his thoughts had been on other matters.

His trembling legs would no longer support his body. He sank down to earth, almost unable to move.

Chapter

18

Kimba spent the night stretched out where he had fallen, too sick to crawl to any shelter. He awoke at times, his head spinning, only to lapse again into unconsciousness.

He was distantly aware of the dog's presence. Twice he heard its threatening growls as it warned off some lurking carnivorous animal.

Kimba's body shook with chills, then seemed to burn with the fury of the sun. His brain pitched like a twig in a whirlpool. But one thought prevailed: He must rejoin the Tribe.

By morning he was able to drag himself to the creek. He dashed water on his face, then shakily arose. He began walking, but his feet did not seem connected to his legs. He could not be sure they would stop or if they would bear his weight.

His forehead felt flushed, as though steam were rising from hot coals burning behind his eyes. He must get to the Tribe. He must. That was the single idea which his feverish mind could retain.

His steps grew more certain as the day lengthened. But the poison from the creek water remained in his body. He trembled continually and felt too weak even to speak to the dog. He was gripped by a terrible thirst, but he came upon no more sources of water.

Worse, he knew, was that he had seen no more signs of the Tribe's passing.

Then he reached a low, grassy ridge that pointed outward like a knife blade. Below, the ground dropped sharply, curving into a long stretch of marshy plain.

From here he could see far. His vision was clouded from the siege of illness, but he could make out figures moving on the flatlands.

There were perhaps four dozen of them—a typical tribe. No group that depended on hunting to sustain itself could be larger than that. It would be impossible to find enough game to support greater numbers of people.

So it was a tribe. And not the Others. But he must be absolutely certain . . .

He put his hands over his eyes to keep out the glaring sun. Now he recognized them. He was sure of it.

They entered a grove of scrubby trees, but he had seen them distinctly first.

Utrek. Urda. Narik. Odlag. And many more.

He had seen them clearly.

And Rab? Was Rab there? No, he did not see the Spear-Maker.

A cry burst from his parched lips.

Down the hillside Kimba ran. His legs buckled and he rolled a long distance. He did not care. He wobbled to his feet and ran on.

The Tribe! He had found it!

He held out the piece of ivory from the One-Tusk. He held it high.

"Utrek!" he called. But he was still a long way from them, and his voice was little more than a squawk.

The dog raced ahead, puzzled and excited by the boy's sudden laughter. "See, Tor! The Tribe!"

Onto the marshland he dashed, waving the One-Tusk's ivory. "Utrek! Here!"

The earth was soft and gummy. Again his legs collapsed. The breath whooshed out of him as he stumbled.

The piece of tusk shot from his hand and arched through the air.

It came down upon the black, bubbling crust of a small bog. Frantically, Kimba thrust out a hand. The tusk was too far away.

Then it began to sink below the surface.

"No!" Kimba screamed.

174

He must not lose it! Not now! Not after coming all this way!

On his knees, teetering on the very edge of the bog, he reached outward, extending his fingers to their fullest length.

Still he was just short of the ivory.

And now it had vanished beneath the surface.

The boy stood up. He was desperate. In a moment the magical, healing piece of tusk would be gone forever.

Kimba leaped into the bog.

He landed in mud up to his chest. He scooped in his hand, searching for the piece of ivory. It touched nothing. He plunged his whole arm into the bog. Wildly, frantically, his fingers probed—finding nothing.

Maybe it had been farther away. He attempted to pull his arm out, to try again near the center of the bog. The oozing mud gripped him tightly. For a moment his arm would not move. Only with a great wrench could he yank it free.

But immediately he reached into the bog again, up to his shoulder, so deeply that mud splashed over one side of his face and his hair. His wriggling fingers encountered nothing solid, only the soft and sucking mud.

The piece of tusk could not disappear! The Power must prevent it!

Kimba was sobbing now. With great difficulty he once more pulled his arm free. He spat mud out of his mouth and with both arms half dived into the churning mire.

The dog growled, and then a voice called: "Kimba, come out of there!"

He did not hear it clearly because he was poking so deeply and intently for the ivory that even his ears had filled with mud. But he knew he had heard something and he peered up.

He shook his head, clearing his ears and eyes of the mud. He tried to talk but could not.

Rab stood only a half dozen paces away, looking surprised but impatient.

"Kimba, come out of there," he repeated.

He strode forward and extended the butt of his spear. Kimba grasped it and, fighting the tight embrace of the mud, pulled himself back onto the grass.

"What are you doing?" Rab demanded.

Kimba again attempted to speak but did not know how to begin to explain. He gestured at the bog and then at Tor—and noticed suddenly that the dog was gone.

Rab looked over Kimba, encased almost entirely in mud. And then he burst out laughing.

He dropped his spear and clasped the boy warmly with both arms. "Kimba!" he shouted, happily. Then he saw that mud had gotten over him, too, and once more he broke into rich waves of laughter.

"Rab," Kimba said. He felt intense joy and, all at once, extreme weariness. He had come so far. He had seen so much. He had been so sick. He had so many things to tell them.

Against his will, his eyes closed and his body went limp.

When he awoke it was to see Urda gazing at him, smiling as he spoke her name.

"Kimba!" she answered. "Welcome!"

He felt warm and dry and discovered he was wrapped in thick skins. They had taken him to a stream and washed the mud from his body. But he remembered none of this. And Urda had trimmed his wild and tangled hair, but he did not remember that either.

It was late afternoon, and he saw that the Tribe had already set up camp.

"Rab?" Kimba asked.

He was with some other hunters, Urda replied. He had gone after finding Kimba. The men had had bad luck and no game had been seen since the Tribe had left the cave.

Rab, she said, had heard a wolf or a wild dog and rushed to it, hoping it could be slain for its meat. Instead, he had come upon Kimba.

"Tor?" the boy inquired.

Urda shook her head, not understanding.

"The dog," Kimba explained.

"It ran off. Here."

She brought him a few snails, all that she had to offer. He dug the edible portion out of the shells with thorns. Though the snails were tasty, they were small and there were few of them. Kimba ate but was far from filled.

"Rab is well?" Kimba asked, and in his voice there was uncertainty and wonder.

The wound from the Mighty One had brought Rab to the edge of the place where he must begin his final journey, Urda told him. Some had wanted to move from the cave at once, in pursuit of game, and abandon Rab. But

177

she and Utrek had protested, and so they had stayed for a number of days. Rab was strong and healed quickly.

"That is good," Kimba said. "But Utrek said . . ."

Utrek was surprised at the recovery, Urda went on. The sorcerer said he had never seen a hunter with such a serious injury survive. Rab had been weak on his feet at first. He was still far from recovered. But each day he grew more vigorous.

Kimba nodded, relieved and joyful at the news.

The question that had for so long dominated his thoughts—Did Rab still live?—had been answered. Now his mind was free of it. He felt as he had when he found himself once again in sunlight after escaping the dark underground lake.

"That is good," he repeated. "But Utrek said only the tusk of the Mighty One would save Rab. Where is Utrek?"

He had gone off by himself as soon as camp had been set up, Urda said. He would use the Power to determine what the Tribe must do to find more herds of game in this time of scarcity.

"I know where there is much game," Kimba said. "I must tell Rab and Utrek. The Tribe must take a new trail, to the Forbidden Mountains."

"No, Kimba," Urda said, gently. "Not there."

"Yes!" Kimba insisted. "There is game there!"

He began to say more to Urda, but she put a finger to her lips and pointed. Kimba had a visitor. His friend Tabok had been hovering nearby, waiting for Kimba to wake up.

"Welcome," he greeted Kimba, solemnly and formally, as veteran hunters would when meeting after a long absence in pursuit of game. Then Tabok became shy, pleased at Kimba's return but not knowing what to say to him. He sensed a great change in Kimba.

Had he become a hunter? Tabok asked.

Kimba hesitated. Sabo's tribe had forced the One-Tusk off the cliff. Kimba had had nothing to do with it. Yet he had tracked the One-Tusk; he had faced it; he had risked his skin to pursue it.

Still, a hunter is one who slays game. No, Kimba said at last. But . . .

And he began to tell of his experiences. As he talked, Tabok's mother came over and then other women of the Tribe. Each touched Kimba, welcoming him back, and then they sat in a circle, listening to his words.

It pleased Kimba to see them assembled about him so. The role of storyteller was Utrek's and would someday be Kimba's, too, if he assumed the role of sorcerer. It was a part of the Power, one that Kimba had not considered before now.

Every hunter had his stories to tell. But it was only the individual who possessed the Power who could command such full and close attention from all in the Tribe.

It was right to be a hunter, Kimba thought. But there was much about the Power to be savored also, much that hunters would never know.

He found himself injecting into his tale some events that had not actually occurred, and he found himself pausing significantly when the women's attention was at its peak. He enjoyed the quick nods and the whispers of "Yes! Yes! Go on!"

He prolonged the story of his adventures so that he had not even reached the part about the death of the One-Tusk when Rab and the hunters returned.

Kimba noticed the huge, swollen scars on Rab's shoulder. But on the Spear-Maker's face was his familiar, wide smile. He sat beside Urda, letting Kimba continue.

The hunters also gathered around to hear the boy. Many looked friendly, and they signaled their greetings to him. But Narik and his son, Mrodag, stood apart with a few others. They stared sullenly at Kimba. To them, he knew, he was still the outsider. Now they would be muttering that he had returned and had likely brought his bad Power with him.

For the benefit of the hunters, Kimba went back to a part of his story that he had already touched on earlier. It was his description of Tor and how the dog had become his companion. As he talked, he wondered if Tor was still nearby, keeping just outside of camp as it had when he was with Sabo's tribe.

Rab broke into Kimba's recitation. No animal is a companion, he said. All are to be hunted.

Tor is a friend, Kimba said. And Tor must live with the Tribe.

No animal lived with the Tribe, Rab maintained. It had never been so.

Let Tor be the first then, Kimba persisted.

Rab looked increasingly baffled. Let it be up to Utrek, he said. Only the sorcerer could make such a decision.

With the weight of that problem gone, Rab's perpetual grin reappeared.

"Utrek," someone said. Kimba looked past his audience to see the sorcerer approaching.

He looked older and more frail than Kimba remembered. The sorcerer's eyes dwelled on the boy a long while. He did not touch Kimba, nor did he smile, nor, indeed, did any sign of emotion flicker over his face.

"You are back," he said simply. "I knew it would be so."

The boy propped himself up on his elbows. "The piece of the One-Tusk. I brought it. You said—"

"You brought it?" Utrek asked. For the first time, an expression passed over his face. It was one of surprise and, Kimba thought, of sadness.

"Yes. But when I saw Rab—"

"You brought it?" the sorcerer asked again.

"Yes. I do not have it now, but—"

"From the One-Tusk?"

"Yes. I followed the One-Tusk until it was slain. I took from it a piece of its tusk. All these days I carried it. Only that piece of tusk, you said—"

Utrek interrupted, lifting a skinny arm. "I will speak to Kimba alone," he told the members of the Tribe. "Come, Kimba."

The sorcerer shuffled away. Kimba got to his feet and made his way through the group. Once out of earshot of the Tribe, Utrek stooped to sit on a boulder. His legs creaked louder than ever as he did.

"It was the tusk of the Mighty One that stabbed Rab?"

181

He pulled at his beard, his face very long and very ancient.

"Yes. Because you said that was all that would save Rab."

The old man's voice was slow and deliberate. "Kimba, it is time for you to be told certain things. Because you will soon take my place. I will tell you this and only you will I tell this: A sorcerer knows many things. Many, many things. But not as many as the Tribe believes."

Kimba squatted down beside the boulder. Never before had he heard Utrek speak like this.

The sorcerer, Utrek continued, must make the Tribe believe he knows more than he does. When Rab was hurt, Utrek was sure he would make his final journey. All that Utrek knew of wounds and healing—and that was much—pointed to the fact that Rab would not remain with them much longer.

But he could not *say* that Rab was beyond all help. A sorcerer must not confess he is helpless. Such admissions create doubt and confusion in the Tribe.

So Utrek had announced that all that could save Rab was the tusk of the Mighty One that had attacked him. He had said that because he had known there was no chance of obtaining a piece of the tusk. So, if Rab left them, he could say it was for lack of the tusk, not because the sorcerer was unable to be of any help.

The old man chewed on a tuft of beard. He looked very uncomfortable.

"I did not know you would go after the tusk. I did not know you would believe so strongly that you would go after it. I thought no one would go. If they did I was sure they would not find it."

"The tusk . . ." Kimba faltered. "It has no Power?"

"No. None. I said it only so the Tribe would believe in me. Not because the tusk had any Power."

Kimba felt as he had when he had plunged into that underground lake: cold, shocked, drowning.

It had been for nothing! All the dangers he had faced, all the pain he had endured! For nothing!

Kimba jumped to his feet.

"It is all a trick!" he shouted. "All that you do! All the Power you speak of! All that you have trained me for! It is all a trick!"

He tore off the wolf-tooth amulet that Utrek had given him. Angrily, he hurled it at the sorcerer's feet.

Chapter

19

He could be a hunter now, Kimba told himself grimly. No more need to submit to Utrek's instructions and his disciplines. Now he could be like the rest.

Kimba stood far away from the fire, seeing the members of the Tribe as small silhouettes against the flames.

He had to be alone at this time. There were too many strange and difficult feelings whirling within him.

That Rab lived he was gloriously happy.

But that his efforts to destroy the One-Tusk had been useless goaded him to fury. He thought of the One-Tusk, of Sabo, of the Others. All had filled him with fear. Yet he had confronted them all because he had believed in Utrek.

Two yellow dots gleamed in the darkness. The boy tensed, but he knew instinctively there was no cause for alarm. A moment later, the red-speckled dog padded up to him.

Kimba rumpled Tor's shaggy coat. He realized that now he could not bring the dog into the camp. The Tribe was famished and would certainly kill Tor. How foolish he had been to think it could be otherwise. They would not listen to explanations. They would instead quickly plunge their spears into the animal.

So Tor must be an outcast. This, too, angered him.

One person left the Tribe and started toward Kimba. It was, he knew, Utrek. He had avoided the sorcerer since he had learned that his pursuit of the One-Tusk had been totally unnecessary.

At once the dog left, melting into the blackness of the night.

Utrek leaned heavily on his staff. "Kimba," he began, "you will hear me whether you wish to or not. You will soon wear my robes. There are many more things I must teach you."

"No," Kimba said. "I will be a hunter."

"Do not be misled because I sent you after the One-Tusk. I have the Power. And you have it, too."

"There is no Power!" Kimba cried out.

185

He thought of Sabo, and how he had tried to deceive his tribe into thinking his Power was genuine. Was Utrek any different? Was he not just more skillful at deception than Sabo had been?

"It is all a trick!" Kimba shouted. "The Tribe does not need your tricks! The Tribe needs meat!"

He darted past the sorcerer and ran back to the fire. "Hear me!" he called to the Tribe. "Come hear what I have to say!"

There was authority in his voice, and at once they began to assemble about him. Good-natured curiosity showed on the faces of many; others were suspicious of Kimba.

"What is it?" Rab asked.

"Who summons us now—Utrek or this whelp?" Narik demanded of no one in a loud, grumbling voice.

"I will lead you to where there is meat!" Kimba declared.

"Where?" a half-dozen voices cried.

The boy pointed toward the faraway peaks, cloaked now in darkness. He described the green valley he had found, and its great herds.

Those were the Forbidden Mountains, Narik growled.

He had traveled through a cave under one of those mountains, Kimba went on. And he had returned.

But it was forbidden to go there, said another hunter.

There was game to be had there, Kimba insisted. And the Tribe was hungry.

This was the boy's bad Power again, shouted Narik. He wished to lead them to their doom. The hulking, gray-bearded hunter glowered down at Kimba. "Your Power is bad," he asserted.

Then Rab faced Narik squarely and asked: What choice had they? They had found no game in a long while. A few small creatures, true. But these were not enough, not for the entire Tribe. The large herds had left the region of their cave. They must look elsewhere or soon they would grow too weak to continue.

If the boy knew where there was game, Rab said, they must go after it.

Some murmured agreement. But Narik repeated that it was forbidden to go near those peaks. It had always been forbidden. Back when he had been a child and there had been another sorcerer—even then it had long been known that those mountains were forbidden. Evil dwelled there.

Mrodag, Narik's son, nodded vigorously. None of the Tribe had ever approached that dreaded area, others said.

"I have," Kimba stated.

"I say you are not of the Tribe!" Narik thundered.

"I am of the Tribe and I will lead the Tribe to game."

"You were not bred of the Tribe and you have never been of the Tribe!"

"Let it be up to Utrek," Rab said quietly.

The sorcerer moved into the firelight. Voices babbled, telling him of Kimba's suggestion. Utrek silenced them by waggling his staff.

"I heard," he said.

It was forbidden to go there, Narik persisted. It was a place of bad Power.

187

There was much game in that valley, said Kimba impatiently. "The Tribe has great hunger. What has your Power done?"

His question was insolent, he knew. Once he would not have dared to speak that way to Utrek.

The muttering voices ceased abruptly. No one had ever questioned Utrek in such a tone before.

For many long moments the old man's eyes bored into Kimba's. The boy suddenly turned away, feeling his new-found defiance crumbling.

"I will lead you to fresh meat," he repeated, stubbornly but softly, almost to himself.

At last Utrek spoke. The boy had the Power, he said. He felt the Tribe being called to those mountains. What was forbidden once might not be so now. He felt that Kimba had been sent to lead them there. He felt that there his own Power again would be strong; there he would summon more game than they could eat. And his Power, he was sure, would counter any bad Power of the mountains.

The sorcerer hobbled slowly into the shadows. Kimba realized that he had stood up to Utrek and forced the old man to give in.

It was well, he thought. He and Rab would see to it that the Tribe was fed soon. Their courage and skill would do it—not any of the ancient sorcerer's worthless tricks.

Progress was painfully slow for the next four days. Gaunt and hungry, the men, women, and children toiled along with effort, bowed under the sacks that held their possessions. The loads were carried either on their backs or slung from head straps.

Kimba had refused to carry Utrek's equipment, and the sorcerer had accepted this refusal without a word. A boy who had not yet seen ten summers was instead recruited for this purpose. Rab was displeased with Kimba's attitude, but he would not interfere in matters between the sorcerer and his assistant.

The rest of the Tribe knew that all was not well between the two. But neither Utrek nor Kimba would discuss the cause of it. Tabok walked beside Kimba throughout the long day, but he said little to his friend. He was awestruck by this unfamiliar sense of tension between those who had the Power.

Only Narik and a few others talked about the subject among themselves in low and surly voices, seeing it as dissension that could lead to disaster. They also frowned apprehensively at the pinnacles of the Forbidden Mountains. Often they looked searchingly over the empty tundra. If only they could sight fresh game, they told each other. Then they need not complete this foolhardy journey.

Kimba, too, glanced frequently about. He was concerned that he might glimpse Tor—and that the hunters of the Tribe might also.

Almost as much, he feared that Tor was no longer nearby, cautiously trailing them.

But there was no sign of the wild dog.

Each day they fed only on nuts, roots, bark, and a few snails. Though the pace of their march was slow, a woman called Mota could not keep up with the rest. She was soon

to become a mother. Her mate had been one of the hunters killed by the One-Tusk. Exhausted and weak, she
continually lagged behind.

Urda fell back frequently to keep her company, smiling
and gossiping. But Mota would seldom look up. On the
morning of the fourth day, as they crossed a ridge, Mota
stubbed her toe on a rock. She was thrown off balance
and pitched into a ravine.

The woman was attempting to stifle cries of pain as
the members of the Tribe hurried to her. One leg had suffered a deep, wide gash. Her body writhed in spasms of
agony.

Utrek ordered a fire made, while he went to gather
some creeping purple and white flowers that were just
coming into bloom. He tore off a few tendrils, ground
them up, and began boiling them in a horsehide con-
tainer.

He pointed to some squat, prickly hawthorn bushes
that grew on a hillside. "Go, Kimba," he said, instructing
the boy to pick off the tiny, just-reddening berries.

Kimba set his mouth into a hard line. He did not
move.

"Go," Utrek repeated.

The boy shook his head. It was as though he were
being sent again after the ivory of the One-Tusk. It would
not help. It was another trick. Utrek could become out-
raged if he chose, but Kimba was determined not to be
deceived once more.

Utrek only turned away, his face expressionless. He
walked, very stiffly, the long way to the hawthorns him-

self. When he returned, he told Mota to drink the water that the flowers had been boiled in.

Then he reduced the tiny berries he had picked to a pulp, heated them also, and thoroughly soaked a thin piece of doehide in the mixture. This poultice he applied to the leg wound.

Kimba looked on skeptically. The woman's pain and her injuries were severe. They must either spend several days here with her—while they all became more desperately hungry—or they must abandon her.

But soon her spasms ended and she went peacefully to sleep. More poultices were applied during the night, and by the next dawn the bleeding and swelling had subsided. The healing was well along. She was able to walk, and so the Tribe set out again.

As Mota resumed her place in the column, Utrek came over to Kimba.

"The Power is not all a trick," he said simply.

A hard rain began after midday. It lasted all the way to the base of the Forbidden Mountains. Narik and a few others complained constantly, convinced that this was an evil sign. Kimba noticed that Tabok looked up often, measuring the heights above. His mouth gaped open and his eyes were wide with wonder.

That night they huddled, shivering, under a projecting boulder while the rain continued. They were too famished and weary to talk, but fear of this strange and mysterious region shone in their faces.

Kimba knew he should tell them of the cave they must

go through to reach the valley: the cave which the Others inhabited.

But the Others might be gone when they entered the cave the next day. They might all be out hunting or they might have moved to wherever else they camped during their migrations.

Still, Kimba knew, he should tell the Tribe. But if he did, would they still follow him? And if they would not, how could he convince them that they should? He could not say it was because he had the Power. He was not sure now there was any such Power.

He saw Narik studying him with distrust. If something went wrong on the mountainside, he knew he would be blamed. Even Utrek could not save him from the wrath that would follow.

And why—it occurred to him suddenly—would Utrek even care to defend him now?

He reached up to touch the magic wolf tooth and then remembered he had thrown it away. At that moment, he wished he had it back.

At a very late hour that night, as he attempted without success to sleep, he heard the snarl and growl of two animals in the far distance. It was a brief battle, and then there was only the sound of the steady downpour. But he was certain he had recognized one of the growls.

"Tor," he whispered. May Tor have won that fight and may Tor remain nearby.

The rain ended as they began their climb in the morning. But the day was damp and dark.

Like Tabok, many of the Tribe stared at the towering

shafts of the peaks above, dazzled and fear-stricken. The rest were too terrified even to raise their eyes.

Kimba had sighted the entranceway to the cave, and so he scrambled ahead first. Most of the climb would not have been difficult if they had been well fed and confident. But because of their exhaustion, the belongings they carried, and their dread, progress was slow.

Hugging the mountainside closely, Kimba crept to within a stone's throw of the ledge outside the cavern. He saw nothing, and he heard nothing. Rab appeared and Kimba motioned to him to keep down.

For the first time, the boy mentioned the Others.

Rab looked surprised and, for an instant, angry.

"Is there more you have not told us?" he snapped.

No, Kimba replied. A valley filled with game awaited. Through that long chamber.

Rab's face was grim. He looked upward and then to the slopes below. Kimba knew he was asking himself if it might be best to leave now, before they were discovered.

"We will continue," he said. The Tribe had come too far to turn back. And where would they go, and what game would sustain them? He signaled to the hunters, waving them upward.

As they climbed to join Rab and Kimba, a burly, shambling figure came into view on the ledge. It was a lookout for the Others.

He glanced down, and then his hoarse shout brought a dozen of his comrades on the run.

Rab and the hunters clambered up to the attack. The Others rushed to a row of boulders they kept on the ledge to ward off enemies. Yelling to work up their courage, they strained and pushed.

With a roar, the first boulder rolled down the slope toward the approaching hunters. Then a second hurtled after it.

Chapter

20

Grabbing Kimba, Rab flung himself to one side. The rest of the hunters also reacted quickly and jumped out of the way. The first boulder streaked past, scraping one man's back, smashing another's elbow.

Then the second boulder thundered by, just missing the women and children farther down, setting off a small avalanche as it bounced to the bottom of the mountain.

Several of the Others got behind a third boulder, ready to roll it, too. The rest began hurling smaller rocks.

Narik, hit on the knee, let out a mighty howl. The rest of the hunters ducked, shielding their heads with their hands.

The third boulder wavered on the edge. The hunters frantically slipped and slid down the slope. They rejoined the remainder of the Tribe, and all descended rapidly to a large, shelflike rock out of the Others' sight.

Those who were hurt rubbed their wounds and gritted their teeth. Utrek inspected the injuries briefly, but there was no time to offer treatment.

They must leave here at once, said an old woman. "The Power of this mountain is bad."

"His Power is bad!" Narik yelled, pointing accusingly at Kimba.

"It is bad!" his son, Mrodag, echoed.

The boy had brought them to this evil place, another hunter agreed.

"His Power is bad!" Narik shouted. He extended his hands as if to clasp Kimba and hurl him down the side of the mountain.

"No," said Rab. "He will lead us to fresh meat."

"We must go back," the old woman whined.

"Go back! Go back!" many began chanting.

"Wait!" Rab called out. "Hear me!"

They could not go back, he told them. They had found no large herds thus far in their usual hunting areas. They must continue on, to the valley Kimba had described.

196

But the Others would destroy them, one of the hunters insisted.

"He is right!" Narik said.

Ordinarily, they knew, the Others would be no match for them. But their position on the ledge above gave them an advantage over an enemy that must climb upward, exposed and vulnerable all the while.

The Tribe could not attack, Odlag declared flatly. They could not get close enough to use their throwing sticks effectively before more boulders rolled down on them. There was no chance.

Heads nodded. There were weary grunts of assent.

Then Utrek rose. He had been squatting on the far corner of the shelf rock. The climb had weakened him, and he had been silent and slumped over.

But suddenly he appeared tall and stalwart as a young man. His voice was vibrant and assured. He held his staff up high and turned his face to the top of the peak.

"My Power is mighty! This mountain speaks to me!"

As still as a column of stone Utrek stood, seeming to listen to the message of the mountain.

The people of the Tribe stared, startled by the old man's transformation. And then they flinched in further surprise at the shout that exploded from his throat.

It was a strong, sharp howl, like the victory cry of a dire wolf.

Immediately, Utrek began stamping and spinning in a frenzied dance. His piercing howls continued. They excited the Tribe. Within moments, some of the hunters were dancing, too. The rest nodded, standing straighter, brandishing their weapons.

"The Power! The Power!" Utrek called out. "They cannot stop us! We have the Power with us!"

The women and children were suddenly swept up in the spirit. And now all of the hunters were howling, blending their voices with the sorcerer's.

Kimba alone remained seated. He watched Utrek, puzzled. Was not the Power a deception? Had he not discovered that Utrek was no more than a trickster? What was this that the old man told the Tribe?

Their shrieks grew into a steady, powerful din, drifting up to the Others. Even the wounded hunters danced with abandon, jumping, bellowing, flinging their arms about, forgetting their pain.

Utrek halted abruptly. "They have no Power!" he screeched. "My Power is good! They cannot touch us! They cannot stop us!"

The hunters gripped their throwing sticks, long spears, clubs and knives. They leaped up the steep wall of rock that led to the Others.

Gone were the doubts, the complaints, the weariness of a few moments before. They felt that nothing could stop them. The mountain was their friend! They would overwhelm the Others! They had nothing to fear!

They shouted as they surged upward, roaring with courage, challenging their enemies to meet them again.

Kimba's forehead creased in confusion. Was there a Power at work here? It seemed beyond him to sort it all out.

But one thing he knew. Rab and the other hunters could use another spear in their attack. He started after them, but a hand dug deeply into his shoulder.

"No, Kimba," said Utrek.

"But I will be a hunter now."

"No. You must take my place when I am gone."

"No! I will be a hunter!"

"You have the Power! You must not risk your life in battle!"

"The Power!" the boy exclaimed. "Always it is the Power!"

"Yes," Utrek said softly. "That is so."

In their initial charge some of the hunters, led by Rab, almost reached the bottom of the Others' ledge. They whipped their throwing sticks and the javelins flew into the ranks of the Others. There were screams of pain and fright.

Several of the Others managed to push another boulder off. But the hunters, seeing the path it would take, had swung around to approach from both flanks. The boulder rolled harmlessly between the two columns of attackers.

The hunters' yells reached a shattering pitch. They swarmed up the escarpment and onto the ledge.

A few of the Others threw rocks or thrust vainly with their spears. But they were demoralized. The fierce cries of the hunters, their bold charge, their feeling of invincibility—all these melted the valor of the defenders.

The Others shouted in panic and fled. Some scrambled higher up the mountainside. Some dashed deeper into the cave, there to hide, quaking, in dark recesses. A few were slain on the spot.

The fight was over in moments. The hunters—none of whom had suffered any serious injuries—cheered and waved to those below.

While the women and children hastened to join the hunters, Utrek and Kimba remained where they were. The sorcerer's eyes glittered so brightly they seemed to radiate heat.

"That is the Power!" he declared. "The Power to make the Tribe believe. The Tribe can do what it believes it can do. That is the greatest Power: to make the Tribe believe in itself. You have that Power, Kimba."

The boy was unable to meet the awesome gaze. "Yes, Utrek," he said.

At last he thought he understood. The hunters were no mightier the second time than they had been during the first attack. But because they believed that they were unconquerable, they succeeded.

Perhaps he did have this Power, he reflected. His skill at sketching, his ability to charm small animals, the guiding dreams he experienced at times—these were mysteries to the Tribe. And so its members thought he had other, greater Powers. And if they believed this, they would believe whatever he told them about themselves. By telling them what would stimulate their bravery and confidence, he would make their lives more than they had been. And so the Tribe would be stronger and more vigorous.

That, Kimba saw now, was the role of the sorcerer.

"The Summoning Rite . . ." he said hesitantly. "Does

200

what you draw in the cave cause game to appear? Or do the hunters only think so—and so hunt harder and with more sureness?"

Utrek's mouth curved in a very faint smile. "There is more for you to learn, Kimba," he would only say. "Come."

Together they climbed to the cave entrance where the Tribe waited.

Chapter

21

With torches lit, the Tribe filed into the winding corridor that cut through the mountain. Kimba, in the lead, remembered how fearful he had been when first he had traveled this way, when he and Tor had been pursued by the Others.

Now, in the presence of the Tribe, he felt secure. But he missed the big dog. He had sighted it keeping pace with them to the foot of the mountain. But he doubted it had come far up the slopes. It was not natural for a dog or a wolf to climb so high.

True, Tor had accompanied him this way once before. But it had been different then. He and Tor had grown used to each other and had been somehow dependent on each other. Now Kimba was with the Tribe, and he felt certain the dog would be extremely wary of so many two-legged beings. It might follow them cautiously through the plains and woodlands it inhabited, but not up these strange and precarious heights. Not through this dank and threatening cave.

In guiding the Tribe to fresh game, he realized he had probably lost Tor.

"Through here," he told the Tribe as they came to the tiny slit in the wall of the long tunnel.

They skirted the lake and he heard them murmur as their torches illuminated that cold, black, silent expanse of water. Then they saw the sunshine ahead. As if by signal, they broke into a run.

A few moments later they stood in the long, wide valley that Kimba had discovered.

No words were spoken for a long while. There were sighs and grunts as they marveled at the endless carpet of grass, the delicate green of the hills, the thick forests.

But most of all they stared at the distant herds of animals.

Then they were laughing and scampering about like children. Urda hugged Kimba as tears coursed down her cheeks. Rab, whooping, pulled the boy away and twirled him around joyously.

203

Other hunters, beaming, slapped Kimba's back. Their silence gave way to an excited hubbub.

"Good, Kimba!"

"You see, just as he told us."

"Tonight we feast!"

"Utrek, he has the Power, as you said!"

Even Narik was smiling. "It is good you are of the Tribe," he said softly. Mrodag, too, approached the younger boy. "We are friends," he told Kimba. Awkwardly, respectfully, he touched Kimba's shoulder, as he would touch something magic.

"It is the Power," Kimba said to Narik and Mrodag. "My Power is good. Remember that. In times to come, remember that—both of you."

Rab pointed out the many smaller caves on this side of the mountain. They would serve as shelters. The women, he said, must select which ones they wanted for their families, while the men went out to hunt.

Some grazing bison were the nearest game. It was time to pursue them. The members of the Tribe, so long without meat, suddenly felt their appetites could not be contained another moment.

The hunters shook their weapons eagerly. Kimba raised the new spear that Rab had given him. Surely, now that he had led the Tribe to game, he would be granted the opportunity to participate in his first real hunt.

The men looked to Rab for a signal. But the Spear-Maker turned to Kimba.

Utrek would need help, he said. The sorcerer must find

a cave of his own and prepare it for its sacred uses. And the old man was very tired. Kimba, as Utrek's assistant, must stay here and aid him.

Kimba opened his mouth to protest, but Rab quickly motioned him to keep quiet. "Your place is with Utrek."

It was unfair! Kimba had to bite his lip to keep from saying the words aloud. After all he had accomplished, he was still not a hunter. And now to be deprived of the chance again!

True, he had the Power. True, he would learn more of Utrek's teachings.

Yet the urge to be a hunter still pounded in his veins.

"You have done well." Rab grinned.

Then he and the rest were off. The boy could only watch them growing smaller as they spread out to surround the bison.

The women made a great clamor, inspecting the caves and squabbling about who would get which. But there was a lightheartedness to their bickering, for they knew they had found a safe refuge and there would soon be meat in abundance for all.

Kimba kicked a clump of dirt. If he must assist Utrek, so he must.

A sorcerer required a larger cave than anyone else, and a cave removed from the central area of activity. Utrek was nowhere to be seen. Had he already begun searching for such a place?

Kimba recalled from his earlier visit to the valley that there were other cave openings to the eastward, although he had not had time to explore them. He wondered if these might have attracted Utrek, and so he started toward them.

Stepping through a field of high grass that was already the vivid green of summer, he heard a sound that stopped him in his tracks. It was a familiar sound, but frightening: the angry growl of a wild dog.

He knew that growl. He knew it well. He had heard it only last night, on the far side of the mountain. It was Tor.

The boy dashed forward. Tor! How had the dog entered the valley? Perhaps there was some other way, some passage Kimba had not noticed. That would be good. It meant the Tribe could come and go by another route, if enemies should ever block them in the great cave. He had guessed that there must be another such way in and out. Now Tor would show them where it was!

The dog was barking, loudly and viciously.

Then Kimba heard a rumble that grew in pitch and intensity. He knew the fight must be a terrible one. For it was the roar of a cave bear.

It came from an entranceway just ahead. Kimba ran up to the wide hole and as he did so heard another sound that struck terror even deeper—a cry for help.

He recognized the voice as Utrek's.

Kimba stepped into the cave. For a moment his eyes could not adjust to the dimness. But the rank smell of the cave bear was strong and unmistakable.

And then he saw it, standing upright on its stubby legs.

The beast almost seemed overbalanced by its massive fore-
paws, shoulders, and head.

Utrek lay sprawled behind the bear. Kimba could guess
what had happened. The bear had been disturbed and
had cuffed the sorcerer. But it must have been a glancing
blow. For one solid swat of those long, curved claws
would have killed the old man instantly. Before the bear
could finish the job, Tor must have appeared.

The dog leaped forward, snapping. The bear showed
its fangs and roared. Tor dodged away out of reach of its
claws.

But the dog could never drive off so gigantic a beast.
Kimba knew the bear would shortly turn back to Utrek.
When it did, the battle would be over in one bloody
moment.

He yelled, as the hunters had in attacking the Others.
He lunged with his spear.

The bear batted the spear aside, slamming Kimba onto
the cave floor. The animal fell to all fours, its huge jaws
gaping. Tor again darted in, snarling, distracting. Kimba
jumped back to his feet.

Again he thrust. The spear tore in and out of the bear's
mighty shoulder.

Infuriated, the bear reared up on its hind legs. The boy
backed away as the beast came toward him.

"Kimba, run!" Utrek called feebly.

But he did not turn to flee. He poked the spear at the
advancing beast, feinting, probing. Suddenly he felt his
back against the cold wall.

Once more the dog flew in, biting furiously. The bear whirled to brush Tor aside and Kimba struck again.

The spear stuck in the bear's chest muscles. The animal's roar was deafening. The boy had to tug hard to pull out the weapon.

But the wound was not fatal. Bellowing with pain, the bear waddled closer, raising a thick forepaw. Its oversized head sank low on its chest; its teeth were bared.

The dog flashed in to take another nip. The bear ignored it.

Kimba knew he had only one brief moment. With both hands on the shaft, he heaved the spear upward, putting all his strength into the thrust.

The bear gurgled, and then its mountainous body collapsed heavily against him.

That night several large fires crackled outside the caves. The smell of roasting meat floated over the camp.

Kimba sat beside Urda and Rab. Little was said until they finished the meal. Rab grinned and rubbed his stomach. Urda offered him another chunk of the sizzling bison flesh, but he shook his head. Another bite, he grunted, and—his two hands flew apart in a gesture indicating an explosion.

Although Utrek lay near the fire, he had pulled a robe over himself. He had said his old bones required much warmth if he were to recover quickly. He had treated his own wound, covering it with foul-smelling herbs. He could not move his right arm, but he assured the Tribe that he would in time be well.

Kimba wrenched loose a large piece of meat and flung it into the far shadows. A black shape materialized and they heard a loud, gnashing sound.

Tor had already eaten well, but Kimba could not resist rewarding the dog further.

Tor was welcome in the camp. Utrek had decreed it because of the dog's battle with the cave bear, because it had befriended Kimba.

But Tor distrusted the Tribe and would venture only near Kimba at first. Soon it also would come to Tabok, who had taken an instant liking to it. But most of the members of the Tribe were suspicious of the animal. Odlag, in particular, had cause to remember how Tor had once attacked him, and he did not look kindly on his son's new friendship with this creature.

It did not matter, Kimba told himself. They would know each other better in the future, Tor and the Tribe, and the uncertainty between them would slowly disappear.

The boy rose and went to Utrek. Would he like more meat? Kimba inquired.

"No, Kimba. But you . . ." Wisps of his beard blew into Utrek's mouth and garbled a lengthy flow of words.

"Now that you are a hunter" was all that Kimba could make out.

A hunter?

Kimba had not thought of that when he had killed the cave bear. He had thought only of saving Utrek.

But it was true. The realization swept over him. It *was* true. He had slain one of the most formidable of creatures. He was a hunter now, and all the Tribe knew it.

It was an honor which he had long desired. It was a good feeling, a satisfying thought: He was Kimba, the hunter!

Kimba, the hunter!

No more need he think there was something lacking in him.

Yet he felt no desire to march about boasting of his feat—not as he had seen Narik do after killing game. Somehow it did not instill in him the intense and glowing pride he had thought it would. After all, every man in the Tribe became a hunter.

It was fine to be a hunter and to be accepted as one. But he was still not like the other hunters. And he enjoyed the thought that he was not.

He remembered Nupa and how wide-eyed she had been to learn that he was to become a sorcerer. One day he would go back for her—and display more of the Power for her.

He thought of the cave Utrek had chosen. It was larger than any of the others in this valley, though the Grotto in their home cave was still bigger.

In time, they would return to that other cave that had so long been their home. There, in the secret den, was much of Utrek's magical gear. And also the impressive bison costume he had given to Kimba.

Yet this new cave would be used for many rites. And here Kimba would be taught all that the Power was—and all that it was not.

That would be the biggest thing to grasp, Kimba thought: the difference between what the Power was and what it was not. There was so much Utrek must teach him. He found himself eager to begin once more. He remembered with shame his actions of the past few days.

"Utrek," he said, "the wolf tooth . . ."

He wanted to apologize, but could not bring himself even to speak of how he had thrown it at the sorcerer's feet.

"I have it. In the cave. It is yours again. Get it now."

"Yes, Utrek!" The boy's green eyes sparkled.

"The Power will be strong in that cave, Kimba."

"Yes, Utrek." The boy started away, then thought of something else.

"But its walls are bare."

"They will be filled. Someday."

"Yes, Utrek," Kimba agreed, lighting a torch and hurrying off. But he knew Utrek would not be ready to paint until his arm had healed. Suddenly the boy felt a yearning to create the images he saw in his mind. He had not done so for what seemed a long while.

He entered the cavern that would become the new Grotto. The empty walls looked inviting.

What he would like to do was put a Mighty One on the wide expanse near the entranceway: a woolly mammoth bigger than any Utrek had ever drawn. Then, next to it, a wild horse, galloping, its mane blowing in the breeze. Then, perhaps, a reindeer . . .

But first of all he would depict Utrek himself!

He would show him in his eerie sorcerer's costume of antlered mask, bear claws, and wolf tail. It would be a perfect likeness!

He was aware that never had Utrek made paintings of anything other than animals upon the walls of a cave. Only these were of use to the Tribe, he often said.

But Kimba yearned to show so many other things, whether they were of practical value or not. Might this not, he thought, be part of his Power? Perhaps his portion of the Power was different, in this way, from Utrek's. Perhaps the Power did not work its wonders in the same manner with every sorcerer.

Perhaps, at last, he understood something that Utrek did not. Could he not draw what he wished—and dream his own dreams—and still be true to the Tribe?

The materials needed for painting—the colored powders, the animal fat to mix them with, the palette made of the shoulder blade of a musk ox, the brush of raven feathers—all had been placed at the base of the cave wall.

The walls would be filled someday, Utrek had said.

Someday? Why not, the boy asked himself, make a beginning this very day?

Eagerly, he went to work. Let Utrek be surprised to see this in the morning, he decided. Perhaps the old sorcerer would be angry. But it would be too late. Perhaps Kimba would be punished, but he could not restrain himself.

He had almost finished drawing the face of the sorcerer when a question popped into his mind: Why had

the painting materials been so carefully laid out . . . as
though awaiting Kimba's appearance?

Was the boy doing what he was doing because Utrek
had wanted it so? He remembered that back at the fire
the sorcerer had smiled at him, very, very slyly.

Kimba frowned. The Power of a sorcerer could be a
puzzling thing.

Then he resumed work on his picture.

Author's Note

This story takes place toward the end of the last Ice Age—a time when winters were longer and more severe than at any period since. Great glaciers covered much of Europe and forced many animals—and the hunters who pursued them—southward into areas that border what we now call the Mediterranean Sea.

The earliest of these hunters are known as Neanderthals. They are the "Others" of this book.

In time a more advanced people appeared in the territory so long dominated by the Neanderthals. These newcomers are now termed Cro-Magnons. Kimba's and Nupa's tribes are modeled on what we know of the Cro-Magnons. They were people of high intelligence and great physical dexterity. They were, in fact, the first "modern" human beings.

Eventually the Neanderthals disappeared, leaving the Cro-Magnons the masters of the Ice Age world.

Considerable mystery still surrounds the people of that long-ago time, even though every effort has been made in this book to be true to the facts that archaeologists and paleontologists have uncovered. Knowledge of the Cro-Magnons has come to us through the discovery of objects they had so skillfully fashioned—tools and weapons of animal bones and flaked stone of the sort that are mentioned in this story. Even more revealing, perhaps, are the magnificent paintings that have been discovered on the walls of caves.

Cro-Magnon paintings and engravings have been found in more than one hundred caves in southern France and northern Spain. Many of these caves are near the Pyrenees Mountains, which are called the Forbidden Mountains in this story. Most frequently, the paintings show animals that were vital to the existence of prehistoric peoples—the woolly mammoths, reindeer, bison, wild horses, and giant stags.

These ancient picture galleries were lost to history for tens of thousands of years and have only been rediscovered during the past century. The first was found in 1879 in a cavern near Altamira, Spain.

The leading scholars of that day angrily insisted that these paintings could not have been the work of Ice Age humans. They could not believe that primitive "cavemen" could possess such artistic sensitivity and talent.

But more and more caves containing similar paintings were discovered, and every scientific test confirmed the remarkable age of the pictures. There could be no doubt: They were authentic.

In addition to Altamira, some of the most famous of these caves are Lascaux, Trois Frères, Rouffignac, and Les Eyzies in France and El Castillo and Minateda in Spain.

Today visitors are able to go deep into many of them. There they can see for themselves the very pictures painted so long ago by artists such as Kimba and Utrek. And there too the visitor might reflect that, despite the passage of centuries almost without number, these were people not so very different from ourselves.

Thomas Millstead

was born and grew up in the Midwest. As a child, he says, he became fascinated with prehistoric times after seeing the movie *One Million B.C.* with Victor Mature and Carole Landis. "It was about man versus dinosaur, though to my disappointment I soon learned that the dinosaurs had been extinct for millions of years before anything resembling people had evolved."

Mr. Millstead was a newspaper editor and has written mystery-suspense stories and magazine articles. He now works in public relations and lives in Chicago. This is his first book for young readers.

◆ ANCIENT WORLD LEADERS ◆

ALEXANDER THE GREAT

ATTILA THE HUN

JULIUS CAESAR

CHARLEMAGNE

GENGHIS KHAN

SALADIN

JULIUS CAESAR

Samuel Willard Crompton

CHELSEA HOUSE
PUBLISHERS
A Haights Cross Communications Company

Philadelphia

Frontispiece: Roman leader Julius Caesar, the dictator who oversaw the end of the Roman republic, is one of the most legendary figures of the ancient world. Few before or since have matched his reputation both in politics or on the battlefield.

CHELSEA HOUSE PUBLISHERS

VP, New Product Development Sally Cheney
Director of Production Kim Shinners
Creative Manager Takeshi Takahashi
Manufacturing Manager Diann Grasse

Staff for JULIUS CAESAR

Associate Editor Benjamin Xavier Kim
Production Editor Jaimie Winkler
Picture Researcher Pat Holl
Series Designer Takeshi Takahashi
Cover Designer Takeshi Takahashi
Layout 21st Century Publishing and Communications, Inc.

A Haights Cross Communications ✦ Company

http://www.chelseahouse.com

First Printing

1 3 5 7 9 8 6 4 2

Library of Congress Cataloging-in-Publication Data

Crompton, Samuel Willard.
  Julius Caesar / by Samuel Willard Crompton.
     p. cm.—(Ancient world leaders)
Includes index.
Summary: A biography of the Roman general and statesman whose brilliant military leadership helped make Rome the center of a vast empire.
  ISBN 0-7910-7220-7
  1. Caesar, Julius—Juvenile literature. 2. Heads of state—Rome—Biography—Juvenile literature. 3. Generals—Rome—Biography—Juvenile literature. 4. Rome—History—Republic, 265-30 B.C.—Juvenile literature. [1. Caesar, Julius. 2. Heads of state. 3. Generals. 4. Rome—History—Republic, 265-30 B.C.] I. Title. II. Series.
DG261 .C84 2002
937'.05'092—dc21
                                                        2002015928

921
CAESAR

◆ TABLE OF CONTENTS ◆

07028 2927

ON LEADERSHIP

Arthur M. Schlesinger, jr.

Leadership, it may be said, is really what makes the world go round. Love no doubt smoothes the passage; but love is a private transaction between consenting adults. Leadership is a public transaction with history. The idea of leadership affirms the capacity of individuals to move, inspire, and mobilize masses of people so that they act together in pursuit of an end. Sometimes leadership serves good purposes, sometimes bad; but whether the end is benign or evil, great leaders are those men and women who leave their personal stamp on history.

Now, the very concept of leadership implies the proposition that individuals can make a difference. This proposition has never been universally accepted. From classical times to the present day, eminent thinkers have regarded individuals as no more than the agents and pawns of larger forces, whether the gods and goddesses of the ancient world or, in the modern era, race, class, nation, the dialectic, the will of the people, the spirit of the times, history itself. Against such forces, the individual dwindles into insignificance.

So contends the thesis of historical determinism. Tolstoy's great novel *War and Peace* offers a famous statement of the case. Why, Tolstoy asked, did millions of men in the Napoleonic Wars, denying their human feelings and their common sense, move back and forth across Europe slaughtering their fellows? "The war," Tolstoy answered, "was bound to happen simply because it was bound to happen." All prior history determined it. As for leaders, they, Tolstoy said, "are but the labels that serve to give a name to an end and, like labels, they have the least possible connection with the event." The greater the leader, "the more conspicuous the inevitability and the predestination of every act he commits." The leader, said Tolstoy, is "the slave of history."

Determinism takes many forms. Marxism is the determinism of class. Nazism the determinism of race. But the idea of men and women as the slaves of history runs athwart the deepest human instincts. Rigid determinism abolishes the idea of human freedom—the assumption of free choice that underlies every move we make, every word we speak, every thought we think. It abolishes the idea of human responsibility, since it is manifestly unfair to reward or punish people for actions that are by definition beyond their control. No one can live consistently by any deterministic creed. The Marxist states prove this themselves by their extreme susceptibility to the cult of leadership.

More than that, history refutes the idea that individuals make no difference. In December 1931 a British politician crossing Fifth Avenue in New York City between 76th and 77th Streets around 10:30 P.M. looked in the wrong direction and was knocked down by an automobile—a moment, he later recalled, of a man aghast, a world aglare: "I do not understand why I was not broken like an eggshell or squashed like a gooseberry." Fourteen months later an American politician, sitting in an open car in Miami, Florida, was fired on by an assassin; the man beside him was hit. Those who believe that individuals make no difference to history might well ponder whether the next two decades would have been the same had Mario Constasino's car killed Winston Churchill in 1931 and Giuseppe Zangara's bullet killed Franklin Roosevelt in 1933. Suppose, in addition, that Lenin had died of typhus in Siberia in 1895 and that Hitler had been killed on the western front in 1916. What would the 20th century have looked like now?

For better or for worse, individuals do make a difference. "The notion that a people can run itself and its affairs anonymously," wrote the philosopher William James, "is now well known to be the silliest of absurdities. Mankind does nothing save through initiatives on the part of inventors, great or small, and imitation by the rest of us—these are the sole factors in human progress. Individuals of genius show the way, and set the patterns, which common people then adopt and follow."

Leadership, James suggests, means leadership in thought as well as in action. In the long run, leaders in thought may well make the greater difference to the world. "The ideas of economists and political philosophers, both when they are right and when they are wrong," wrote John Maynard Keynes, "are more powerful than is commonly understood. Indeed the world is ruled by little else. Practical men, who believe themselves to be quite exempt from any intellectual influences, are usually the slaves of some defunct economist. . . . The power of vested interests is vastly exaggerated compared with the gradual encroachment of ideas."

But, as Woodrow Wilson once said, "Those only are leaders of men, in the general eye, who lead in action. . . . It is at their hands that new thought gets its translation into the crude language of deeds." Leaders in thought often invent in solitude and obscurity, leaving to later generations the tasks of imitation. Leaders in action—the leaders portrayed in this series—have to be effective in their own time.

And they cannot be effective by themselves. They must act in response to the rhythms of their age. Their genius must be adapted, in a phrase from William James, "to the receptivities of the moment." Leaders are useless without followers. "There goes the mob," said the French politician, hearing a clamor in the streets. "I am their leader. I must follow them." Great leaders turn the inchoate emotions of the mob to purposes of their own. They seize on the opportunities of their time, the hopes, fears, frustrations, crises, potentialities. They succeed when events have prepared the way for them, when the community is awaiting to be aroused, when they can provide the clarifying and organizing ideas. Leadership completes the circuit between the individual and the mass and thereby alters history.

It may alter history for better or for worse. Leaders have been responsible for the most extravagant follies and most monstrous crimes that have beset suffering humanity. They have also been vital in such gains as humanity has made in individual freedom, religious and racial tolerance, social justice, and respect for human rights.

There is no sure way to tell in advance who is going to lead for good and who for evil. But a glance at the gallery of men and women in ANCIENT WORLD LEADERS suggests some useful tests.

One test is this: Do leaders lead by force or by persuasion? By command or by consent? Through most of history leadership was exercised by the divine right of authority. The duty of followers was to defer and to obey. "Theirs not to reason why/Theirs but to do and die." On occasion, as with the so-called enlightened despots of the 18th century in Europe, absolutist leadership was animated by humane purposes. More often, absolutism nourished the passion for domination, land, gold, and conquest and resulted in tyranny.

The great revolution of modern times has been the revolution of equality. "Perhaps no form of government," wrote the British historian James Bryce in his study of the United States, *The American Commonwealth*, "needs great leaders so much as democracy." The idea that all people should be equal in their legal condition has undermined the old structure of authority, hierarchy, and deference. The revolution of equality has had two contrary effects on the nature of leadership. For equality, as Alexis de Tocqueville pointed out in his great study *Democracy in America*, might mean equality in servitude as well as equality in freedom.

"I know of only two methods of establishing equality in the political world," Tocqueville wrote. "Rights must be given to every citizen, or none at all to anyone . . . save one, who is the master of all." There was no middle ground "between the sovereignty of all and the absolute power of one man." In his astonishing prediction of 20th-century totalitarian dictatorship, Tocqueville explained how the revolution of equality could lead to the *Führerprinzip* and more terrible absolutism than the world had ever known.

But when rights are given to every citizen and the sovereignty of all is established, the problem of leadership takes a new form, becomes more exacting than ever before. It is easy to issue commands and enforce them by the rope and the stake, the concentration camp and the *gulag*. It is much harder to use argument and achievement to overcome opposition and win consent. The Founding Fathers of the United States understood the difficulty. They believed that history had given them the opportunity to decide, as Alexander Hamilton wrote in the first Federalist Paper, whether men are indeed capable of basing government on "reflection and choice, or whether they are forever destined to depend . . . on accident and force."

Government by reflection and choice called for a new style of leadership and a new quality of followership. It required leaders to be responsive to popular concerns, and it required followers to be active and informed participants in the process. Democracy does not eliminate emotion from politics; sometimes it fosters demagoguery; but it is confident that, as the greatest of democratic leaders put it, you cannot fool all of the people all of the time. It measures leadership by results and retires those who overreach or falter or fail.

It is true that in the long run despots are measured by results too. But they can postpone the day of judgment, sometimes indefinitely, and in the meantime they can do infinite harm. It is also true that democracy is no guarantee of virtue and intelligence in government, for the voice of the people is not necessarily the voice of God. But democracy, by assuring the right of opposition, offers built-in resistance to the evils inherent in absolutism. As the theologian Reinhold Niebuhr summed it up, "Man's capacity for justice makes democracy possible, but man's inclination to justice makes democracy necessary."

A second test for leadership is the end for which power is sought. When leaders have as their goal the supremacy of a master race or the promotion of totalitarian revolution or the acquisition and exploitation of colonies or the protection of greed and privilege or the preservation of personal power, it is likely that their leadership will do little to advance the cause of humanity. When their goal is the abolition of slavery, the liberation of women, the enlargement of opportunity for the poor and powerless, the extension of equal rights to racial minorities, the defense of the freedoms of expression and opposition, it is likely that their leadership will increase the sum of human liberty and welfare.

Leaders have done great harm to the world. They have also conferred great benefits. You will find both sorts in this series. Even "good" leaders must be regarded with a certain wariness. Leaders are not demigods; they put on their trousers one leg after another just like ordinary mortals. No leader is infallible, and every leader needs to be reminded of this at regular intervals. Irreverence irritates leaders but is their salvation. Unquestioning submission corrupts leaders and demeans followers. Making a cult of a leader is always a mistake. Fortunately hero worship generates its own antidote. "Every hero," said Emerson, "becomes a bore at last."

The single benefit the great leaders confer is to embolden the rest of us to live according to our own best selves, to be active, insistent, and resolute in affirming our own sense of things. For great leaders attest to the reality of human freedom against the supposed inevitabilities of history. And they attest to the wisdom and power that may lie within the most unlikely of us, which is why Abraham Lincoln remains the supreme example of great leadership. A great leader, said Emerson, exhibits new possibilities to all humanity. "We feed on genius . . . . Great men exist that there may be greater men."

Great leaders, in short, justify themselves by emancipating and empowering their followers. So humanity struggles to master its destiny, remembering with Alexis de Tocqueville: "It is true that around every man a fatal circle is traced beyond which he cannot pass; but within the wide verge of that circle he is powerful and free; as it is with man, so with communities." ■

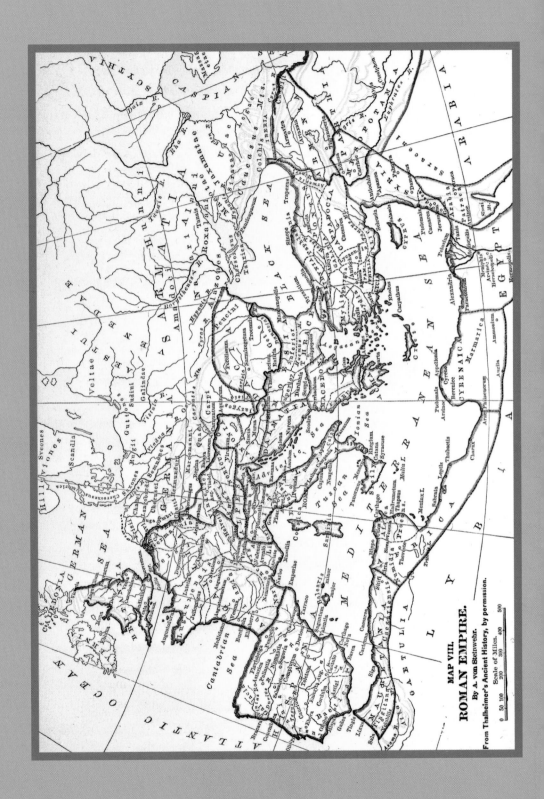

MAP VIII.

ROMAN EMPIRE.

By A. von Steinwehr.

From Thalheimer's Ancient History, by permission.

Scale of Miles.

0 50 100   200   300   400   500

1

ROMAN
YOUTH

Gaius Julius Caesar and his wife Aurelia had a son on July 13, 100 B.C. The Romans knew it as the thirteenth day of the month Quintillus, in the year 653 of the founding of Rome. July thirteenth was also the principal day of the games devoted to the god Apollo. Caesar and Aurelia already had two daughters; this would be their only son. They named the child after his father.

The younger Gaius Julius Caesar grew up in a family that prided itself on being *patrician*—that is, descended from among the early founders of Rome. The family had played a role in Roman politics for centuries. There were also military leaders in the family. The very name "Caesar" came from an ancestor who had killed an elephant in the First Punic War waged between Carthage and Rome.

We know little of Caesar's first ten years. His education was directed by two persons: his mother, Aurelia, and a tutor named Marcus Antonius Ginipho. Ginipho had studied at the city of Alexandria,

Perhaps the most widely recognized of ancient Rome's many powerful figures, Gaius Julius Caesar transformed a thriving city-state into a fledgling empire, expanding Rome's influence into Gaul and Britain.

Egypt, where he had absorbed much of the great Greek learning we now call "Hellenistic." From an early age, young Caesar knew about the temples and pyramids of Egypt, the city-states and rivalries of the Greeks, and of the heroic conquests of Alexander the Great of Macedon. This early learning appears never to have left him; for the rest of his life, Caesar remained a more worldly and well-read man than most of his political contemporaries. The typical Roman of the time knew a great deal about Rome, its people, and its politics, but Romans were often ignorant about the customs and politics of other lands— but not Caesar. Years later, he would see many of the sites that were described to him by Ginipho.

Aurelia, Caesar's mother, appears to have had a profound influence on the boy. Born in the hilly area north of Rome where the Etruscans had ruled some centuries earlier, Aurelia was less upper-crust than her husband but more ambitious. She "married up" when she married Julius Caesar the Elder, but she generally showed more drive and determination than her husband. Aurelia was a conservative mother in that she raised Caesar to revere the Roman Republic and its grand history. She doubtlessly instilled in him a scorn for most forms of luxury and a desire to prove himself both in politics and in war. This was not unlike the mothers of ancient Sparta, who told their sons as they departed for war: "Come home with your shield [victorious] or on it [dead]."

Caesar's father, Gaius Julius Caesar the Elder, is more of a mystery than his wife. Born into one of the old patrician families, Caesar the Elder did not accomplish a great deal, though he spent many years in political life. He appeared to be on his way to finishing a rather undistinguished career when opportunity came his way—and indeed to the entire Julii family. Caesar's aunt Julia was married to Gaius Marius, then the most powerful man in Rome. Suddenly, when Julius Caesar the Younger was about nine years old, his father had the opportunity to serve Rome in an important capacity.

Marius was the outstanding military leader of his generation. Born in Cereatae, 60 miles southeast of Rome, he was the son of a prosperous farmer, but he was not a patrician. Throughout his long career, Marius was seen as the leader of the Popular (Populares) Party, which was opposed to the Conservative (Senatorial) Party. Marius fought the Gauls, the Germans, and North African tribesmen. Marius also reformed the Roman

Caesar's uncle, Gaius Marius, was the outstanding military leader of his generation. Leader of the Popular Party and a superb general, Marius fought in Gaul, Germany, and North Africa and greatly increased the size and the power of the Roman army.

army, opening it to men who were of age, regardless of their background. Previously, a young man had to be a Roman citizen and own property in order to serve in the legions; Marius changed this and greatly increased the size and the power of the Roman army.

Marius married Julia, a sister of Aurelia, around 112 B.C. Years later, Marius was in early old age, but he commanded Roman armies against those of several Italian city-states in what were called the "Social Wars" of 90–88 B.C. Just before the

Social Wars began, Marius helped to have his brother-in-law, Julius Caesar the Elder, made *praetor* (or governor) of the Roman province of Asia, which really meant a portion of what is now Turkey. Caesar the Elder went east in 91 B.C. In his father's absence, Caesar the Younger began to look upon his uncle Marius as something of a substitute father.

Almost as soon as the Social Wars were concluded, Marius announced he wanted another command. He wanted to go east to fight Mithridates, the King of Pontus, in Asia Minor. Mithridates considered himself a successor to the legacy of Alexander the Great and sought to expand Greek rule through-out the eastern Mediterranean at the cost of Rome.

Marius therefore ran in the elections for *consul* (a top executive position in the Roman government) and won an unprecedented seventh term. He was preparing to go east when a civil war broke out between Marius and Lucius Cornelius Sulla.

Sulla, who had been born in 138 B.C., considered himself the defender of the conservative tradition in Rome. He wanted to deprive Marius of further glory and to be the conqueror of Mithridates. Sulla's men chased Marius and his followers out of Rome, and Sulla went east in 87 B.C. with a large army to chastise the King of Pontus.

Almost as soon as Sulla had departed, Marius and Cinna (his chief colleague) returned to Rome. They carried out a purge of Sulla's supporters and made grand preparations of their own. One aspect of Marius' plans was the further cementing of the relationship between himself and his party and the Julii family. He was already married to Julia. Now he arranged a marriage between Julius Caesar the Younger and Cornelia, who was the daughter of Cinna.

Caesar was willing and ready to marry. He also was able to make his own decisions because his father had died suddenly and unexpectedly, probably of a heart attack. Gaius Julius Caesar was now leader of the Julii family in his own right. It suited his plans and his future ambitions to cement the alliance between the Julii family and the leaders of the Popular Party. He married Cornelia in 85 B.C. They were, by all accounts, a happy and devoted couple.

But tragedy, as the Greeks knew so well, can ruin even the best plans.

Marius died suddenly in 86 B.C. Leadership of his group passed to Cinna. Cinna, however, died while on campaign in Greece in 84 B.C. Suddenly, the Popular Party, as Marius' followers had come to be known, was without a leader. Suddenly, Julius Caesar's boldness in marrying the daughter of Cinna appeared to be a liability.

The day of reckoning came on November 2, 82 B.C. On that frightful day, Caesar, his wife, and indeed all of Rome heard the dreaded words "Sulla *ad portas*! Sulla *ad portas* (Sulla is at the gates)!"

The words *"ad portas"* had a special meaning for most Romans. During the wars between Carthage and Rome, the Carthaginian general Hannibal had once come within sight of the walls of Rome. Though he had never captured the city, Roman mothers still frightened their children into obedience with the words, "Hannibal *ad portas* (Hannibal is at the gates)!"

Sulla had returned from the east, landed his men at Brindisium on the southeast coast of Italy, and marched to Rome. Now the city lay at his feet. Sulla had returned in a vindictive frame of mind. He wanted vengeance for the indignities he had suffered in the past, *and* he wanted to wipe out the leadership of the Popular Party. Therefore, Sulla published a list of those who were proscribed, meaning they were to suffer banishment or death. About 40 Senators and 1,200 knights were eventually put to death under this proscription.

Julius Caesar was on the list. He was, after all, both the nephew of Marius and the son-in-law of Cinna.

Caesar was found and brought before Sulla. The 56-year-old man, who had recently been named Dictator of Rome, frowned at the 18-year-old Julius. Caesar, Sulla announced,

The chief rival of Gaius Marius was General Lucius Cornelius Sulla, defender of the Rome's Conservative Party. As the power struggle between Marius and Sulla raged, Sulla placed his enemies, including a young Julius Caesar, on a death list.

must divorce Cornelia and act as if the marriage had never occurred. Then, and only then, Caesar would be left in peace.

The younger man refused. He refused the most powerful Roman of the day, the first Roman to be made Dictator in nearly 130 years. Perhaps Caesar was inspired by some of the stories told to him by Ginipho of Greek heroes who defied tyrants. Perhaps Caesar was motivated by pride. Perhaps his actions were caused by love. Many other Romans were brought before Sulla and told to divorce their wives who had associations with the Popular Party. Most of them promptly did so.

But Caesar would not. Sulla did not order Caesar's death, but he did confiscate the wealth from Cornelia's family, including all that would have gone to Caesar. Perhaps Sulla hoped that Caesar would change his mind and realign himself with the Conservative Party. If this happened, Caesar could be a valuable asset.

Caesar went into hiding for some time. During the months that he struggled from one cave to another in the hills of central Italy, his relatives made impassioned pleas to Sulla on his behalf. The boy was young, they said. His marriage to Cornelia had been arranged, but now he was in love with her. If Sulla allowed him to live, Caesar might become a valuable Roman in the future. Finally Sulla relented. He did not return the property that had been confiscated, but Caesar's name was removed from the list.

Tradition has it that Sulla remarked to those who pled for Caesar's life, "Keep him since you so wish, but I would have you know that this young man who is so precious to you will one day overthrow the aristocratic party which you and I have fought so hard to defend. There are many Mariuses in him."

Caesar had lived to fight another day. Even Sulla, the most fearsome tyrant of the time, had not been able to tame the lion that lay within Gaius Julius Caesar.

A POLITICAL
EDUCATION

The Roman government of 80 B.C. was much the same as it had been 300 years earlier. Rome was proud of, and famous for, her consistency. The Roman government was composed of two executives, a legislature called the Senate, a large number of magistrates, and the Popular Assembly. Two men called *consuls* filled the executive function. Consuls were elected each year by the Senate. The term was for one year, and there were numerous limitations on how old a man had to be to serve as consul, and how many years had to elapse before he could once more run for the office.

There were two consuls, rather than one, because the Romans believed in a balance of power. They had thrown out the last Etruscan King in 509 B.C. and had no wish for future kings. Having two consuls ensured that one man would not dominate the State. Two consuls also meant that one could govern the city of Rome while the other ran the armies in the field. It was a practical division of

Republican Rome was composed of two executives (called *consuls*), a legislature called the *Senate*, a large number of magistrates, and the *Popular Assembly*. The two consuls shared executive authority in the hope that no one leader could seize too much power.

power, and the Romans were an extremely practical people.

Three hundred men made up the *Senate*. The primary qualification to become a *senator* was to have previously served as a magistrate in some capacity. The Senate therefore was made up of men who had political experience. This was a good thing since the Senate ran most of the day-to-day affairs of Rome.

Ten *tribunes* served as a check on the senatorial power.

Long ago, perhaps as early as 400 B.C., the lower classes of Rome, known as *plebeians*, had revolted against the upper classes and demanded a form of redress against the Senate. The upper class had granted the lower class the right to have ten tribunes, who were elected annually by the Popular Assembly.

The ten tribunes sat in the Senate. They did not vote on legislation, but they had an important power which they could exercise by standing up and shouting *Veto* ("I forbid")! By doing this, the tribune could prevent the proposed legislation from going forward. In fact, the Senate was required to immediately cease all discussion on the subject. In this way, the tribunes were supposed to protect the power of the lower classes.

There were a large number of magistrates. The *censors* guarded the public morals. They inspected the streets, kept immoral material out of the public hands, and watched over the attitudes of the Roman people. The *aediles* guarded the treasury. Each aedile had a different section of the treasury that was his responsibility. The *questors* published the news of the government functions and presided over the courts. Even the *Vestal Virgins*, who technically were not magistrates, had important functions. They guarded the public morals, and they held all the wills and deeds of the Roman people.

Finally, at the bottom of this government, was the *Popular Assembly*. From time immemorial, the Assembly had technically held all the power in the Roman State, but as Rome had grown larger and greater, it had been necessary to delegate most of the responsibility to the 300 members of the Senate.

The historian Polybius wrote that if one looked at the consuls and their powers, then Rome would appear to be a monarchy with two heads, rather than one. If one looked at the Senate and its vast powers, then Rome would appear to be an aristocracy, because very few Senators came from other than the top families. And finally, if one looked at the tribunes, their veto power, and the Popular Assembly, then one could only conclude that Rome was truly a Republic.

Rome's strength lay in the diversity of her political institutions. At the root, all the institutions were designed to prevent the rule of one person or one faction. Yet one person, Sulla, had come forward to rule, and he represented one faction—the reactionary members of the Senate.

After he purged Rome of the followers of Marius and Cinna, Sulla relaxed into a form of retirement. He was still the Dictator of Rome, and he continued to watch out for the Conservative interests, but he did not run the day-to-day matters of the city. After 81 B.C., when Sulla had reluctantly spared his life, Caesar spent most of his time in the Kingdom of Bithynia in Asia Minor, waiting for the political winds to change.

Sulla died of natural causes in 78 B.C. Caesar soon returned to Rome and began to play a role in the city's politics. Caesar's first major speech came on the occasion of his aunt Julia's funeral. She was the widow of Marius, and Marius' name had been banned in Rome for the past ten years. Caesar, however, gave a stirring speech in honor of his aunt, and, by implication, in honor of his uncle Marius. Images of Marius were paraded through parts of the city for the first time in ten years. Through this one speech, Caesar showed himself to be a coming man.

Caesar's wife Cornelia died in 68 B.C. Caesar soon married Pompeia, who was a granddaughter of Sulla. The marriage surprised many people who remembered Caesar's previous defiance of Sulla. Caesar had already become a devious and skillful politician, one who could change direction when it suited his cause.

In 63 B.C., Caesar ran for the elected office of Pontifex Maximus ("Chief Priest") of Rome. Many people were offended by Caesar's candidacy. He seemed too young and too worldly to head the Roman religion. Caesar had staked everything on this political contest. Knowing that the office was for life and that it carried great prestige, he ran up enormous debts during the campaign and used every bit of financial and political capital available to him. When he left

Rome's Senate was made up of 300 men with a proven history of political experience. Together, they were responsible for managing most of the day-to-day affairs of Rome.

home on the morning of the election, Caesar told his mother that she would see him either become the Pontifex Maximus or that he would go into exile. Caesar won the vote by a very close margin. He had paid a high price, but it was a position that was held for life, and it became one of the important bases of support upon which he could draw.

One year later, in 62 B.C., scandal struck the home of Julius

Caesar. During the festival of the *Bona Dea* ("Good Goddess"), a minor politician named Clodius snuck into Caesar's house dressed as a woman. This was not unusual, in that Clodius was both a friend of Caesar and an admirer of Caesar's wife Pompeia. The timing was atrocious. The festival of the Bona Dea was celebrated by women only, and Caesar, as the Pontifex Maximus, was careful to observe such rituals. Clodius was first discovered in the house by the watchful eye of Aurelia, Caesar's mother. Unfortunately the story spread rapidly throughout Rome. Soon everyone in the city knew that the home of the Pontifex Maximus had been violated by the presence of a man during the festival. What was worse, many tongues wagged that Caesar was unable to keep his wife content and that she actively sought the advances of Clodius.

Caesar now showed his great ambition and unscrupulous methods. When the news broke and Clodius was brought to trial, people expected Caesar to denounce Clodius as a vile man, but this did not happen. Instead, Caesar was quiet throughout the early stages of the trial. Only when he came to the witness stand did he testify that he had no knowledge of the affair between Clodius and Pompeia. Incredulously, the prosecutor asked, "Why then did you divorce your wife?"

"Because I insist that my wife should be above suspicion," Caesar answered in a nonchalant manner.

The divorce had already taken place. Caesar had acted quietly and effectively to stem the damage to his reputation. The expression "Caesar's wife must be above suspicion" remains an important political saying to this day. Clodius was found innocent (the jurors were bribed) and then became a quiet but effective ally of Caesar.

Soon after the scandal and trial, Caesar went to Spain as the praetor for that province. Caesar had previously served as the questor for Spain; now he returned as the governor and military leader.

We know little about the extent of Caesar's military experience to this point. He had served under the King of Bithynia, and he had shown his alacrity in the way he handled a group of pirates who had captured him in the eastern Mediterranean. None of these early commands, however, had been enough to show whether Caesar was a true army man, or if he was, like many Roman nobles, only to spend a short time in the military before using that career to springboard into politics.

Now Caesar showed his critics that he was no amateur. Almost at once upon his arrival in Spain, Caesar announced the creation of a new legion: the Tenth Legion. Until about twenty years earlier, legions could only be created by the Senate and Popular Assembly. During the time of Sulla and afterward, victorious generals like Pompey had started the new precedent of creating legions, and then having them confirmed by a vote in the Senate. Caesar thus continued this tradition. The new Tenth Legion was added to the other two already stationed in the province. The new Tenth Legionnaires were young men, predominantly Spanish. As a gesture to please them, Caesar gave the legion the bull as its emblem (bulls were popular in Spain, even then).

Caesar then moved against the tribes of eastern Spain. Coastal Spain, along the Mediterranean, had been conquered by Rome nearly 100 years earlier, but inland Spain, extending to the Atlantic Ocean, was still the realm of the Iberian tribesmen. Caesar marched against the tribes, attacking, capturing, and often burning their towns. Though his praetorship extended for only one year, Caesar did much to extend Roman control throughout Spain. By the time he left for Rome, he had enhanced his military reputation and had gained the unswerving allegiance of the men of the Tenth Legion. It was said that he remembered the names of all his centurions, and that he could call upon them to undertake special tasks on his behalf.

Caesar's victories over the Iberian tribesmen were little reported in Rome. Therefore, when Caesar returned to Rome in 60 B.C., he was still considered something of a political light-weight: handsome, charming, gifted with the populace, but not a major player or formidable opponent. Caesar showed his political skill clearly on his return. He had submitted his name for consul for the year 60 B.C. He knew, as all Romans did, that a consul was not allowed to have a military triumph within the city limits. Therefore he was faced with a difficult choice: whether to be consul or to have the adulation of the crowd.

As it turned out, this was an easy decision for Caesar to make. He wanted and needed to be consul. A triumph was a secondary matter.

As events turned out, it was a fortunate time for Caesar to have returned to Rome at this time. There was a situation that called for someone with a silver tongue, a large purse, and mighty ambitions.

THE GREAT
TRIUMVIRATE

At the age of 39, Julius Caesar had achieved things that were considerable, but not great. Due to his charm, wealth, and free-spending habits, he had acquired more friends than enemies. His position as Pontifex Maximus placed him constantly in the eye of the Roman crowd. To make the most of his chances, though, Caesar had to find allies. Caesar knew this when he returned to Rome; so did those in the Senate who wanted to prevent Caesar's continued rise in politics. Had he chosen an obvious path, his foes might have thwarted him, but Caesar took on what seemed like a hopeless and thankless task: to bring together Gaius Pompey and Marcus Crassus.

Born in 106 B.C., Pompey was from a distinguished Roman family. Early in life he had caught the eye and attention of Sulla, who had entrusted important military commands to him.

In 67 B.C., the Senate decided to free the Mediterranean from

Gaius Pompeius Magnus (Pompey the Great) was a skilled military leader. He not only rid the Mediterranean of pirates who threatened Roman shipping, but also defeated King Mithridates of Pontus, who had so far repelled all Roman efforts to overthrow him.

the hosts of pirates who seized ships and held wealthy Romans —like the young Caesar—for ransom. The command was given to Pompey. So great was the public trust that Pompey was given the honor of *imperium* (supreme command) not only on the waters of the Mediterranean but up to 60 miles inland if he needed to pursue the pirates to their lairs. Technically this gave Pompey the ability to bring soldiers right to Rome itself, but this was overlooked in the need to bring an end to the pirate menace.

At the height of his powers and prestige, Pompey rid the Mediterranean of its pirates in a lightning-quick campaign of six months. He organized convoys with military galleys that thwarted pirate attacks; he hunted down pirates in their island lairs; and sometimes he pursued them inland. Half a year after he began, Pompey had won the most complete victory at sea that his fellow Romans could have imagined.

The victory over the pirates was but the beginning. Pompey went to the eastern Mediterranean to fight Mithridates, the King of Pontus. This was the same Mithridates against whom Sulla had fought years earlier. During the course of a long reign, Mithridates had fought three separate wars against Rome. Never had Mithridates succeeded in his grand ambitions, but neither had Rome been able to overthrow him. Now Pompey went against Mithridates.

One Roman general after another had failed to subdue Mithridates, but Pompey succeeded. Pompey was known for his thorough command of logistics and careful planning. He organized campaigns that succeeded because supplies arrived on time, and detachments went where they were supposed to go. All of this was masterminded by Pompey. Mithridates was defeated. He died soon after of natural causes, and his body was brought before Pompey as a sign of submission. The son, Pharnaces, who brought the body, will appear again in our story of Caesar and Rome.

After he defeated Mithridates, Pompey went on further military excursions that can really be called adventures. There was no need, strictly speaking, for Pompey to enter Phoenicia and Judea; he did so because these were lands full of fable and, perhaps, of riches. These lands at the eastern end of the

King Mithridates was a savvy military leader who had fought many Roman generals (including Sulla) to a draw. Pompey, however, used superb planning and organization to defeat Mithridates, who died soon after of natural causes.

Mediterranean never knew a Roman conqueror until Pompey; he was the first Roman to besiege Jerusalem, and the first to enter the holy Temple which was built by King Solomon, destroyed by the Babylonians, and then rebuilt about 520 B.C. Perhaps out of superstitious fear, Pompey left the Temple treasures where they were instead of taking them for himself or in the name of the Roman People.

Additionally, Pompey continued on minor campaigns in the Middle East and reached nearly as far as the Caspian Sea. When he returned to Rome in 78 B.C., Pompey was one of the most traveled of all Romans and was certainly the most renowned.

Pompey returned to Rome in 61 B.C. His foes feared he would come as Sulla had before him, to initiate a reign of iron and blood. But Pompey proved remarkably moderate— perhaps even naive. He disbanded his forces when he landed at Brindisum on Italy's southeast coast and marched to Rome with only a handful of comrades. Pompey presented himself to the Senate as the most successful conqueror Rome had seen in 100 years, and as one of the few who was able to resist the temptation to take over the government. However, he was not rewarded for this. The Senate ignored Pompey to the extent that it could and refused to ratify the promises he had made to his soldiers concerning land grants.

Pompey was furious. To whom he could turn? Certainly not to Marcus Licinius Crassus. He and Pompey were old rivals, whose rivalry had gone over the line to bitter hatred.

Born in 110 B.C., Marcus Crassus came from one of the noblest and most distinguished of all Roman families. Unlike Caesar, who wore his dignity lightly, and who worked to please the Roman crowd, Crassus had a deep and abiding dislike of the common people. He believed it was his right, indeed his mission, to further the cause of aristocratic government, and down deep he despised the type of compromises made by ambitious men like Caesar.

Like Pompey, Crassus had risen because he had caught the attention of Sulla. Crassus and Sulla were very much alike; both of them believed in the rule of the patricians, and both scorned to win the favor of the populace. For these reasons, one might expect that Sulla would favor Crassus. In most cases, Sulla appeared to prefer the services of Pompey, and he would sometimes condescendingly compare Crassus' accomplishments to Pompey's. One of Crassus' most bitter memories revolved around the crisis that had been caused by the slave rebellion led by Spartacus. Crassus had been the Roman who had risen to the occasion. He had received extraordinary powers from the Senate, had mobilized the army, and had won critical victories over Spartacus toward the rebellion's end. For all this, however, Crassus received much less attention than did Pompey, who had had the good fortune to return to Italy in time to play an important last-minute role. Rather than remember Crassus as their savior, the people of Rome turned to Pompey as their hero.

There was one area, though, in which Crassus had no equal. He was a master at making money. During the years he had been one of Sulla's henchmen, Crassus had perfected certain financial techniques. Later, when he struck out on his own, Crassus developed Rome's first fire department. It was not a true municipal service; the department belonged entirely to Crassus. As the years went on, Crassus developed a technique which made him the wealthiest man in Rome. When an alarm sounded, Crassus and his fire engines hastened to the scene of the fire. There, Crassus would make a very low offer to the owner of the home that was burning. Should the homeowner indignantly refuse, Crassus would simply stand by, and the fire engines did the same. But once the owner agreed to sell, nearly always for a rock bottom price, then Crassus would send the engines to work. In this way he became the single greatest owner of real estate within the city.

Crassus' wealth made him the subject of envy, jokes, and downright anger. He used the money to many purposes, not the least of which was to become the bankroller for the political campaigns of many of his colleagues. Nearly everyone who mattered in Rome, it was said, owed money to Crassus.

Crassus was about 55 years old in 60 B.C. The years had brought him great wealth and influence, but little fame. He

Although under-celebrated as a military leader, Crassus (right) was skilled at making money and was one of the wealthiest men in Rome. Crassus and Pompey were bitter rivals until Caesar applied his flattery and persuasion to the situation, reconciling the two men and gaining more power for himself.

ached for a military command with which he could outshine Pompey. The rivalry between the two men had only increased over the years, and Crassus was eager to find a way to bring Pompey down to earth. Therefore, when Julius Caesar came with propositions, Crassus was willing to listen.

Pompey too, was willing to entertain ideas from Caesar. Pompey already regretted his magnanimous gesture in disbanding his troops at Brindisium. If he had them in Rome now, the Senate would not be able to ignore his demands.

Caesar called upon both Pompey and Crassus by turns. He flattered each of them, told them they were the most important Romans of their generation, and that it was shameful that Rome failed to honor them properly. Then Caesar made his proposition. Rather than continue to vie with one another, Pompey and Crassus should join him and form a three-way political partnership. Pompey would provide the military brilliance and the popularity with his men; Crassus had the wealth and the respect of the conservative Senators; and he, Caesar, was beloved by the Roman crowd. Together they would harness the energies of the military, the finances, and the popular will. They would become what has been called ever since the First Triumvirate (it was "first" because Octavian, Mark Antony, and Lepidus formed another one 30 years later).

Only someone like Caesar could have pulled this off. Somehow, he brought Pompey, Crassus, and himself together into an alliance that was able to defy the Senate.

Caesar was doing so much for Pompey, for Crassus, and for the good of the state. What was he getting for himself? Plenty, as it turned out. Caesar was named consul for the year 59 B.C. and granted proconsular power in not one but two provinces, Cisalpine Gaul and Transalpine Gaul. (Cisalpine Gaul was what is now northern Italy, and Transalpine Gaul was what is now southern France.) Anyone who previously had thought Caesar lacked military ambition now knew such an idea was mistaken. Rather, Caesar was trying to set up a base for conquests that might eventually rival those of Pompey. Pompey appeared willing to take the risk because he needed Caesar's support to make sure the land bill got through the Senate.

Now the howls of discontent arose in the Senate. Finding themselves outmaneuvered, the Senators first tried to block Caesar's consulship and then Pompey's land program for his veterans. The historian Plutarch narrates the response of the three men who formed the new Triumvirate:

> And so Caesar was escorted to the consulship, protected and surrounded by the friendship of Crassus and Pompey. He was elected with a clear majority, with Calpurnius Bibulus as his colleague, and as soon as he took up the post he began to introduce the kind of proposals for allotments and grants of land, designed to please the masses, that one might have expected from the most radical of tribunes, but not from a consul.

Tribunes were expected to safeguard the interests of the common people. Consuls were expected to lead the state in military matters and to work for the interests of the patricians.

When the Senate balked at the proposals, Caesar went before the people in the Popular Assembly. With Pompey on his right side and Crassus on his left, Caesar proclaimed the necessity of the new laws. Pompey threatened to back them up with sword and shield. Crassus made no public declaration, but everyone knew he was at one with Caesar and Pompey. Conservative Senators ground their teeth, but the bills were passed.

There was one last piece of business. In 60 B.C., Caesar married his daughter Julia to Pompey. It was designed to weld the two men close together and to prevent treacherous acts by either while Caesar was away from Rome. Pompey was nearly 30 years older than his new bride, but it became, by all accounts, a happy marriage. Some historians even suggest that Pompey's ambition began to ebb at this time, and that he savored the pleasures of home life more than the struggles of political life.

This was Caesar's last season in Rome for many years. He left the great city in January 59 B.C., and headed northward over the Alps to Gaul. Caesar, the glamorous youth, had become Caesar the skillful politician. Would he now acquit himself as well on the battlefield?

CAESAR
IN GAUL

When Caesar arrived in Cisalpine Gaul, he found the Roman legions there in a high state of readiness. These were troops who had to be so ready that they could be dispatched at a day's notice to serve in the Alps or beyond. Even more important, they were the last major body of soldiers between Rome and her foes to the north. The Romans never forgot that Gallic tribesmen had come south in 390 B.C. and laid waste to the city of Rome.

No one expected great things from the new consul. Caesar was into middle age, and previous leaders—such as Marius and Pompey—had gained great laurels by the time they were thirty. Caesar was known as a fine speaker (his training at Rhodes had been beneficial) and an excellent diplomat, but not a battlefield commander. It was expected that Caesar would at most hold the line against the Gauls and Germans to the north.

A Roman legionnaire. Caesar helped refine the capabilities of the Roman legions, using catapults and battering rams to conquer Gaul (an area now occupied by northern Italy and southern France).

The men whom Caesar now commanded were drawn from the best Roman legions, soldiers who followed a military tradition that had been honed to perfection over about 200 years. Rome had developed the legion, a mobile division of 6,000 men, that had proved superior to the Greek phalanx. Each legion was broken down into groups called *maniples* and *centuries*, each of which was commanded by a *centurion*. The commander of 100 men, the centurion was considered the backbone of the Roman military machine.

The Romans had seized upon and improved techniques of siege warfare, including the use of catapults and battering rams. They had also learned to create night camps that were practically forts of their own. Every Roman legionnaire (soldier) carried a shovel as well as his short sword. A Roman legion could stop marching at five in the afternoon and have a trench dug with small fortifications put up by nine that evening. This backbreaking labor prevented the types of ambushes and night attacks for which Rome's enemies were famous.

The single best source for Caesar's campaigns in the north is his own *Commentaries*, published around 50 B.C. Generations of students—both Romans and then Europeans, and finally Americans—learned the first few words of the *Commentaries* by heart:

> All Gaul is divided in three parts. They are inhabited respectively by the Belgae, the Aquitani, and a people who call themselves Celts, though we call them Gauls. All of these have different languages, customs, and laws. The Celts are separated from the Aquitani by the river Garonne, from the Belgae by the Marne and Seine. The Belgae are the bravest of the three peoples, being farthest removed from the highly developed civilization of the Roman Province, least often visited by merchants with enervating luxuries for sale, and nearest to the Germans across the Rhine, with whom they are continually at war.

The areas which Caesar described encompass most of modern France and Belgium. The division between the Aquitani and Gauls, which he places at the Garonne River, remains an important linguistic and cultural divide today.

What Caesar describes as the "Roman Province" was in the very south of France. Today it is called Provence and is known for its hot weather and beautiful beaches.

Caesar found a crisis in Transalpine Gaul in the spring of 59 B.C. The Helvetti, a Gallic tribe located in what is now Switzerland, wanted to migrate south and west through the Roman Province. The Helvetti were hemmed in by the lack of room in their homeland and needed to migrate to find better lands. At another time, and under the command of another leader, the Romans might have allowed this migration. Julius Caesar knew that to allow one such movement would encourage others to follow. Therefore, he demanded that the Helvetti return to their ancestral lands.

The Helvetti tried to cross the Rhone River, which flows from north to south and empties into the Mediterranean. They found Caesar's men watching the fords, and even the use of boats was to no avail. Caesar had stopped the Helvetti just in time. The tribesmen turned and moved as if to return to their native area, but Caesar followed them; he wanted to be sure they would not change their minds. The Helvetti leaders sent diplomats to Caesar, urging him to leave them alone, but he continued to pursue.

About two months after the Helvetti first began their march and about one month after they began their retreat, Caesar fought a great pitched battle against them. The fight was close in many respects, and there were moments when it became desperate for sections of Caesar's army. At the crucial moments, however, Roman discipline and Roman organization prevailed. The centurions could manage their centuries in a way that no Gallic or German tribal leader could, and by the end of the day, the Helvetti were flying in full retreat. Caesar later wrote that some 380,000 Helvetti began the march of migration, and that only 110,000 of these ever returned home. This is almost certainly an exaggeration, but given that Caesar's *Commentaries* is the only history that

Gaul was not a single nation, but three distinct regions, each with its own tribal chieftains, customs, and language. Caesar knew that gaining victory in Gaul would mean fighting each of these groups separately using well-coordinated Roman troops. Shown here is a Gallic tribesman.

survives, one can surmise that he did inflict a great defeat, and that many thousands of the Helvetti were killed.

To say that Rome was surprised would be an understatement. Caesar, the darling of the crowds, the elegant nobleman, had shown himself to be a great general. Just as important, he was ruthless in a way that the Senate and Roman people could appreciate.

A few weeks after his great victory over the Helvetii, Caesar learned of a new, pressing danger. This time it was German tribesmen, led by a king named Ariovistus.

The Germanic tribesmen were distantly related to the Gauls, but there the comparison ended. The Germans were known for being much fiercer and more warlike than the Gauls, and recent incursions into Gaul had shown the Germans how fertile the soil there was. Ariovistus was one of a number of Germanic leaders who claimed the right to sections on the west bank of the Rhine River; now he made his move.

Ordinarily the Gauls would have fought the Germans on their own. Many Gallic leaders, especially their Druidic priests, told the people that if they relied on the Romans, they would end up with a new set of invaders and conquerors. The Gauls were spent from a long series of internal wars between the tribes of Audea and those led by Arverni. Given this weakness, many Gauls solicited Caesar and asked him to stop the German invasion. Naturally, Caesar was only too happy to oblige.

Caesar marched rapidly and confronted Ariovistus on the west side of the Rhine River, perhaps near the border of present-day Switzerland and Germany. The German king was astounded that Caesar had moved so far so quickly, and he asked for peace negotiations. The talks that followed were more a form of sparring between the two leaders than a genuine hope for peace. Ariovistus explained that his people needed more land, for their herds of horses and cattle. Caesar agreed that this was true, but declared the Germans could not enter Gaul, which, he said, was under his protection. Many Gallic tribesmen were happy to hear this at the time, but they did not realize the extent to which Caesar would later use this claim against them.

So the issue would be resolved by force of arms. The Germans had crossed the Rhine in a state of high confidence, but Caesar's quick movements had taken them aback, and they now assumed a defensive posture. Ariovistus brought out his men and aligned the groups according to their tribal heritage: Harudes, Marcomanni, Triboci, Vangiones, Nemetes, Eudusii. Caesar correctly perceived that these tribal divisions were a weakness that he might exploit. The Germans, like the Gauls, fought tribe for tribe, and even man for man, so that they might receive personal acclaim for their deeds. By contrast, Caesar's legionnaires fought as one compact, mass unit. The day that Caesar met Ariovistus was probably the largest clash between two such different military systems since Crassus had defeated Spartacus 15 years earlier.

Caesar began the battle with a charge by his front lines. The Germans at once were thrown on the defensive, and they adopted their shield wall technique that had often worked for them in the past. But many Romans actually jumped on top of the wall of shields and hacked their way downward, causing consternation in the German lines.

Within just a few hours it was all over. The Germans who escaped the battle fled north and west, headed for the Rhine. Ariovistus and a handful of followers found rafts and made their way across to safety. But his army was completely shattered, and the women and children the Germans had brought with them were taken captive; most were later sold into slavery. Like many other Roman commanders, Caesar was an active participant in the slave trade. Thousands upon thousands of the captives from his campaigns were sold in slave markets around the Mediterranean, helping to make Caesar a very wealthy man.

Once again, Rome was astounded to learn of another great victory by Caesar. The Senate voted for several days of thanksgiving, and special tokens of honor were sent to Caesar.

The following spring Caesar marched against the tribes collectively known as the Belgae. The modern-day nation of Belgium takes its name from these tribes, who lived between the Sambre and Rhine rivers. Caesar described them in his

Commentaries as the most warlike of the tribes of Gaul, because of their proximity to the Germans with whom they often fought. Some of the German customs infiltrated into the Belgae as well; the Belgae were the only tribes in Gaul that practiced cremation, a German custom.

Caesar moved against the Belgae, claiming that they had amassed a great army to fight him. Because the Belgae left no written records, it is difficult to say whether they were indeed the aggressors, but as usual, Caesar's speed of movement allowed them no opportunity to take advantage. Caesar was soon crossing the first rivers into their lands.

The area controlled by the Belgae was wetter and swampier than it is today (the dams built by the Dutch over the last thousand years have vastly changed the terrain for the better). The Rhine River splits into many different channels as it nears the North Sea, creating a bewildering mass of water and swampy land. Amidst these channels and rivulets, the Belgae awaited Caesar's advance.

Several of the Belgae tribes yielded as soon as Caesar arrived. He followed the usual custom of demanding hostages to ensure their good behavior, but he soon pushed on because he learned that the Nervii, the most warlike of the Belgae, had gathered a great force of 60,000 warriors.

The battles that followed were a series of close-runs. Caesar had the advantage of his soldiers' discipline and his own decisive leadership; the Nervii had the advantage of the terrain, and their own fanatical (according to Caesar) willingness to resist. In the last battle, Caesar was in serious trouble. The Nervii commanded a river bank, and Caesar and two of his legions were pinned down at the water's edge. The historian Plutarch claims that all was lost until Caesar seized the shield of a dead centurion and, wearing his traditional scarlet cloak, inspired his men with his own courage. The legion that had been hanging back in reserve now came forward with speed, and Caesar won yet another resounding victory.

Caesar used the speed of his legions to out-maneuver the Gallic tribesmen, and in the end brought victory to Rome. Here, a Gallic princess offers wine to her Roman conquerors.

Completely chastened, the Nervii came forward in submission. Caesar took numerous hostages, but he probably knew that this foe would not oppose him again; he had done too much damage to the Nervii. And so, within two years of coming to Gaul, Caesar had defeated the Helvetti, Ariovistus the German, and the tribes of the Belgae. He had fought on the Alsatian plain, near the mountain passes of Switzerland,

and in the swampy marshes of what is now Belgium. Caesar's accomplishments were all the more remarkable considering the different opponents he faced and the different terrain on which he fought. He had become a general of the first rank, and the only Roman who now could compare to him was Gaius Pompey.

How does one account for Caesar's remarkable success? Here was a man who had never commanded in the field until his late thirties, and who had always seemed better at pleasing the crowds than at command. What was his secret?

First, Caesar was extremely ambitious. Even during the times when he appeared to be absorbed in social activities, Caesar was always reading, always planning. Second, Caesar inherited a northern army that had been brought to the peak of its success under the command of Marius 40 years earlier. Caesar did not have to invent the legion, the maniple, the *cohort* (a unit of 600 men), or the *gladius* (short sword). All these were in place by the time he became the commander of Transalpine Gaul.

Perhaps even more important was the army's speed. Caesar never waited for his enemies; he consistently moved faster than his foes. Against another traditional army, as perhaps against the Greeks or Parthians, this would not have been so important, but the mixed tribal groups of Gauls and Germans that Caesar fought were consistently astonished by the speed of his movements.

Julius Caesar was now a force known from Rome to the Atlantic Ocean. Though they might have pronounced his name differently, the Gallic, Germanic, and even British tribes knew that the man in the scarlet cloak was one of the most devastating war leaders ever seen.

CAESAR IN
GERMANY
AND BRITAIN

Caesar made it a practice to return to Cisalpine Gaul every
winter, leaving his troops in their camps in Gaul. He wanted to
be close to Rome, to keep a sounding of which way the political
winds blew. By the winter of 56–55 B.C., Caesar knew that events
were reaching a dangerous point.

Caesar's incredible successes in Gaul had earned him many
enemies at home. The common people of Rome still cheered his
name, but many Senators, especially those who remembered the
dire prediction made by Sulla, now thought of Caesar as the worst of
enemies. He combined the military skill of Marius with the political
skill that was all his own.

So long as Crassus and Pompey did their part to keep Rome calm,
Caesar had little to worry about. But the First Triumvirate was already
beginning to show signs of strain. Crassus was displeased by the
lack of attention to all his services to Rome; Pompey appeared to be in

After his decisive victory in Gaul, Caesar turned his attentions to the island of Britain. Caesar's first invasion attempt was thwarted, however, when ships supplying grain to the Roman legions were blown off course by a storm.

something of a daze. Though he had been an amazing leader in the field and on the sea against the pirates, Pompey seemed at a loss when it came to Roman politics. Rather than lead and develop a strong "Pompey" faction—or even a "Pompey, Crassus and Caesar" faction—Pompey drifted, sometimes taking the advice of a certain group of Senators and sometimes others.

Caesar met his colleagues at Luculla in 55 B.C. Whether or not they still liked each other, the three men committed to another five years of working together. Caesar received his prize; his command in Gaul was extended by another five years. Pompey received command of Roman forces in Spain, and Crassus was granted command of an ambitious expedition against the Parthians, who inhabited the land between the Tigris and Euphrates rivers in what is modern-day Iraq. With matters settled between him and his colleagues, Caesar hastened northward to Gaul.

Caesar had ambitious plans for the upcoming campaign season. Until now, Caesar had been forced to respond to the invasions of the Helvetti and German tribes. Though he had beaten them soundly, it was they who chose when to cross the Rhine River and to invade Gaul. Caesar had been forced to react, rather than to initiate events. That would now change.

Sometime in the early summer of 55 B.C., Caesar approached the Rhine at one of its narrower parts, perhaps near the present-day city of Coblenz, Germany. The German tribes never bothered to defend the right bank of the Rhine. They considered this completely unnecessary, since their neighbors cowered in fear of them, rather than the other way around. Thus there were no German forces on either side of the Rhine.

Caesar had his men start to build a bridge. Romans were excellent builders and engineers, but this was a mighty task because of the swiftness of the current and the depth of the riverbed. The first few efforts all came to naught, but then Caesar's men began to experiment with laying "piles" in the riverbed. Piles, which have been used by engineers ever since, allow a firm, though usually temporary, foundation on which bridges can be built. The piles were made of large planks of wood; there was no lack of wood in the vicinity. Then, on top of the piles, Caesar's men laid wooden planks, knotted together with rope. Within 18 days the bridge was complete, and Caesar and his army marched east over the Rhine. As simple as those words sound today, this was the first time it had been done— previously the Germans always used rafts or simply swam across the great river.

The Germanic tribesmen simply were not ready for Caesar. After he crossed the Rhine, Caesar marched steadily eastward for several days. His progress was slow, because the area was heavily forested (parts of the forest, known as the Black Forest, remain today). Wherever he went, Caesar found that the Germans avoided battle; they fled their towns and dispersed into the woods. This was not at all disappointing to Caesar, for the German reluctance to fight allowed for an easy march with few casualties. The Germans melted away, and Caesar's progress on the eastern side of the Rhine was more like a triumphal procession than a true campaign.

After two weeks, Caesar returned to the Rhine. His army crossed over, and Caesar destroyed the bridge, rather than leave it as an easy road for the Germans to use. He built a strong fort on the west bank of the Rhine and left enough men to ensure that the Germans would know of their presence. Then he headed due west to the waters we call the English Channel today, with the intent to conquer Britain. In his *Commentaries*, Caesar made it sound as if he decided to cross the Channel just after he crossed the Rhine. Historians, who know the complexities of the invasion, are certain that Caesar must have begun planning the Channel crossing months before, and that his lieutenants on the coast of Gaul must have been procuring ships and boats all that spring and early summer.

Caesar assembled his men at the Gallic port town of Gesoriacum, which is present-day Bolougne, on the coast of Normandy in France. Caesar gave it a new name, Portus Itius. There he assembled about 10,000 men in 30 ships. While he awaited a favorable wind and tide, Caesar sent one of his

Knowing that the Germans had left the eastern bank of the Rhine River undefended, Caesar ordered the construction of a bridge at one of the river's narrowest points, thus enabling him to guide his legions easily into Germany. Here Romans destroy German huts.

most favored tribunes, named Volusenus, to reconnoiter the British coast. Volusensus was perhaps the first Roman to see the white cliffs of Dover. He went further and saw the beginnings of shale beaches where Caesar might land. Volusensus returned and gave the news to Caesar, who embarked with his expeditionary force around midnight on August 25, 55 B.C. This departure time sounds strange to us today, but Caesar was making the most of the wind and tide to get out of the harbor at Portus Itius (William the Conqueror would also use an early evening departure time when he invaded Britain more than 1,110 years later).

Late August of 55 B.C. brought blustery weather to the waters between Britain and Gaul. Early autumn was not an auspicious time to cross the waters to Britain, but Julius Caesar seldom backed away from any challenge. He had learned in years of fighting the Gauls and the Germans that decision and speed were among the most important tools in the art of war. Now he brought those tools and his own fearsome reputation across the thirty miles that separated Britain from Gaul. He intended to conquer Britain for Rome.

Historians have ever since debated Caesar's embarkation point. Was it Boulougne in what is now Normandy? Or was it at the Pas-de-Calais, the departure point for the shortest crossing of the Channel? We cannot say for sure, but we are confident that after Caesar and his men departed at midnight, early morning found him in front of the cliffs of Dover, on the southeast side of Britain.

However, the British tribesmen had been alerted and were ready for Caesar. They stood on the white cliffs of Dover and made a menacing sight, brandishing their javelins and making great cries of dread to their enemies. But Caesar had faced many such foes—none were more ferocious than the German tribesmen whom he had recently beaten—and now he planned his landing. It would be foolhardy to set down on the narrow beach and receive the British assault; far better to sail north in search of a better landing spot. Caesar had found his new spot by the next day—a much wider, more open beach without the added danger of cliffs.

One day later the Romans found a beach full of small stones or shingles. The Britons had followed by land, and they came down to the water's edge to oppose the landing. The Romans were the most disciplined and organized soldiers of their day, but they were accustomed to land battles, not to this type of amphibious operation. As the first Romans came ashore they were met by hundreds of Britons, throwing javelins and using occasional chariot charges to disrupt the enemy. For the first hour there was no success in getting ashore, and many Romans were killed or wounded.

A turning point came when a standard bearer inspired his fellow Romans. The man who carried the eagle of the Tenth Legion cried out, "Jump down, comrades, unless you want to surrender our eagle to the enemy. I, at any rate, mean to do my duty to my country and my general." After those words, he leapt into the sea and was one of the first Romans to get a foothold on the beach.

Within an hour, most of the Roman landing force had made it ashore. The Britons fell back in disarray; Caesar's first amphibious landing had been carried out. It was a heady ending to what had been an eventful day. Once ashore, Caesar and his Roman legionnaires utilized their shovels and began making a fortified camp. Within one day, Caesar had a fortified camp in place, and from this position he was virtually invincible.

The Britons had already entertained doubts about the wisdom of resisting Caesar. British emissaries entered Caesar's camp on the third day of his arrival and asked for peace. Caesar was initially harsh toward the emissaries, but then accepted their pleas; he also accepted a number of hostages to ensure the good behavior of their fellows. The invasion of Britain was going splendidly, and then to top things off Caesar learned that the transport ships bearing cargoes of grain had been sighted.

It was the night of the full moon, probably August 31, 55 B.C. Caesar and many of his men watched with eager anticipation as the transport ships appeared and neared the coast. Just minutes before some of the transports would have landed, a contrary wind blew up, and the ships were blown south by southeast, away from the men who anticipated their arrival. The squall turned into a genuine storm, and the tides, heightened by the full moon, carried the ships far off course. Several were wrecked; others limped back to Gaul. It was a naval disaster.

Caesar's second invasion of Britain was not much more successful than his first, but he was able to maintain popular support through skillfully worded letters home.

During his many campaigns in Gaul, Caesar had become famous for his ability to have his men live off the land. The Romans were expert at passing through an area and confiscating the grain and wine they needed. But here in Britain, Caesar had no maps and no trusty guides, and thus did not know where food supplies could be found. The transport ships were therefore extremely important, and their failure to reach the landing spot was a disaster for Caesar's plans.

The Britons appeared to sense Caesar's plight. Just one day after the naval calamity, a group of Romans were caught by Britons while foraging. The Britons made numerous attacks, both with javelins and with men in chariots, and they might have eliminated the Roman cohort had Caesar not arrived with reinforcements. Caesar inflicted a punishing defeat on the Britons in the area, but then withdrew to his beachhead. Even Caesar knew that the omens, the gods, and the season were now against him.

A few days later Caesar re-embarked his army. The Roman ships, piloted by Gallic sailors, went back to Gaul. Caesar's great reconnaissance was something of a failure; he had not penetrated inland and he knew little more about the island than when he had begun. It was in Caesar's nature to learn from his mistakes, and when he returned one year later he would be more dangerous than ever to the men of Britain. Caesar cast a parting shot at these tribesmen in his *Commentaries*. "By far," wrote Caesar, "the most civilized inhabitants are those living in Kent (a purely maritime district), whose way of life differs little from that of the Gauls. Most of the tribes in the interior do not grow corn but live on milk and meat, and wear skins. All the Britons dye their bodies with wood, which produces a blue colour, and shave the whole of their bodies except the head and the upper lip."

Caesar would be back. He never let an initial reverse frighten him off from an action.

When Caesar returned to Portus Itius (Bolougne), he immediately began to prepare for a second invasion of Britain. Caesar had his men gather Gallic carpenters and build ships and boats for the coming year. Caesar then left Gaul and spent the winter in Cisalpine Gaul, as usual. He did not return to

Rome, but the news of his British adventure traveled rapidly and the Roman Senate ordered a thanksgiving session of 20 days to commemorate the event. Some have cast doubt on the Senate's sincerity, but one of the best historians of early Britain affirms that "No one who is versed in Roman literature and gifted with historical imagination will regard the decree as ironical. For Caesar's countrymen may well have felt that he had opened the way for the conquest of a new world."

The new year brought opportunities for all three members of the Triumvirate. Pompey remained in Rome even though he had been made consul for Spain. Crassus went east to take up his governorship of Roman Syria. Because of his immense private wealth, Crassus was able to foot the cost of outfitting more men and legions than would otherwise have been possible. Caesar returned north, eager to do more than he had in 55 B.C.

Caesar's lieutenants in Gaul had done their work well during the winter and spring. By the time Caesar arrived on the coast, he found hundreds of ships built and hundreds more still under construction. Most important from Caesar's viewpoint was that many of the ships could carry horses. Caesar felt that the lack of cavalry had hampered his campaign the previous year.

It was about the tenth of July that Caesar and 30,000 men embarked at Portus Itius. It was close to the time of his birthday, and Caesar was 46 years old. He had come a long way from the aristocratic dandy who had been captured by pirates, and he was determined to go even further. This second invasion of Britain was intended to make his name; he had already secured his fortune through the loot and slaves obtained in Gaul.

THE CONFEDERACY OF VERCINGETORIX

Caesar's second invasion of Britain was not much more success-ful than the first. However, Caesar exaggerated his efforts in his letters to the Senate, and he once again received the applause of the Roman people (the actual conquest of Britain would be accomplished by the Emperor Claudius, in 50 A.D.).

Meanwhile, things changed on the home front. Caesar's appeal to the Roman people remained very high, but his grip on Roman politics was about to slip. The Triumvirate had endured rather well for five years, but it was about to be reduced to the rule of two men. Marcus Crassus died on campaign against Parthia in 54 B.C. Crassus, who long ago had defeated Spartacus and put down the slave rebellion, fell prey to the steppe conditions of Mesopotamia and to his own eagerness for more military glory. Suddenly there was no longer a Triumvirate. Power was now divided between two men: Pompey and Caesar.

Due to his heroic efforts and skill in battle, the Arvernian leader Vercingetorix remains an important symbol of strength to this day, as this statue at Alesia attests. In 52 B.C., Vercingetorix emerged to challenge Caesar and the Roman right to Gaul. Vercingetorix was able to unite Gaul's tribal factions against the Roman army.

In that same year, Caesar's daughter Julia died in childbirth. Pompey mourned the loss deeply, but Julia's death removed one of the key elements that had held Caesar and Pompey together. As his political situation began to worsen, Caesar faced a new foe within an old campaign ground: Gaul.

During the early winter of 53–52 B.C., Caesar appeared to have won virtually all of Gaul. Through the combination of his military ability, the valor of his troops, and his adroit diplomacy, Caesar had split the Gauls into numerous factions, each of which was too weak to oppose him or Roman rule. Caesar noted in his *Commentaries* that the Gauls were generally in favor of factional division which they believed prevented tyranny:

> In Gaul, not only every tribe, canton, and subdivision of a canton, but almost every family, is divided into rival factions. At the head of these factions are men who are regarded by their followers as having particularly great prestige, and these have the final say on all questions that come up for judgment and in all discussions of policy. The object of this ancient custom seems to have been to ensure that all the common people should have protection against the strong; for each leader sees that no one gets the better of his supporters by force or by cunning—or, if he fails to do so, is utterly discredited.

More than any previous Roman leader, Caesar had perceived this weakness among the Gauls and exploited it to his own benefit. But in the late winter and early spring of 52 B.C., a young Arvernian leader emerged to challenge Caesar and the Roman right to Gaul. His name was Vercingetorix, and he remains a powerful symbol to freedom fighters throughout the world today.

Vercingetorix must have been a powerful speaker because the Gauls respected the gift of oration at least as much as did the Romans. Gaul was full of tribal leaders, each of whom maintained some animosities toward some different tribal group. Vercingetorix soothed the hurts of many, and persuaded a large majority of the tribes to enter into a confederacy with him. The goal was simple: to throw the Romans out of Gaul.

The first action in the war—which Caesar called a "rebellion"—was taken by the Carnute tribe, located in what is now northwest France. The Carnutes were warriors, like all other Gauls, but they also made up a large percentage of the Druids who served as the priests and dispensers of justice throughout Gaul. Inspired by some of the Druids, the Carnutes threw themselves against a Roman garrison at Cenabum, on the Loire River. Cenabum was captured, the Romans there were killed, and the great Gallic War or Revolt had begun.

The Gauls had a method of communication that, while simple, was extremely effective. Rather than send courtiers on horseback, as the Romans did, the Gauls "shouted over the trees." The expression means that news was shouted from house to house, from tree to tree, and throughout the wooded areas that were so prominent a part of the landscape. It is believed that Vercingetorix, in the land of the Arverni, learned of the capture of Cenabum the evening of that same day, even though 150 miles stretched in between. The signal had been given; the war began.

Caesar hastened north from Cisalpine Gaul. By the time he reunited with his legions, Caesar found that at least half of Gaul was lost to Gallic control. Vercingetorix had done his work well; the Gauls stayed in their confederacy instead of splitting into the tribal factions that Caesar had previously manipulated.

The Romans consistently won the few skirmishes that followed. Following the advice of his Druidic counselors, Vercingetorix decided that hunger would force Caesar from Gaul. Rather than fight to defend some towns instead of others, Vercingetorix and the Gauls began to burn every village and town that the Romans came near. Within weeks, Caesar's men were hungry.

Vercingetorix's plan failed when it came to the town of Avaricum. The people pled for the right to defend their town, which was dear to them. Against his better judgment, Vercinge-torix allowed them to fight the Romans. Not only did Caesar capture Avaricum, but the supplies he found there enabled him to face the coming campaign.

Now it was Caesar who held the initiative. He pursued

On the advice of Druidic counselors (such as the one shown above, at right), Vercingetorix adopted a policy of burning every Gallic village and crop in an attempt to starve Caesar's legions.

Vercingetorix so fast that the Gauls barely made it to the city of Gergovia in time to shut the gates. Gergovia was a mountain-side fortress, and one of the strongholds of the Arverni tribe. Vercingetorix refused to come outside the city and try the matter in open battle. He kept his men confined to their fortifications, and he methodically planned his defense.

Gergovia was one of the few cities that Julius Caesar besieged but did not capture. In a rare display of insubordination, Roman legionnaires attacked the hillside on which Gergovia was based and did not heed the trumpet calls to retreat. The Gauls had placed stones and boulders there which they now pushed down-ward, crushing many Romans to death. By the time they pulled back, the Romans had lost about 750 men and many centurions.

Soon after the setback at Gergovia, Caesar began to march back to the province. He had seven legions with him, and his men were at a peak state of readiness. Vercingetorix misinter-preted Caesar's movement, believing that it was a true retreat. Under Vercingetorix's lead, the Gauls blocked Caesar's path. A major battle loomed.

Vercingetorix began the day's action by placing his 15,000 horsemen in front of Caesar's army. The Gauls had about a three-to-one ratio against Caesar in cavalry, and Vercingetorix believed this would be his trump card. Instead, it led to his downfall.

Almost as soon as the Gallic cavalry began its attack, Caesar made a counterattack. He sent about 1000 Germanic horsemen, whom he had recently recruited, against the Gauls. Faced by their oldest and fiercest foes, the Gauls panicked. Within an hour of its commencement, the battle had become a rout in favor of the Romans and Germans.

Knowing that his cause had become desperate, Vercingetorix led his Gallic warriors to a hilltop stronghold named Alesia (today the small town of Alise). Even Caesar was daunted when he first saw the white walls and towers of Alesia. He soon found answers to the situation.

Within two weeks of his arrival at Alesia, Caesar had his men build a wall that completely encircled the city. Vercinge-torix could scarcely believe the skill and willingness of the Romans since they used the shovel and pickax as well as they did swords. The Gauls made numerous attempts to break the walls, to no avail.

Vercingetorix had the remnants of his cavalry make a nighttime breakout. Many cavalrymen escaped the walls and made their way throughout Gaul, summoning each and every Gaul to come to the relief of Alesia.

Knowing that Alesia had supplies for only one month, the

Gauls assembled an immense relief army; Caesar later estimated that it was 200,000 strong. Just as the defenders of Alesia were about to give up in despair, they heard the sound of trumpets (Roman) and the songs of the Gauls. The final battle for Gaul was about to begin.

But when the army of relief descended on the valley around Alesia, the Gauls found, to their astonishment, that the Romans had built an entire second set of walls. The second set faced outward, towards the relief army. Realizing what Vercingetorix's cavalrymen would do, Caesar had set his 50,000 men in motion, and in one month they had dug and built an entire second set of walls. It was one of the supreme examples of Roman military engineering.

The relief army attacked from the outside. The Gauls within Alesia attacked the inner set of walls. The attacks went on and on. For two days the relief army battered its head against the outer set of walls. Then Caesar took the offensive.

Once again, his German allies spread terror amidst the Gauls. Thousands of Gallic archers were killed by the German cavalrymen. When the last set of attacks against the outer walls failed, the remains of the relief army dispersed. No one could have fought harder or with more willingness than the Gauls. Caesar's leadership and Roman discipline were too much for them. The Gallic War was over.

Late in October of 52 B.C., Vercingetorix came out to surrender. He rode on a magnificent horse right up to Caesar and made his last public speech. Soon Vercingetorix was in chains, and Caesar had taken Alesia. He had won it all. The Gallic Revolt, as Caesar called it, ended quickly after Vercingetorix's surrender.

Caesar spared the people of Alesia because Vercingetorix had come and surrendered. The Gallic chief was taken to Rome and held as a prisoner for the next three years before he was executed on the day of Caesar's triumphal procession through Rome.

Although he put up a mighty battle, Vercingetorix had to surrender to Caesar in the end.

News of Caesar's victories reached Rome. Though the people of Rome had not seen Caesar in over eight years, they cheered themselves hoarse. Caesar was, without a doubt, the most celebrated leader of his time. Only those who recalled Pompey's successes in the previous decade could remember anything like the adulation that was accorded to Julius Caesar.

The question was whether even the city of Rome would be big enough for the two generals.

THE
CIVIL WAR

The beginning of the year 49 B.C. found Caesar at Ravenna, on the northeast coast of Italy. Caesar appeared happy and confident, but his closest advisers knew that horsemen were galloping from Ravenna to Rome and then back again, because Caesar was engaged in negotiations with the Roman Senate.

Ravenna is just north of the Rubicon River. The Rubicon served as the dividing point between the province of Cisalpine Gaul, of which Caesar was the governor, and the heartland of Italy. Therefore, even though he was a general and a statesman of great renown, Caesar could not legally cross the Rubicon going south with any of his soldiers. If he did, he would have to do so as a private citizen rather than as a general or consul.

This limitation was one of the important rules of the Roman Republic. Rome was frequently at war—sometimes with the Gauls to the north, and sometimes with the Spanish tribesmen to the

 During Caesar's lifetime, Roman battle tactics evolved greatly. When facing an enemy city, Roman legions frequently laid siege, cutting off supplies to the city and weakening both her people and morale, before making an assault.

west. Roman generals accumulated great power during the course of their campaigns outside of Italy. To avoid takeovers and civil wars, the Roman Senate had long since decreed that it was illegal to bring any soldiers from the armies onto the Italian mainland.

Caesar needed to reach Rome, however. His political enemies had gathered against him in recent weeks, and they threatened to undo much of his work of the last decade. Envious of Caesar's battlefield successes, some of his enemies proposed that Caesar be brought to trial on charges of corruption and disobedience to the Roman Senate. It was imperative for Caesar to go to Rome and refute the charges. These many victories had brought Caesar wealth and fame, but they had also earned him many enemies. While Pompey was not an obvious enemy, he listened with great attention to those in Rome who spoke against Caesar, and it seemed now as if Pompey had joined the ranks of those who insisted Caesar disband his forces and return to Rome a private citizen.

All these matters came to a head in the first ten days of the year 49 B.C. Caesar left no diary or record from this time period. We can only make approximations of how and when he made up his mind concerning this perilous situation.

By January 7, Caesar learned that Rome was in a state of tumult. Pompey and his friends were running the day-to-day matters of the city while the Roman Senate was in a state of suspended animation. The tribunes, men who were elected to safeguard the interests of Rome's lower classes, had fled the city. It appeared as if Rome, which was so proficient at mastering other peoples, might fall to the divisions within itself.

It is likely that Caesar made his decision early on the morning of January 10, but he gave no public sign. Caesar was scheduled to attend a banquet in Ravenna that night, and to do otherwise would provoke suspicion because there were many spies from the different Roman factions in the town. Therefore Caesar went to the banquet, and, as was his way, appeared charming and hospitable to all. Years of social life as a young aristocrat and as Pontifex Maximus to the Roman people had given Caesar a sociable personality, and he played this card well on the evening of January 10.

Then, late in the evening, Caesar pled illness and left the banquet earlier than was normal. None of the spies around him took much notice; they may well have been drunk by this time. But, as was his trademark throughout his campaigns in the north, Caesar would act with stunning speed.

Caesar and a few companions left the banquet and headed on the road to their quarters. Before they had gone even one mile, Caesar changed direction, and the small group hastened to the banks of the Rubicon River. There they met nearly 1,500 of Caesar's most loyal troops, men who had been with him through years of campaigning. The rendezvous had been arranged prior to the banquet; Caesar had sent the secret orders sometime in the afternoon of that fateful day.

Caesar and his men crossed the Rubicon in the middle of the night. Morning found them well past the other side of the river; they had reached and occupied the city of Rimini. There Caesar paused. He had accomplished his goal of crossing the Rubicon. It was a decision from which there was no turning back.

Fifteen hundred men was a tiny force with which to invade Italy. Pompey had two legions totaling approximately 12,000 men on the peninsula, and he boasted he could summon thousands simply by "stamping my foot." Almost from the day that Caesar crossed the Rubicon, Pompey did not act like "Pompey the Great," the man who had defeated the pirates and Mithridates. As soon as he learned Caesar had invaded Italy, Pompey began to make plans to flee Rome. The conservative Senators, who had backed him just weeks before, now found Pompey was made of straw. On January 18, he abandoned Rome and crossed the peninsula, headed for the coastal city of Brindisium.

Since their commander had fled, Pompey's legions put up only half-hearted resistance to Caesar. His 1,500 men swelled

To avoid military takeovers, the Roman Senate had forbidden any general (including Caesar) to lead troops from a province onto the Italian mainland. By crossing the Rubicon River (the boundary between Cisalpine Gaul and Rome), Caesar sparked a civil war.

to double and then triple that number as he advanced south. Rather than march on Rome, Caesar pursued Pompey all the way to Brindisium. As he moved south, Caesar gathered the support of many townspeople and villagers along his way.

There was a brutality and a callousness about some of the Senators with Pompey that turned people against his cause and in favor of that of Caesar. But Caesar did suffer one notable defection from his ranks: Titus Labienus. Labienus had been Caesar's chief legate (virtually the number two man in command) throughout the campaigns in Britain and Gaul. Labienus and Caesar had collaborated on military plans and had been an excellent team. Now, as Caesar moved further south, he learned that Labienus had deserted his camp and joined that of Pompey.

Caesar arrived in time to blockade the city of Brindisium, and started to build siege engines. Rather than stay and fight, Pompey embarked what soldiers he had, what conservative Senators had chosen to remain with him, and sailed from Brindisium. Pompey crossed the Adriatic and landed on the northwest coast of Greece.

Lacking ships, Caesar could not pursue Pompey, but the entire Italian peninsula was now his. Caesar went to Rome and spoke before the Senate, the very body that had been ready to declare him an outlaw and an enemy of the state just six weeks earlier. Caesar made a magnanimous gesture, offering to make peace with Pompey if he would agree to disband his forces in Greece. Caesar asked a group of Senators to carry the offer to Pompey. When the Senators refused, Caesar quit Rome. Disgusted by the political process, he determined to seek out and destroy his enemy's support in Spain.

Pompey had been the proconsul for Spain for five years. One of his sons was in Spain, and several of his legions there declared for Pompey in the Civil War. Knowing that he could not cross the Adriatic Sea until ships were built, Caesar went by land to what is now Southern France and began the war against Pompey's forces in what was called "Nearer Spain" and "Farther Spain."

Caesar arrived at the city of Massalia (today it is Marseilles, France), where the Rhone River met the Mediterranean Sea.

Though they were not Roman citizens and had no special reason to favor Pompey, the people of Massalia resisted Caesar more fiercely than any Italian city had done. After two weeks of building siege towers and constructing battering rams, Caesar left the siege of Massalia to his lieutenants and hastened on to Farther Spain where Pompey's legions resided.

Though they were able troops and commanded by committed officers, Pompey's forces in Spain were not able to contain Caesar. He knew the ground well, having held a governorship there over 12 years earlier. As usual, Caesar made alliances with local tribesmen that allowed him to surprise and outmaneuver his foes. Within three months, the Pompeaian forces had surrendered, and Caesar returned by land to Massalia.

The citizens of this city, who were of Greek descent, still resisted more stoutly than almost any fortified place that Caesar had ever encountered. After about four months of siege, the Massalians capitulated to Caesar. He might have wished to teach them a harsh lesson for their resistance, but he knew that it was more important to appear merciful than vengeful at the time. So he did not destroy the city, but rather accepted the surrender and hastened back to Rome.

Caesar found Rome obedient when he returned at the end of 49 B.C. His exploits in Spain had confirmed his reputation as a dangerous enemy. The Senate practically prostrated itself before him and voted him the title of Dictator for the duration of the Civil War. This was important because Caesar could now face Pompey with the support of the Roman government. Far from being an outlaw, Caesar could now claim he was the hope and savior of the Republic.

Early in January, Caesar made another bold move; perhaps it was one of the few times that he acted too hastily. Arriving at Brindisium, Caesar found that ships had been built, but only enough to carry about 25,000 men across the Adriatic Sea. Rather than wait for more to be built and for the better weather that would come with spring, Caesar made a daring crossing of the Adriatic Sea in winter. He arrived safely in northern Greece and immediately sent his ships back to Brindisium to ferry across the second half of his army. By then Pompey's fleet had been fully aroused. Pompey's ships blocked any further movement by sea, and Caesar's army was cut in two: half in northern Greece and half in southern Italy.

Caesar was in a difficult position, but Pompey made no move to attack him. The news of Caesar's many victories made Pompey extremely hesitant, and he failed to take advantage of the situation. Instead it was Caesar who moved against Pompey, besieging the city of Dyrrachium.

Pompey had about twice as many men as Caesar. Many of Pompey's troops were drawn from the eastern provinces which remembered Pompey's astonishing successes in the decade of the 60s. But Pompey allowed himself to be besieged at Dyrrachium. Caesar's men showed all their customary resourcefulness in digging ditches and building redoubts, and soon Pompey was blocked in.

Early in July, Pompey attempted a breakout. Not only did Pompey have twice as many infantry as Caesar, but his advantage in cavalry was even greater. Taking advantage of this, Pompey broke out from Dyrrachium in a one-day battle. Caesar lost over 900 men, many of them from the centurion rank.

Pompey's circle of advisers immediately named him "Victorious General." He was, after all, the first person to have won a battle over Caesar in many years. But rather than continue to contest the ground on the northwest coast, Pompey withdrew inland, with Caesar following.

The two armies moved at a brisk pace, and at the beginning

of August they were on a level area of ground on the border between Greece and Thessaly. The area where the two armies converged was called Pharsalus, or sometimes Pharsalia. It seemed an excellent place for Pompey to fight since the level ground would favor his cavalry force. Pompey seems to have doubted the wisdom of meeting Caesar in open battle, even after the partial victory at Dyrrachium. The circle of Conservative Senators who had accompanied Pompey to Greece demanded, however, that he meet and crush Caesar now. Just as important, General Labienus appears to have assured Pompey that this was the right moment for the decisive battle. In his *Commentaries*, Caesar attributes these words to Labienus:

> Do not think, Pompey, that this is the army which conquered Gaul and Germany. I took part in all the battles and my view is not put forward without consideration or based on facts beyond my knowledge. A very small fraction of that army remains; a large proportion has died, many fell victim to disease in the autumn in Italy, many have gone home, and many were left behind on embarkation. . . . These forces you see have been reconstituted from the levies of recent years in Cisalpine Gaul.

With the benefit of hindsight, we can assert that Labienus spoke a half-truth. True, many of the veterans from the Gallic Wars were dead or had gone home, but their indomitable leader and the core of his army—the centurions—remained. If Pompey were to win now, he would have to overcome the aura of invincibility that had grown around Caesar.

One of Caesar's centurions named Crastinus began the day saying, "Follow me, you men who were in my company, and give your general the aid you have promised. This is the only battle left; once it is over, he will regain his position and we our freedom." Crastinus then looked at Caesar and said, "I shall do things today, general, that you will thank me for, whether I live

While Caesar was at war in Gaul, the business of running Rome fell to Pompey, who had the backing of many Roman Senators. When Caesar crossed the Rubicon with 1,500 troops, however, that support dissolved, and Pompey chose to flee rather than face Caesar's small but fiercely loyal army.

or die." Crastinus then ran forward, followed by about 120 picked volunteers. Crastinus' loyal attitude was something that Pompey could only long for. This does not mean Pompey was inadequate to the task; rather it suggests that Caesar had an extraordinary ability to coax loyalty from his men.

The Battle of Pharsalus raged all day on August 9, 48 B.C. Pompey began the battle well, with a cavalry charge against Caesar's right flank. Caesar had prepared a special reserve force—which, even though it was on foot, met and defeated Pompey's cavalry. Pompey's entire army then fell back to a wall of fortifications, but the blood was up in Caesar's men. They stormed the forts and captured them in the second part of the battle that raged all afternoon.

As the situation worsened, Pompey's mood gave way to panic. He tore off his general's uniform, mounted a horse, and escaped out the rear entrance of the fortifications. Riding hard, Pompey reached Larissa that night. Accompanied by only about 30 horsemen, he reached the coast of the Aegean Sea a day or so later and took a ship, first for Miletus and then for Alexandria, Egypt.

The day after the battle, Caesar received the surrender of thousands upon thousands of Pompeian soldiers. Many had been killed in the battle, but those who remained came forward and professed allegiance to Caesar. Knowing the value of clemency, Caesar urged them not to be downcast. He assured them he still considered them faithful Romans, and said they would be repatriated home as soon as possible.

Caesar also made a speech to his victorious soldiers. Caesar knew that these men were weary of war and of travel. They had been with him from Gaul to Germany, from Britain to Rome, and now to Greece. Now Caesar promised them that the war would soon be over. He mentioned generous grants of land and money to each and every veteran in the near future. These men did not forget.

Caesar then set off in pursuit of Pompey. Among the hundreds of men Caesar had lost at Pharsalus was the centurion Crastinus, killed by a sword thrust in the mouth. Whether Crastinus had a family, and whether any such family received money and honor for his action, is not noted. But Crastinus stands out as one of the few men mentioned by name in Caesar's *Commentaries*. He stands for the thousands of Romans who fought and died for Julius Caesar.

8

EGYPT AND CLEOPATRA

Caesar pursued Pompey first to Miletus and then to Egypt. Early in October, Caesar arrived in the harbor of Alexandria, located at the northwest corner of the Nile Delta.

Rome was undeniably the superpower of the Mediterranean world, but it still had competition from Alexandria. Founded by Alexander the Great around 330 B.C., Alexandria had become one of the major centers for learning in the Mediterranean world; teachers, scholars, and translators flocked to the Museum and Library at Alexandria. Then too, there was the architectural marvel of the Pharos Lighthouse, one of the Seven Wonders of the Ancient World. Built around 280 B.C., the lighthouse shone a light powerful enough to be seen 27 miles out to sea.

Caesar had never been to Alexandria, but he knew a good deal about its politics from afar. During his time as consul, and then while he was proconsul in Gaul, Rome had often had occasion to

Upon his arrival in Alexandria, Caesar was presented with the head of Pompey by Alexandrians who believed this a showing of loyalty to Caesar and Rome. Casear is reported to have wept at the offering, remembering the great man Pompey had been and their once close alliance.

debate its policies toward Egypt. The country of the pharaohs and the pyramids was no longer ruled by a native dynasty. Now it was governed by the Ptolemies who were descendants of Ptolemy Soter, one of the Macedonian generals of Alexander the Great.

The early Ptolemies had been capable military men and excellent administrators, but over the centuries the line had declined. While Caesar was in Gaul, the Ptolemaic throne was held by Ptolemy XII, usually called Ptolemy Aleutes (which meant "flute player"). Ptolemy Aleutes seems to have been a thoroughly incompetent ruler who enraged the people of Alexandria with his policies. Twice he fled his nation and went to Rome; twice he won over the Roman Senate which helped to reseat him upon his throne. Therefore, Caesar could claim with some legitimacy that he was not only a stranger chasing the defeated Pompey, but that Caesar had a right to arbitrate in the matters of Egyptian government.

Ptolemy Aleutes died in 51 B.C., and was succeeded by the joint rule of his daughter Cleopatra and his son Ptolemy XIII. Cleopatra was about 22 when Caesar came to Egypt; Ptolemy XIII was about 10 or 11. The brother and sister had recently gone to war with one another. When Caesar arrived, Ptolemy and his advisers held Alexandria, while Cleopatra and her followers were at a fortress on the eastern side of Egypt.

Caesar landed on October 2, and almost at once was presented with a gift: the head of Pompey. The advisers of Ptolemy XIII had killed Pompey upon his arrival so that they could present the head to Caesar as a gift and as a token of their allegiance to him. It is said that Caesar wept at the sight. Pompey had been his son-in-law, and Caesar remembered the former greatness of the man. Though he had been a lackluster opponent in the Civil War, Pompey had once been the greatest man in the Roman world.

His quest was finished—Pompey was dead. Caesar could have returned to Rome at once, and many of his critics suggest that he should have done so. But Caesar appears to have been interested in Egyptian affairs; he tarried a while, and during that time he met Cleopatra.

Virtually all sources agree that Cleopatra made a dramatic entrance into Caesar's life. Since Alexandria was held by her brother's forces, she had herself wrapped into a merchant's carpet as if she were the wares. The queen of Egypt was brought before Caesar in a carpet, and when it was unrolled, there she was.

Both the coins that were struck and the reports written indicate that Cleopatra was not a beauty. She had a large

Cleopatra, queen of Egypt, had to use her ingenuity to gain an audience with Caesar. Hiding in a rolled carpet to sneak past Alexandrian guards, she surprised and soon charmed the Roman leader. In the days that followed, the two became lovers.

nose and features that could change from benign to fierce. She also had consummate charm, feminine wit, and intelligence; she had mastered at least seven languages. Whether it was her appearance, her youth, or her ability to speak in Egyptian, Greek, and Latin, Cleopatra charmed Caesar from the first meeting.

The two probably became lovers within a matter of days.

Caesar had always been an amorous man. Cleopatra may have been smitten by the Roman leader, but whether or not she loved this man 30 years her senior, she needed his help. Cleopatra wanted Caesar to arbitrate between her and her brother, and hopefully to award the crown of Egypt to her alone.

Caesar was not initially inclined to favor Cleopatra's desire. It made much more sense to keep Egypt a land divided between the rule of two relatively weak rulers. That had been Roman policy until now, and Caesar was at first ready to continue that policy. But the advisers of Ptolemy XII, especially Achillas, the head of the royal bodyguard, decided that Caesar would indeed favor Cleopatra. Therefore they began to incite the crowd of Alexandria against the Romans.

Caesar had brought only about 3,000 men with him. It was a tiny force with which to defend himself against the Alexandrians, much less the entire Egyptian army. This was one of the times when Caesar's impetuous spirit and daring worked against him. Within two weeks of arriving in Alexandria, Caesar was a prisoner within the northernmost part of the city, surrounded by the Egyptian forces.

The Alexandrian attacks affirmed Caesar in his favor for Cleopatra. She became his political client as well as his lover, and her astute knowledge of Egypt made her an important asset to Caesar in his defense of the Roman position. In his *Commentaries*, Caesar described the physical location:

> The Pharus is a tower of great height and of amazing architectural construction, standing on the island from which it takes its name. This island lies off Alexandria and created its harbour . . . Moreover, on account of the narrow channel, it is impossible for a ship to gain entrance to the harbour against the wishes of those who hold Pharus. This was Caesar's immediate fear, and while the enemy was occupied with the fighting he landed soldiers, seized the lighthouse, and stationed a garrison there.

Caesar and his 3,000 men were boxed up in Alexandria by about 22,000 Egyptians, led by Achillas, head of Ptolemy XIII's bodyguards. Caesar deployed his men in such a way as to maintain their position. His small group of ships also attacked the Egyptian fleet, using flamethrowers to spread fire amongst the enemy ships. During one such attack, flames spread into the city, and the famed Library of Alexandria was consumed in fire. We have no way to know exactly how many scrolls and volumes perished that day, but the Library had been the most important seat of learning in the ancient world. The Torah, which had been translated from Aramaic to Greek by the Library scholars, and other numerous great works were destroyed. It was a serious loss to Alexandrians, and an even greater loss for future historians.

Caesar managed to get messages out of Alexandria. Within weeks, Roman troops were marching from Syria on their way to Egypt. When the Roman reinforcements entered Egypt, King Ptolemy and Achillas broke off their siege of Caesar and went to meet the new foe. In the Battle of the Nile that followed, the Egyptians were defeated. The young king escaped on a boat that sank, and Ptolemy XIII drowned in the Nile.

Cleopatra and Caesar were triumphant. She was elated, believing he would soon chose to marry her and align Egypt's destiny with that of Rome. Caesar had other ideas. Fond as he may have been of Cleopatra, Caesar wanted to finish off the Civil War for good. He had to leave Egypt soon.

Cleopatra used all her charm and persuaded Caesar to take a vacation with her: his first vacation in at least 12 years. The Roman general and Egyptian queen floated down the Nile on Cleopatra's elaborate barge; it was equipped with all the comforts of the time, including no less than five restaurants. As they floated south along the Nile, Caesar may well

In a rare respite from battle and politics, Caesar was persuaded by Cleopatra to vacation aboard her elaborate barge, which was equipped with all the amenities befitting a queen, including no fewer than five restaurants.

have relaxed for the first time in more than a decade. He was victorious, he was in love, and soon he would be the father of Cleopatra's child. He learned of her pregnancy before he left Egypt in the early summer of 47 B.C.

However, the wars were not yet over. Despite his triumph over Pompey and his victories in Egypt, Caesar still had enemies to fight. There were still Pompeian troops in Spain. Closer to hand, though, was the danger presented by Pharnaces, the King of Pontus in Asia Minor.

Pharnaces was a son of King Mithridates, who had finally been defeated by Pompey in 65 B.C. Pharnaces was a sworn enemy of Rome, but no one had troubled to fight him during the early part of the Civil War. Now with Pompey dead, Caesar marched out of Egypt and then past Jerusalem on his way to Asia Minor (what we now call Turkey). Pharnaces marched south to meet Caesar and the two armies collided at

Zela. The Battle of Zela lasted only four hours; Pharnaces was completely defeated, and suddenly there was no further threat to Rome's eastern frontier. Caesar commemorated the event in a now-legendary dispatch to Rome, saying "Veni, Vedi, Vici," meaning "I came, I saw, I conquered."

THE
LONGEST
YEAR

When Caesar returned to Rome in the autumn of 47 B.C., he found three pressing problems: revolt, the Civil War, and calendar difficulties. In typical Caesar fashion, he attacked all three problems at once.

Over the past 14 years, Caesar had proved adept at recruiting good men for the legions—the centurion Crastinus being a prime example. Most of them fought for him with both discipline and ardor, but the time had come for them to be released. Prior to the Battle of Pharsalus, Caesar had promised many of his oldest legionnaires that it would be their last battle. Now he returned to Rome and found many of his best troops in revolt. Their pay had gone unmet, the terms of their enlistment had expired, and they wanted to go home.

The men of the Eighth, Ninth, and Tenth Legions were united in their determination—they had had enough of soldiering. Caesar

After returning from Alexandria, Caesar and his legions had more battles to fight. Not until all of Caesar's political enemies had been defeated could he discharge the soldiers who had served him so loyally.

went to Naples, where the three legions were stationed. He mounted a podium and addressed them in something like these words:

"Men of the legions. I understand you wish to go home. Very well, I release you. You are disbanded from your legions."

Men gasped. Caesar continued, "Not only do I release you from service, but I will make good on the promises I made to you after the Battle of Pharsalus. I will settle you on bountiful lands in the future, *after* I make provision for those legions with whom I shall finish this war."

Now men started to shift about, uneasily. Who knew what Caesar might do, or when he might do it?

Then Caesar began to speak again. He said one word: "Citizens . . ."

Now the shifting and grumbling turned into fear, almost panic. Someone shouted, "No Caesar, we are still your soldiers! We belong to you!"

Minutes later, Caesar accepted the renewed loyalty of all three legions. He had frightened them with his iron will, his apparent fearlessness, and with the idea that other legionnaires would earn greater glory and larger rewards in the future.

Danger from outside enemies was now over. Caesar then learned that the Civil War was not yet over. In the days and weeks after their defeat at Pharsalus, many of Pompey's soldiers had regrouped and moved to the west coast of Greece. Employing the fleet that Pompey had used, his shattered legions had taken ship for North Africa. Now, in the area that once was known as Carthage, Pompey's former army had been rebuilt to the size of about nine legions. Scipio, Pompey's father-in-law, was the new commander, and Scipio had found an ally in King Juba of Numidia. The Numidians of North Africa had long been known to Rome—sometimes as allies and sometimes as fierce enemies. Caesar knew that if Scipio had Juba as an ally, Scipio would bring elephants and the fast-riding Numidian horsemen into any future contest.

None of this news seems to have daunted Caesar. He left Asia Minor and took ship for Rome. Sometime in the autumn of 47 B.C., Caesar returned to the city had had so seldom seen in the past 12 years. There he was welcomed as a conquering hero and the savior of Rome. Celebrations were held, and the

Although one of Caesar's most trusted lieutenants, Mark Antony was not a great administrator. When Caesar returned to Rome, he quickly removed Antony from his post.

Senate renewed Caesar's title as Dictator of Rome.

Caesar could almost certainly have remained in comfort in Rome. His legions and generals were by now so well-accustomed to battle that he might have sent them off to North Africa on their own. To do so, however, would have compromised Caesar's reputation, which was fast growing into a legend. He would have to go to Africa in person.

During his short time in Rome, Caesar found that Mark Antony, one of his most trusted lieutenants, was not a good administrator. Antony had alienated many members of the Senate, and a mutiny by some of the legions that guarded Rome had occurred on his watch. Caesar therefore removed Antony from his position and replaced him with Mark Lepidus, the Master of Horse for Rome. Caesar sailed from Sicily toward the end of December and was on the coast of North Africa on the first of January 46 B.C.

Upon arriving in North Africa, Caesar found the situation even more dangerous than he had been led to believe. Scipio had compiled a very large army, and one of his most trusted lieutenants was Titus Labienus. Caesar's former trusted second-in-command had escaped from the Battle of Pharsalus and made his way to Africa. Knowing Caesar's style of battle as well as he did, Labienus was an excellent adviser to Scipio.

Early on in the campaign, Caesar and an advance guard of about 1,000 men were trapped and cornered by cavalrymen under Labienus. For several hours, the Pompeian forces rode around Caesar's men, throwing javelins and taunting their victims. Outnumbered and lacking fresh water, Caesar was in what was probably the worst spot he had ever seen. However, Labienus was wounded in the afternoon fighting, and without him to urge them on, his men began to lose their spirit. Labienus and his men rode off, having badly damaged Caesar's pride and confidence, but the luckiest Roman—as men often called him—was still alive.

On April 6, Caesar met his foes at the Battle of Thapsus. Scipio and Juba had built a series of earthen fortifications on a desert plain, and Caesar's men began the fight without orders, forced into battle by events. Juba's Numidians made the first major attack. Their movement was almost immediately shorn of its largest aspect, however. Caesar's men confused Juba's elephants by shouting, and then threw spears at the elephants' flanks, hoping not to kill, but rather to enrage them. The technique had been handed down from 202 B.C. when another Roman general, Scipio Africanus, had defeated Hannibal's

Carthaginians at the Battle of Zama.

Not only did the elephants stop their forward movement; they turned around and caused great confusion in the Numidian lines. Caesar's men were trained to take advantage of such moments; they moved forward and inserted themselves into the openings caused in Scipio and Juba's lines. Soon the battle had become complete mayhem; because of the dust and noise it was often difficult to tell friend from foe.

Caesar's men excelled at this type of close, hand-to-hand fighting. By the time the sun went down, Scipio and Juba's forces were either destroyed or in full retreat across the desert. The battle was one of Caesar's greatest victories, though this time it had been won through the impetuosity of his men, rather than any tactical plan on his part.

King Juba committed suicide in the desert. Scipio escaped to the coast. When his ship was kept in the harbor by Caesar's ships, Scipio also took his own life. Labienus, however, escaped the battle, and disappeared for the moment.

Caesar was back in Rome by midsummer. The Roman crowds turned out in great numbers to celebrate his special triumph, commemorating his victories in Egypt, Asia Minor, and North Africa.

All was well—except for the Roman calendar. Caesar took the opportunity to introduce a calendar he had brought with him from Egypt. Based on the sun rather than the moon, this new calendar was accurate to within 11 minutes per year. In order to make up for the time missed during the Civil, War, Caesar prolonged the year 46 B.C. until it stretched to 445 days. In his book *Calendar*, David Ewing Duncan wrote, "The entire year of 46 B.C. ended up stretching an extraordinary 445 days. Caesar called it the '*ultimus annus confusionis*,' 'the last year of confusion.' Everyone else called it simply 'The Year of Confusion.'"

On January 1, 45 B.C., the new calendar took effect. Designed by the Egyptian Soignes, the new calendar had a year that was much more accurate than the previous one. Until then, Rome had to insert a thirteenth month of varying days every year in order to keep the calendar accurate. During the mayhem and confusion of the Civil War, no one had inserted the intercalary month, and by now the calendar and the seasons were off by two months. Caesar's new calendar, soon called the Julian, was one of his most long-lasting effects; it remained the primary calendar for the Western world until 1582, when Pope Gregory VII brought in the new Gregorian calendar that is still used today.

All seemed secure until Caesar learned that two of Pompey's sons had escaped the debacle in North Africa and set up operations in Spain. That, after all, had been Pompey's province for five years, and his sons, Gnaeus and Sextus, enjoyed considerable support. Making matters worse, two legions Caesar had left in Spain had deserted en masse, going over to the two brothers. Gnaeus and Sextus had already captured Cordoba and were winning over most of Andalusia, what is now central-southern Spain.

Once again, Caesar decided to handle the matter in person. He left Rome and marched through Cisalpine Gaul, the Province, and entered Farther Spain as autumn began.

Gnaeus and Sextus retreated before Caesar's advance. The brothers knew of Caesar's battlefield ability, but they too had aces up their sleeve. Soon after he arrived in Spain, Caesar was shocked to learn that two more legions had defected and gone over to the Pompeian army. These were both legions recruited in Spain, and they were near the end of their tether. Caesar had made numerous promises of pensioning them off, and he had never lived up to the promises. Now some of his best veterans had joined Gnaeus and Pompey. Fortunately the Tenth Legion, Caesar's favorite, had remained trustworthy.

Even though he was outnumbered, Caesar employed his usual method: advance, attack, advance. The Pompeian forces retreated before him. Several sharp skirmishes were fought

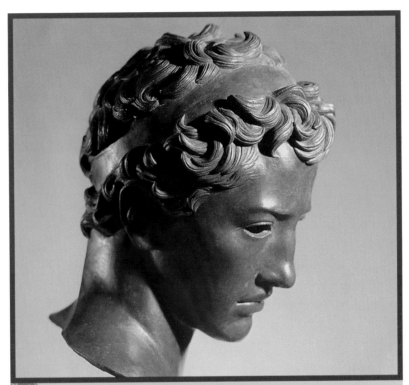

Generals and soldiers loyal to the slain Pompey joined forces with King Juba of Numidia (above) in an attempt to defeat Caesar. In the end, all of Caesar's political enemies were dead, either killed during battle or by their own hand after crushing military defeats.

before Gnaeus and Sextus decided to stand their ground in front of the town of Munda, in southern Spain.

By now Caesar knew that Titus Labienus was with the enemy, advising the two young sons of Pompey. Labienus had endured one failure after another since he had decided to fight against Caesar in the Civil War, but just one victory here in Spain might redeem all the missteps at Pharsalus, Thapsus, and elsewhere.

Whether or not Labienus was their chief adviser, the brothers chose their ground wisely. On the morning of March 17, Caesar's 30,000 men had to advance five miles across a level plain and cross a stream in order to reach the hillside where the Pompeians awaited. Caesar advanced with confidence, believing that the superior experience of his men would tell in any face-to-face encounter. The confidence was probably warranted; only a few thousand of the Pompeian forces were truly battle-hardened veterans.

The Battle of Munda began shortly before noon. Caesar's men advanced up the hillside to be greeted by waves of javelins hurled through the air. Many men fell in the first two advances, and Caesar observed his men wavering. There was no outright panic, but his men refused to advance again. Caesar is said to have seized a shield from one of his men and made a short advance up the hill. Inspired by their leader's bravery, his veterans sprang once more to the attack, and the Battle of Munda quickly became a hard-fought, hand-to-hand struggle.

Gnaeus Pompey ordered a large section of his cavalry, located on his right flank, to cross behind his infantry and reinforce the men holding the hillside. As soon as he saw this motion, Caesar ordered his own horses—7,000 in number— to attack Gnaeus' weakened right flank. Meanwhile, the Pompeian infantrymen were dismayed to see their cavalry make the move behind them. Believing that some type of retreat had been ordered, many of the younger members of the Pompeian army threw down their arms and fled.

Many stood and fought to the death. Titus Labienus met his end on the hillside at Munda. Thousands of Pompeians died that day, and the remainder were put to rout.

Now the Civil War was well and truly over. Gneaus Pompey was hunted down and killed a few weeks after Munda. His brother Sextus was pardoned. Caesar had no remaining military rivals. He returned to Rome to be greeted by the greatest celebrations ever seen in the city.

Cleopatra and her son Caesarion were now in Rome. Egyptians and exotic animals (such as a giraffe from Africa) competed with Gallic warriors and defeated Pompeains for attention. Caesar celebrated all his numerous triumphs in one immense celebration. It was by far the greatest ever seen in Rome.

The occasion was marred by two murders. On the day of his triumph, Caesar had the Gallic chieftain Vercingetorix executed. Such vindictiveness was not in keeping with the training of Caesar's youth. Second, Cleopatra had her younger sister murdered on the same day. Cleopatra wanted no one to come between her and Caesar.

THE REPUBLIC IS DEAD, LONG LIVE THE EMPIRE

Caesar returned to Rome at the beginning of 45 B.C. Many people found it difficult to believe that it was only four years since the Civil War had broken out. In those 48 months, Caesar had defeated Pompey's forces in Spain, Pompey in person in Greece, Ptolemy XII in Egypt, Pharnaces in Asia Minor, Scipio in North Africa, and Pompey's sons in Spain. This was, perhaps, the single greatest string of successes ever achieved by a Roman leader. When one added to this Caesar's prior subjection of Gaul and two invasions of Britain, there seemed little doubt that Caesar was among the greatest military leaders of all time. Only the record of Alexander the Great could rival that of Julius Caesar.

Clearly there was more to Caesar than military leadership. He had shown an adroit combination of mercy and forgiveness toward many of his foes; now, in the full flush of his power, Caesar wanted to change Rome itself.

More clearly than most of his contemporaries, Caesar recognized

With the end of Rome's Civil War, she was now well on her way to becoming a true empire. Although Caesar had unified the country and declared himself Dictator for Life, he publicly refused the crown of laurels offered to him by Mark Antony. The gesture set in motion events that would lead to Caesar's death.

that the Roman Republic was a spent force. Once it had been the best government available anywhere in the Mediterranean world, with its combination of consuls, senators, tribunes, and the like. That government had been designed to govern first a city-state and then to rule over the Italian peninsula. The Roman government had proved unable to manage the business of an empire, and Rome had truly become *the* empire of its day. The time had come for governmental changes to adjust to Rome's new position in the world.

First came changes in land ownership. Caesar was determined to provide for the legionnaires. He remembered the chaos that threatened Rome when Pompey's troops had not received their land grants in 62 B.C. Therefore Caesar proposed, and the Senate rapidly accepted, that new colonies would be created in North Africa and Spain, and that these colonies would consist of veterans who would receive regular payments from the state.

Then came the threat of political changes. So far Caesar had acted within the boundaries of his consulship and his temporary post as Dictator. But on February 14, 44 B.C., the Senate voted to make Caesar *Dictator Perpetuas*, meaning Dictator for Life. Caesar gratefully accepted the honor. He began to prepare for yet another military campaign, this time against the Parthians in Mesopotamia. They had crushed Marcus Crassus in 53 B.C., and Caesar wanted to punish them for their actions against Rome.

Just two days after he was voted Dictator for Life, Caesar presided at the feast of the Lupercalia. Caesar sat on a golden chair while the half-naked Luperci ran through the streets in their enactment of the fertility rites. During the festival, three of Caesar's associates, one of them being Mark Antony, came to Caesar and tried to crown him. Caesar took off the wreath and threw it among the crowd; this was the type of gesture that had always made Caesar popular. But there were some in the street that day for whom this laurel crown was a final insult. They now prepared to kill Caesar.

Though he was one of sixty men who conspired to kill Caesar, Marcus Brutus has been named and discussed the most of the conspirators. Born in 85 B.C., Brutus lost his father at an early age and had a substitute father in Staberius Eros, a Latin grammarian. Brutus went to Athens to complete his education, where he was influenced by the many Greek philosophies of the day: Academic, Peripatetic, Epicurean, and Stoic. Brutus was a serious student who took to heart the Stoic warning against undue emotion, either in joy or sorrow. By the time he returned to Rome, Brutus was considered a "coming man."

When the Civil War began in 49 B.C., Brutus fought for Pompey, because he believed Pompey was more likely to restore the Roman Republic to its former self. Brutus, like Caesar, knew that the old Republic was only a shadow of what it had once been; unlike Caesar, he hoped to restore and renew the Republic.

The day after Caesar won the dramatic Battle of Pharsalus, Brutus was brought before him. Caesar had a special interest in Brutus, considering him one of the most promising members of the younger generation. Caesar pardoned Brutus, and the grateful Brutus became one of Caesar's strongest adherents for the next three years.

Brutus never wrote memoirs, but had he done so, he might have indicated that he believed in Caesar the man, but not Caesar the King or Emperor. Once he decided that Caesar truly intended to complete the destruction of the Republic, Brutus became one of the ringleaders in the group of 60 men who would strike Caesar down.

Caesar rose early on the Ides of March (March 15). He intended to meet with a group of Senators in the late morning and then move to the preparations for his military campaign against Parthia. Caesar's wife, the faithful Calpurnia, begged him not to go to meet the Senators that day; she had had bad dreams and feared treachery. Caesar laughed off Calpurnia's fears, as he nearly always did. It was not that Caesar was blind to danger; rather, he seems to have known that he was a marked man and refused to cave in to the fear. Caesar had actually sent his best bodyguards back to Spain a month or so earlier; he did not believe that excessive precautions could save anyone from fate.

Caesar and Mark Antony went to the Senate House. Caesar walked in alone, reading a document, while Mark Antony was delayed by some of the conspirators. Once he was seated, Caesar was handed a petition for clemency for a relative of one of the Senators. Caesar curtly refused clemency, upon which a group of about 20 Senators came close and surrounded him. Caesar did not yet fear anything, but one of them put his hands on Caesar's shoulder and began to pull at his robe.

"This is violence!" protested Caesar.

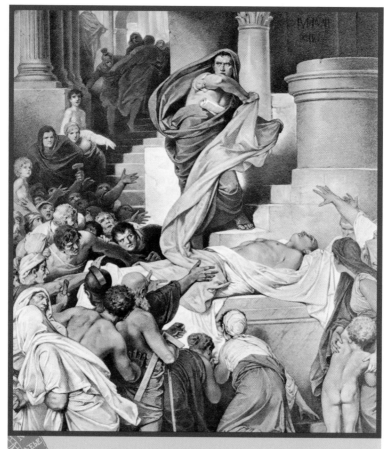

In all, 60 men conspired to kill Julius Caesar. Their plans came to fruition on the Ides of March (March 15), 44 B.C., when 20 armed men, including Brutus, surrounded Caesar and stabbed him to death with daggers.

Then they came at him. Twenty men and twenty flashing daggers did their work. Caesar went down fighting, grabbing one of the knives and inflicting some wounds before he fell on the floor, his life bleeding away. As he looked up, Caesar saw Marcus Brutus with a knife in his hand. Caesar's last words were "*Et tu* (you too), Brute?"

Caesar died on the floor. The Senators, overwhelmed by their action, fled the chamber, and the body lay there for some time, undisturbed.

Caesar was dead. Who now would pilot the ship of state?

Cleopatra fled Rome. She and her son Caesarion reached Egypt and safety. Mark Antony delivered Caesar's funeral oration. A year later, Antony hunted down Brutus and Cassius, two of the men who had murdered Caesar. They took their own lives rather than surrender.

Gaius Julius Caesar was, beyond doubt, one of the most important figures in the history of Rome and of the Western world. In 56 years, Caesar created a new standard for military prowess; he was, and is, among the top military leaders of all time, on anyone's list.

Caesar also altered the political history of Rome. We do not know whether he ever actually wanted to become a King or Emperor, but we do know that he saw that the ancient Republic could not be restored. Caesar had lived through the Civil War of Sulla's day and had won his own Civil War. He had no wish to return Rome to anarchy.

Caesar's life and career represent a turning point: the point on which Rome ceased to be a Republic and became an Empire.

Caesar possessed to a supreme degree the following qualities: courage, capacity, vigor, speed, and ruthlessness. He had worthy opponents, many of whom had some of these qualities, but none of them encompassed them to the degree that Caesar did.

Caesar was, in many ways, the last ruler of the Roman Republic. His adopted son, Octavian, would become the first ruler of the Roman Empire. He and Antony were fierce rivals for Caesar's mantle. Finally, in 32 B.C., Octavian won the naval Battle of Actium and became the new Caesar. Antony and Cleopatra both committed suicide rather than become Octavian's prisoners.

Octavian, who later was called Augustus (the Revered One) was the unofficial ruler of Rome from 32 B.C. until his death in 14 A.D. Augustus never called himself King or Emperor (he preferred the title of "First Citizen"), but he wielded power as if he were. Upon Augustus' death, leadership went to his stepson Tiberius, who became the first Roman to take the actual title of Emperor. From 14 A.D. until the final collapse in 476 A.D., Rome was an Empire.

100 B.C.	Julius Caesar is born in Rome.
85	Marcus Brutus is born in Rome.
84	Caesar marries Cornelia, daughter of Cinna.
82	Sulla arrives in Rome and becomes Dictator.
78	Sulla dies in Rome.
73	A slave rebellion begins in Italy, led by Spartacus and the gladiators who escaped from Capua.
71	Crassus defeats the slave rebels; 6,000 are crucified.
68	Caesar enters political life with his funeral oration for his aunt Julia, the widow of Marius.
67	Pompey receives a command to fight the pirates.
66	The pirates are vanquished.
65	Pompey becomes the first Roman to enter Jerusalem.
63	Caesar is elected Pontifex Maximus of Rome.
62	Caesar divorces Pompeia after a scandal involving her and Publius Clodius.
62	Caesar goes to Spain, his first command.
62	Pompey returns to Rome after an absence of five years.
60	Caesar forms the Triumvirate with Crassus and Pompey.
59	Caesar serves as consul.
58	Caesar becomes Governor of Cisalpine and Transalpine Gaul.
58	Caesar defeats the Helvetii and the Germans.
56	Caesar, Crassus, and Pompey renew their alliance.
55	Caesar crosses the Rhine and attacks the Germans; crosses the English Channel and invades Britain.
54	Caesar invades Britain for a second time.
54	Crassus dies while on campaign in Mesopotamia.
53	A Gallic confederacy is formed by Vercingetorix.
52	Caesar loses a battle at Gergovia, but defeats the Gauls at Alesia; Vercingetorix becomes his prisoner.

49   Caesar crosses the Rubicon River in northeast Italy.

48   Caesar crosses the Adriatic Sea. He loses a battle at Dyracchium, but defeats Pompey at Pharsalus; arrives in Egypt and becomes embroiled in the civil war between Ptolemy XIII and Cleopatra.

47   Caesar wins the Battle of Zela and writes to the Senate, "Veni, Vedi, Vici."

46   Caesar wins the Battle of Thapsus in North Africa.

46   The Roman year lasts 445 days.

45   Caesar inaugurates the new Roman calendar which is based on the sun rather than the moon.

45   Vercingetorix is executed.

45   Caesar defeats the Pompeian brothers at Munda in Spain.

44   The Senate makes Caesar "Dictator for Life"; senators attack and kill Caesar on March 15.

42   Brutus and Cassius are hunted down by Mark Antony in Spain.

41   Power in Rome is shared by the members of the Second Triumvirate: Octavian, Mark Antony, and Mark Lepidus.

31   Octavian defeats Mark Antony and Cleopatra at the Battle of Actium; Antony and Cleopatra both commit suicide.

27   Octavian offers to resign all his offices and retire, but the Senate begs him to remain.

14 A.D.   Octavian dies; is succeeded by his stepson Tiberius, who is the first to call himself Emperor of Rome.

Balsdon, J.P.V.D. *Julius Caesar: A Political Biography*. New York: Atheneum Press, 1967.

Bradford, Ernle. *Julius Caesar: The Pursuit of Power*. London: Hamish Hamilton, 1984.

Caesar, Julius. *The Battle for Gaul*. Translated and edited by Anne and Peter Wiseman. Boston: David R. Godine, 1980.

Clarke, M.L. *The Noblest Roman: Marcus Brutus and His Reputation*. Ithaca: Cornell University Press, 1981.

Dando-Collins, Stephen. *Caesar's Legion: The Epic Saga of Julius Caesar's Elite Tenth Legion and the Armies of Rome*. New York: John Wiley & Sons, 2002.

Duncan, David Ewing. *Calendar: Humanity's Epic Struggle to Determine a True and Accurate Year*. New York: Avon Books, 1998.

Greenhalgh, Peter. *Pompey: The Roman Alexander*. London: Weidenfeld and Nicolson, 1980.

Holmes, T. Rice. *Ancient Britain and the Invasions of Julius Caesar*. Oxford: Clarendon Press, 1907.

Keaveney, Arthur. *Sulla: The Last Republican*. London: Croom Helm, 1982.

Leach, John. *Pompey the Great*. London: Croom Helm, 1978.

Meier, Christian. *Caesar: A Biography*, translated from the German by David McLintock. New York: Harper Collins, 1995.

Plutarch. *Roman Lives*. Translated by Robin Waterfield. Oxford: Oxford University Press, 1999.

Polybius. *The Rise of the Roman Empire*. Translated by Ian Scott-Kilvert, selected by F.W. Walbank. London: Penguin Books, 1979.

Sihler, E.G., Ph.D. *Annals of Caesar: A Critical Biography with a Survey of the Sources*. New York: G.E. Stechert & Company, 1911.

Caesar, Julius. *The Battle for Gaul.* Anne and Peter Wiseman, translators and editors. Boston: David R. Godine, 1980.

Dando-Collins, Stephen. *Caesar's Legion: The Epic Saga of Julius Caesar's Elite Tenth Legion and the Armies of Rome.* New York: John Wiley & Sons, 2002.

Polybius. *The Rise of the Roman Empire.* Translated by Ian Scott-Kilvert, selected by F.W. Walbank. London: Penguin Books, 1979.

Bloggus Caesari—Julius Caesar's Weblog
http://www.sankey.ca/caesar/

Julius Caesar Web Directory of Online Resources
http://www.virgil.org/caesar/

Guide to the play *Julius Caesar* by William Shakespeare
http://juliuscaesar.future.easyspace.com/

page:

13: Archivo Iconographico, S.A./ Corbis
15: Hierophant Collection
18: Bettmann/ Corbis
21: Stapleton Collection/ Corbis
24: Hierophant Collection
29: Hulton Archive/ Getty Images
31: Hulton Archive/Getty Images
34: Hulton Archive/Getty Images
39: Araldo de Luca/ Corbis
42: Gianni Dagli Orti/ Corbis
46: Bettmann/ Corbis
49: Hierophant Collection
52: Hierophant Collection
55: Hierophant Collection

59: Bettmann/ Corbis
62: Christel Gertenberg/ Corbis
65: Vanni Archive/ Corbis
67: Bettmann/ Corbis
70: Bettmann/ Corbis
75: Archivo Iconographico, S.A./ Corbis
79: Bettmann/ Corbis
81: Bettmann/ Corbis
87: Bettmann/ Corbis
89: Hierophant Collection
93: Roger Wood/ Corbis
97: Bettmann/ Corbis
100: Catherine Karnow/ Corbis

Cover: Bettmann/ Corbis
Frontis: Hierophant Collection

SAMUEL WILLARD CROMPTON has a deep interest in the Classical world of Greece and Rome. He has written *Gods and Goddesses of Classical Mythology* as well as *100 Military Leaders Who Shaped World History* and *100 Battles that Shaped World History*. Mr. Crompton teaches both American History and Western Civilization at Holyoke Community College in Massachusetts. He has twice served as a Writing Fellow for Oxford University Press in its production of the 24-volume *American National Biography*. He has written several other books for Chelsea House, including *Waterloo, Hastings*, and *Tenochtitlan*.

ARTHUR M. SCHLESINGER, JR. is the leading American historian of our time. He won the Pulitzer Prize for his book *The Age of Jackson* (1945) and again for a chronicle of the Kennedy Administration, *A Thousand Days* (1965), which also won the National Book Award. Professor Schlesinger is the Albert Schweitzer Professor of the Humanities at the City University of New York and has been involved in several other Chelsea House projects, including the series REVOLUTIONARY WAR LEADERS, COLONIAL LEADERS, and YOUR GOVERNMENT.